BLOOD on the RAVEN

Also by Michelle Winkler

A Lighter Shade of Darkness trilogy
Dust on the Altar
Blood on the Raven
Shadow on the Heart (coming soon)

Sign up for my monthly newsletter with the QR code below, or on my website at mwinklerbooks.com, to be the first to know when my next book launches.

Blood on the Raven

Michelle Winkler

Mariposa Bookworks – Arizona

Published by Mariposa Bookworks, Glendale, AZ.
mariposabookworks@gmail.com

First edition: October 2024
Second edition: November 2025

Cover design by Jake Clark
Edit by Tammy Salyer
Interior design by Mariposa Bookworks

MARIPOSA
BOOKWORKS

ISBN 979-8-9931828-2-7 (eBook)
ISBN 979-8-9931828-0-3 (paperback)
ISBN 979-8-9931828-1-0 (hardcover)

To the neurodivergents. Always remember when the world says you can't, you actually can... it just might take you longer to finish.

CHAPTER 1

Jade dropped to the ground and covered her head with her hands, as flames shot over her and the ground shook from the blast. The heat across her back subsided, and she slowly sat up. Feeling around her head, she half expected to find patches of burnt hair. Luckily, she seemed unscathed. She looked over at Charlie standing a few feet to her right. For a moment, neither of them moved.

"What the hell was that?" Charlie shouted, breaking the silence. He ran toward her over the frozen, bare ground as Jade stood and brushed dirt off her jeans and the hem of her cloak. He reached out and untangled a twig from her wavy brown hair. "We're supposed to be training, not having a full-on battle." As he stepped back, the worry lines eased and his expression softened.

"Well, it's your fault for not being more specific. All you said was 'Think fire.'"

"Yeah, fire. As in, light it on fire, not blow it to smithereens." As Charlie looked around them, Jade followed his gaze.

Bonfire Field was the site of fire festivals going back generations, and the earth in the center of the clearing had been permanently scorched free of any greenery. With no grass or plants to catch fire and the nearest trees a good fifty feet in any direction, it was the best place in the township to practice fire magic.

There were pieces of splintered and charred wood scattered around them, still smoking in the frigid November air. Charlie had cobbled together the makeshift statue from deadwood to represent the enemy. Supposedly any enemy, but Jade had seen Raven's sadistic smile grinning out from the bark of the headpiece. It was the same smile she'd loved only weeks before, when her friend April had been the only spirit inhabiting her body.

Jade's anger and frustration had taken over, and she'd released a fireball much bigger than she'd intended. It spun out of control, whipping around her and finally barreling toward the target. The kindling hadn't stood a chance, but without control, Jade couldn't be sure the spell would be as effective against Raven. Worse yet, she couldn't be sure she wouldn't unintentionally hurt someone she cared about.

Charlie dipped his head to catch her eyes. His rich brown curls framed his face and contrasted his blue eyes, making them almost seem to glow. "Hey, it's okay. You've been doing really well at reconnecting to your magic. You just need to work on your control." His crooked grin teased a smile from her, and he pulled her into an embrace.

She relaxed into him, letting his warmth create a bubble of safety around her. "Mmm. This is nice." She felt she could forget everything and stay in his arms forever.

"Yeah, it is, but we can't get distracted. We need to start Katie's initiation soon." He pushed her away. "After that, I'm all yours."

She leaned back into him. "Promise?"

He grinned back at her and spoke in an exaggerated British accent. "Your wish is my command, m'lady." She giggled, and he continued in his normal voice. "Let's do the breathing exercise, then we can try it again."

Jade rolled her eyes. "I can't stop in the middle of a fight and say 'oh, can you wait a minute, I've got to breathe.'"

"Of course not, but it does help you calm your mind. A calm mind means better control. Practice with the breathing enough now, and you won't need to think about it when you're in battle. It'll be a habit."

"Fine." She closed her eyes and tried focusing on her breath.

The last month had been a traumatic time for Jade, to say the least. Her Aunt, and last remaining family member, was murdered; her best friend was sacrificed in a dark magic ritual; her father figure betrayed her; the most powerful dark Witch in generations was back from the dead; and on top of it all, she was now responsible for an entire township of over a hundred magic and nonmagic folk. She was definitely in need of some counseling.

Luckily, Sophia was a trained healer. She'd been helping Jade with a breathing exercise called box breathing. The simple act of counting slowly to four with each inhale and exhale tricked her nervous system into thinking she was safe. Its effects were short-lived, but they were a positive trigger to focus her mind on the here and now, allowing her logical side to gain control.

Jade stood in the field, acutely aware of Charlie watching her. But as each breath came and went, her awareness of him faded. Her anger subsided, and her tension eased the slightest bit. It did help her feel calmer, but that's not what she wanted right now. She wanted her best friend back. Since that wasn't possible, she'd settle for beating Raven until she was a bloody pulp.

Unrecognizable.

Dead.

"You're panting." Charlie's matter-of-fact voice.

Jade opened her eyes. "What? No, I'm not." She definitely wasn't calm though. She closed her eyes. "Shut up and let me focus." Breathe in, hold, breathe out, hold.

Charlie whispered, "Stop trying so hard. Let go."

Easy for him to say. She took an extra deep breath and pushed it out hard. When her breath returned to normal, she opened her right hand. Pulling the residual heat from the burnt kindling around her, she drew it into a small ball of fire. She opened her eyes and looked for the target. A small piece of bark remained untouched on top of the stump. She shrank the fireball to a less dangerous size and tossed it at the wood.

There was no explosion this time. The fire dropped onto the stump top and disappeared, leaving the wood chip unchanged.

"Great. Now I'm throwing duds."

"You'll find the balance. Try again."

She did. Same results. Jade turned and glared at Charlie. "This is ridiculous."

"Have patience. You've only been at this for a month. Try again."

"Patience? I can light a candle fine. Ask me to heat some water? No problem. The minute you ask me to fight with it, I'm a tragic mess."

"It's your emotions."

"You better not tell me I'm too emotional."

"No, but you don't have very good control of them."
He raised his hands in surrender. "You know I'm right.
It's not always a bad thing, but magic can't be toyed
with. Especially at your level."

"But I never had a problem with controlling it when
I was a kid. Well, almost never." Several spells that had
gone haywire came to mind, her parent's table turning
blue being one of them.

"But you're not a kid anymore. You're a different
person. A Witch's connection to magic changes over
their lives. Even someone as powerful as Willow has to
make adjustments every so often."

Willow. There was a perfect example of how bad
Jade's lack of control could be. Her anger toward
Richard had blinded her to everyone around her, and
poor Willow had ended up in the crossfire. She'd
survived, but without her eyesight, she was no longer
the most powerful Witch in Sugar Hill. It was all Jade's
fault.

Charlie took her hand gently in both of his,
interrupting her shame spiral. Warm, comforting
energy flowed into her. "It wasn't your fault."

"I appreciate your support, but it was. If I hadn't
been so angry at seeing Richard there, I wouldn't have
thrown that energy and Willow would still have her
sight. I didn't mean to, but it was my fault." She pulled
her hand away and turned back to the stump.

Charlie wrapped his arms around her. She leaned
her head back against him and closed her eyes. He
murmured in her ear, "He'd kidnapped your best
friend. You were worried he might have hurt her, or
worse."

She tensed at the memory, but Charlie held her
tighter and kissed her cheek. She laid her arms on his,
pulling them closer.

"If he hadn't been so desperate to bring his daughter
back from the dead, he never would have tried that

spell, never would have even been there for you to attack."

"Well, then I guess it's really Richard's fault," Jade said. She hadn't spoken his name since finding out he was her uncle and the one responsible for sending her on the crazy quest for the ascension keys.

Charlie chuckled. "Okay, it's Richard's fault, but you can't let that blame turn into hatred and control your power." He turned her toward him and held both her hands firmly. "You are the only one who can control your power. So breathe." He turned her around to face the stump and the last piece of untouched bark. He spoke quietly in her ear. "Focus on the target"—he stepped back from her—"and control your power."

Jade glared at the burnt stump and one piece of untouched bark, mocking her. They had been practicing for over an hour, with the sky slowly brightening. Now the sun had just cleared the horizon, and the whole field was lit up in a golden glow. She told herself this was not Raven before her. This was a stubborn piece of bark. But Jade was more stubborn.

She grinned as she lifted her hand and drew the heat into it. *I have the power,* she thought. *I am in control.*

She formed the fireball and threw it at the bark. The flames exploded, and when they cleared, there was nothing left. Not even smoldering pieces. The bark and stump were both gone.

Jade could feel Charlie's eyes burning into the back of her head. She put on a resigned face and turned toward him. "I really am trying."

He was struggling to keep a straight face. "I know you are. And you're getting better. You only completely obliterated the target this time." Unable to hold it in any longer, he burst out laughing.

Jade tried to stay serious, but his laughter was contagious. She wondered how he could always cheer her up. One look at his lopsided grin and she couldn't help herself. She thought it must be that his cheerful presence pushed at the boundaries of her negativity. She'd spent half her life not knowing who had killed her parents, only to find out that the man responsible was a distant family member. While looking on the bright side and staying positive was not her strong suit, Charlie made her want to try.

Charlie's laughter subsided. "We should head to the chapel. It's almost time." He turned toward his car parked on the edge of the field, and Jade walked beside him. "You know, this coven meeting is gonna be kinda fun."

"Fun?"

"Well, interesting. It'll be your first official coven ritual since becoming High Priestess. And from what I've heard of Katie, she's been wanting to be a coven member for a long time."

"Yeah, Sophia said Katie was thrilled to find out she'd sponsor her petition." Jade noticed him glance at the car and edge in front of her. A smile briefly tugged at the corner of his mouth.

Jade squinted at him, quickening her pace to just pass him. He was definitely grinning now as he matched her stride. They quickly gained momentum until they were racing the last few feet to the car.

Jade was about to touch it when Charlie grabbed her arm and pulled her back. A wrestling match ensued with them pulling and shoving each other away from the car, laughing the whole time. Jade ended up between Charlie and the car, pushing against his chest with both hands in a desperate bid to keep him from reaching it over her shoulders. Her feet were slipping though, and it was only moments before he'd touch it.

Not one to give in, she planted her lips squarely on his, thinking she would distract him just enough to reach for the car herself. But he kissed her back and sent warmth racing through her. She wrapped her arms around him, and she soon felt his hands on her. She pulled him closer, deepening their kiss. After several moments of bliss, they parted, staring into each other's eyes.

Charlie glanced over her shoulder. "Should we call it a tie?"

Jade realized she was leaning against the car, but Charlie's hands were behind her, so she couldn't be sure who'd touched it first. "No. I definitely won." She kissed him briefly, then flitted away from him and jumped in the passenger seat.

"Hey! No fair!" Charlie yelled good-naturedly. He looked in the window at her. "You're just gonna cut me off like that?"

"We're gonna be late for Katie's Initiation." She didn't really want to stop, but there'd be time later. They had responsibilities to attend to now.

Charlie grumbled something about a likely excuse and got in the driver's seat. They drove across town and up the winding dirt road toward the chapel.

**

After they parked, they walked the path through the woods hand in hand. Their attraction was palpable, but they'd never done more than kiss. It wasn't because Jade didn't want to, exactly. The week after the Ascension, Jade and Charlie had talked it out. Jade definitely wanted to be with him. She loved him and she could sense Charlie felt the same. The problem was Raven. The dark Witch was out there somewhere, in April's body. Jade couldn't move on until she'd dealt with her. Charlie had said he accepted that, insisted he understood and she should take as much time as she needed. Jade still felt bad about it. And times like this morning, she thought maybe she was ready. But then something always interrupted.

A huge, twisted tree came into view, its dark trunk resembling a human form. The Green Man Tree. Jade had forgotten she used to call it that when she led April on this path. It seemed ages ago when the three of them had been here together. Charlie had seemed a stranger then, so different from the young boy she'd known as a child. April had been her anchor, supporting her without question. Her best friend and her childhood friend. She missed the uneasy alliance the two of them had formed to assist her through the trials. She hadn't realized then how much their combined presence had comforted her.

They arrived at the tangled underbrush that formed a hillside of sorts: the entrance to the Sugar Hill Chapel. Eight of the current coven members were nearby, chatting in small groups. Jade and Charlie nodded to them as they passed through and approached the chapel door. The small solid-wood door sheltered behind a wrought iron gate, mostly hidden behind vines and bushes. It was easy to miss if you weren't looking for it. Charlie whispered the words to unlock them and pushed through, Jade following close behind.

The contrast between the dark, tangled mess outside and bright-patterned beauty inside never ceased to amaze Jade. She took a moment to look around the hall and felt some of her tension drain away. From the moss-and-lichen mosaic floor to the sparkling canopy of leaves and crystals far overhead, the entire structure had the appearance of the most beautiful cathedral, but created naturally from the forest. Straight tall tree trunks grew in two rows, leading to a larger trunk at the end, which formed the altar. Jade could just make out the tinkling of dripping water coming from the small pond at the base of it.

"Ready?" Charlie asked at her side.

She turned back to the face the doorway. "Ready."

Greeting the coven members before a meeting was a routine Jade had dreaded at first. A necessary obligation to get through and be done with. But it only took a couple of times before she started looking forward to it. Each Witch who met her sent their unique energy toward her: strength, warmth, even sweetness. Each added to her, shoring up her soul like pillars under a roof. She began to do the same for them. Unsure how they would perceive her energy, she sent a gentle welcome, thankful they were present.

The simple unspoken exchange of energy turned out to be another one of those things Jade had done instinctively, which she later found out was part of a Witch's training to become High Priestess. The connection between coven members and coven leaders was a sacred one, strengthened over time, little by little, every time they gathered in a circle. As each member passed through the entrance and greetings were made, Jade felt more content. These were her people. This was her coven. She was right where she belonged.

Sophia entered next and greeted Jade with a gentle hug, as was the custom with the elder ladies in the coven. "Merry meet, dear." She removed her cloak and hung it next to the others on one of the short branches of the nearest tree trunk. Her long ivory-and-pink dress reminded Jade of those worn a century ago. The lace and silk decorative hems and ribbons around her waist and collar fit perfectly with her silver curls pinned under a small floral hat.

Sophia turned back and held her hand out to the young, shy-looking girl who entered behind her. "Jade, Charlie, this is Katie, your new initiate."

Katie dipped her head, then looked up at Jade sheepishly. Her jet-black hair hung down past her shoulders, and her long bangs partially covered her eyes like a hooded cloak. Her dress was simple, dark purple with tiny white flowers scattered across it.

Sophia continued. "Katie, this is Jade, our High Priestess, and Charlie, our High Priest. They will be deciding if you'll be allowed into our coven officially."

Jade said, "It's a pleasure to finally meet you, Katie. I'm sorry Charlie and I have been so busy lately, but we've heard good things about you and your abilities. Are you ready?"

Katie nodded, then quickly stepped past them and walked down the hall to join the others at the end.

Sophia said, "She's a bit shy until she gets to know you. I hope you won't hold that against her."

"Of course not." Jade grasped her hand gently. The unplanned move reminded her of when April would take her hand in support. Jade quickly pushed down the sorrow that threatened to rise. "I told Charlie what you said about her being able to talk to faeries. We're thrilled she wants to be in the coven. I'm sure she'll be a great fit. Don't worry." She watched Sophia walk down to meet the others and gave Charlie a grin. Katie seemed a good balance to the energy already present.

An old woman's voice sounded behind Jade, warm as honey with the strength of the tallest oak tree. "Merry meet, child."

Jade turned to greet Willow and the young woman guiding her. "Merry meet, Willow, Crystal."

Crystal was dressed all in black, her bleached-blonde hair and pale skin set in stark contrast. "I'm sorry we're late. We . . . I lost track of time." She looked worried as she paid close attention to Willow's footsteps.

Jade said, "You're not late at all."

Willow's head turned toward Jade, her white eyes seeming to burn into her. She reached out with her wrinkled hand. It fluttered like a leaf, but her posture was tall and regal. Jade firmly took her hand, surprised by the strength with which Willow squeezed. She had always been strong, her dark brown skin radiating a youthful glow, despite her wrinkles. Now, it was thin and stretched tight over her bones. She had aged years in the weeks since she'd lost her sight. Despite the talks she'd had with Charlie, Jade still felt sorrow and shame over being the cause of it.

"Well then, no harm done." Willow turned toward her right, still gripping Jade. "Thank you, Crystal, for your guidance here, and for waiting at the altar to stand with me during the Initiation."

Crystal smiled tiredly. "Of course, Grandma Willow." She nodded to Jade and scooted away down the hall.

Once she had left, Willow leaned close. "I know she means well, but that child is tramping on my last nerve." She looped her arm through Jade's, and they walked to the altar together. "I'll be glad when she finally gets her power back and has something to do besides fret over me."

"She's still struggling to receive any messages from the Goddess?"

"Unfortunately." She patted Jade's arm. "There's no cause for worry yet, child. Our coven went through a lot. It will take time before everyone is completely themselves again."

The coven members were gathered in a circle in front of the altar. Jade guided Willow to a seat placed for her in front, to the right side. As soon as she was settled, Jade took her place next to Charlie in front of the altar pond, facing the coven, and looked around the room. She had gotten to know her coven pretty well over the last few weeks. They were an eclectic mix of talents and personalities. Aiden and Selene were a power couple, water and fire equally matched. Selene's tall stature and flaming red hair contrasted Aiden. His short curly locks were similar to Charlie's, except they were jet black. The tall, beautiful, auburn-haired warrior and her short, hairy, alchemist husband. Together they were almost unstoppable.

Ms. Scrivener was there in her usual neat-as-a-pin suit. Her magical ability was average, not excelling in any one discipline, but as the coven's Justice her legal talent was unmatched. Crystal stood next to her, the coven's Diviner. Being able to receive messages directly from the Goddess could prove invaluable, but she'd not received any clear messages since the former High Priestess, Joy, had crossed over.

Sophia, on the other hand, was a great healer and her magic seemed to be strong as ever. Being one of the Crones of Sugar Hill meant she was also part of the most powerful group of Witches in the township. A mini coven within the coven. Together with Mrs. Keepsake, Willow, and Madame Belle, the quartet was a formidable force of experience and power. Jade was uncertain how Willow's loss of sight had affected the group as a whole.

And then there were Daisy and Mr. Flannerly. Jade didn't know much about either of them. Mr. Flannerly was the coven's Historian. A hermit for all intents, he only attended coven meetings and rituals when required. He always wore an old baseball cap, so beat-up and worn you couldn't see the team logo anymore. His salt-and-pepper gray beard was often unruly, as if he'd just woken up, and he always wore denim coveralls over a flannel shirt, even in the summer. Sophia had told Jade his grumpy nature was concealing a heart of gold, but Jade hadn't gotten to know him that well yet.

Daisy was even more of a mystery. A coven's Ghost was the Witch most adept in deception, finding hidden things, and stealth. While they were living members of the coven, their name was a little on the nose. Supposedly, they could walk down the most crowded street and never be seen. In fact, if she was here, Jade hadn't seen her enter.

She continued looking over the gathered coven, scanning every face. They were all waiting patiently. Jade finally saw Daisy in the middle of the group. It was as if there was a shadow over her. She grinned knowingly at Jade, a twinkle in her eye. Jade literally blinked and she was gone. She looked for her but couldn't find her, even in the small gathering.

Jade began the ceremony. "We call upon the elements, protect us in our rites."

Charlie said, "We call upon the Goddess and God, guide us in our rites."

In unison the coven members said, "In perfect love and perfect trust, so mote it be."

Jade took a step forward. "Our coven has been through a lot lately. While the threat is not completely over, today we celebrate. Today our coven becomes whole once again, with a full thirteen members. Will the sponsor please make their case." She nodded to Sophia, who stood.

"I'd like to petition for our newest potential coven member, Katie. Her cousin was coven member Harmony, who crossed over during the battle with the North Devonshire coven a few years ago. Since then, she has been studying hard in hopes of joining us in her cousin's place as the Earth Key holder."

Jade said, "Thank you, Sophia. We recognize Katie as potential initiate and Earth Key holder. Katie, please step forward."

The young Witch stepped to the center and stood before the altar with her head bowed.

Charlie said, "Katie, I hear you would like to bring a new talent to our coven. Would you please tell everyone what your expertise is?"

Katie glanced between Charlie and Jade several times, then looked at Sophia. Sophia nodded and Katie took a deep breath. "I . . . well, it's not something many would think of as a weapon. It's not really a weapon at all . . . I just—" She looked down at her hands in dismay.

Jade leaned forward and spoke quietly. She focused her most comforting, loving energy toward her, this poor girl who was visibly trembling. "Katie." She waited a moment, and when she didn't look up, said again softer, "Katie." She looked up timidly, peeking out from under her straight bangs. "You've been training to be a coven member for a while?" Katie nodded. Jade continued. "You know what? There's one thing they don't teach you." She glanced at Charlie. In an almost whisper, she said, "When you join a coven, you gain a family." She smiled and was pleased to see Katie smile in return. "We all look out for each other. We take care of our own."

Katie stood a little straighter. Jade said, "Please, tell us about your gift."

Katie nodded and began. "I can talk to faeries. I believe that's called a Marrow? They can be particular about who they trust. The faeries, I mean. But I've been talking to them for as long as I can remember, so they trust me. A lot. And they're strong, and powerful, and . . . and fast. They can help. They want to help."

Charlie said, "That's awesome, Katie. I've tried reading up on faerie folk, but unfortunately there's not a lot of books about them. Not many people have ever been able to communicate with them beyond the most superficial greetings. I'm sure Sophia told you we would need to see a demonstration of your power. Are you ready?"

Katie nodded, and after glancing to her left, giggled. "I brought one of my closest friends, but he . . . well, he's a little sensitive." She looked to her left again and said, "Yes you are. Behave."

Jade noticed when she spoke to the invisible faerie her posture changed and her voice took on a calm yet assertive tone. There was power in this timid girl. The challenge would be to build her confidence up so she could access it reliably.

Katie said, "Sorry. He doesn't like that you're asking for a demonstration. He said it feels like he's performing on command, and he doesn't do that. I can ask him to show you one of his favorite tricks if you'd like though."

Charlie said, "That would be appreciated. If he doesn't mind."

After taking a shaky breath, Katie spoke softly. She only said a few words, but they were lyrical and flowing, almost like music.

One of the exposed roots in front of Jade grew into a small branch. It kept growing, sprouting leaves and more branches as it went. All around her and Charlie branches were sprouting from the ground, growing up around them and becoming a cage.

A shimmer was flying around them, and where it went, more branches grew. After a few moments, the cage stopped growing and Katie stood triumphant before them, the shimmer settling on her shoulder.

Charlie reached out and grabbed one of the branches. He shook gently at first, then harder. It didn't budge. He tried several spells, but nothing moved the branches. They were in a prison.

Jade beamed at Katie. "A powerful friend indeed. Your gift will be very helpful, Katie. Please give our thanks to your faerie."

The shimmer on Katie's shoulder materialized into a small being, not bigger than a thumb. He wore varying shades of green, which nicely complimented his dark brown lacy wings. His head was the shape of an acorn, and he had two pairs of arms, which were very buglike.

Katie said, "This is Boon. It's good he's revealed himself to you. It means he likes you."

Boon immediately disappeared again, not even a shimmer left behind. Charlie glanced at Jade before saying, "We like him too, but would you ask him to remove the cage, please?" Before he'd even finished speaking, the branches were already shrinking back the way they'd come. "Thank you. Now, as a coven member you are expected to help us, but as Jade said, we are family. We would be happy to help you as well. Is there anything you need help with?"

Katie shook her head.

"Well, perhaps another time." He nodded to Jade.

She looked around the circle. "If any coven member objects to initiating Katie as a full member, speak now."

They waited in silence for several moments. Willow said, "Of course no one objects, child. Do get on with it."

Jade glanced at Charlie, who nodded. "The High Priestess and High Priest are in agreement. Katie, with the blessings of the Lord and Lady, we gladly accept you into the Sugar Hill coven. So mote it be."

Charlie repeated, "So mote it be."

The coven repeated in unison, "So mote it be."

Katie squealed with joy, then immediately restrained herself and gave a timid, "Sorry."

Jade said, "Don't be. It's something to celebrate. In fact, will everyone please gather at the mayor's house. I think it's high time we let the township in on the party."

CHAPTER 2

The township arrived in twos and threes, and soon the mansion was vibrating with the energy of a hundred people celebrating one Witch's inclusion. Jade's heart warmed at the sight. While it was tradition for a newly initiated Witch to be presented to the township in a ceremony at Bonfire Field, Jade thought Katie's shy nature might do better with a more informal, cozy gathering.

Not that the mayor's mansion was cozy. The high ceilings, marble floors, and expansive rooms screamed stately opulence. A gift from Sun City, it was meant to inspire awe in anyone who entered. A statement piece signifying how important the Citizens considered Sugar Hill's mayor. At least, that was the official description. In reality it was just a waste of material. Witches valued their people, not their things, and it was well-known Citizens held no love for Witches, or the figurehead mayors who represented them.

Mrs. Keepsake had sent word through the grapevine to all of Katie's friends and family to meet at the mansion. She'd also delegated setting up refreshments and entertainment so that by the time they arrived, the party was already in full swing. The coven members each gave Katie some small magical gift: a leather pouch from Madame Belle for collecting herbs, a Holy Stone from Daisy for seeing into hidden realms. Katie accepted each with glee. She was still so young. Jade wondered if she was too young to endure the dangers the coven would soon face. Jade was grateful she had Charlie to lean on.

He was there across the room, watching her while Mrs. Keepsake enthusiastically relayed some story to him. He grinned and Jade smiled back. The days they'd spent together immediately after the Ascension had solidified an unfinished bond between them. At times it felt like they were kids again, sharing secrets without a word and sensing each other's presence.

A brief scream and a thud echoed from the dining room. Jade dashed across the hall, stopping just inside the door. She was greeted with laughter, loud and rambunctious. A young man of about twenty was being pulled up off the floor. He held Katie's hands tightly as she helped him up, and as he straightened, they shared a moment of close eye contact before being pulled in opposite directions, as Katie was guided to the next well-wisher.

The young man turned away and waved his hand, and the glowing orbs which had formed a pathway over the dining table disappeared.

Charlie slid his hand in Jade's and whispered in her ear, "Reminds me of when you tried to make a stepping-stone bridge over the creek. We were, what, seven?"

"Eight." She grinned and squeezed his hand, still watching Katie make her rounds through the room. She was laughing, seemingly at ease. Jade gave herself a moment to be glad her decision had worked. If only every choice went this well. "And what do you mean 'tried'? It worked."

"If by 'worked' you mean the stones fell just as I was about to reach the shore, sure, it worked." He winked at her.

She turned toward him. "Well, you were taking your sweet time to cross. If you hadn't been such a scaredy cat, you wouldn't have gotten your feet wet. You could have easily jumped the last gap."

He rolled his eyes at her. "I wasn't a scaredy cat, I was just being cautious. Rightfully so, it turned out."

Jade gazed up at him and mumbled an agreement. He smiled down at her and tucked a strand of hair behind her ear. It was a perfect moment.

A loud boom startled Jade. In the time it took for her to spin away from Charlie, she realized it was a drum beat. Someone had found the wet bar off the family room and started a drinking song. It was only moments before the whole room had joined in. Soon the verse was weaving through the whole house, rattling the windows and walls, the chandelier jiggling to the beat.

Willow and Crystal came up to Jade. "And that's my cue to make a graceful exit."

"Must you?" asked Charlie. "Jade and I were hoping to spend some time with you this evening."

"Child, I can barely hear you above this din. No, let the young ones have their fun tonight. We can discuss your concerns tomorrow." She turned toward Crystal. "Home now, child. I need some rest."

Jade and Charlie watched them leave, then found their way into the living room among the crowd. The fireplace was still ablaze, and the room was getting stifling with so many people. Charlie waved his hand at the flames. "Exstingue." *Extinguish.* The flames shrank and disappeared; soon not even coals remained.

He was persuaded to join the line dance with several other young men, and Jade stood by and watched, clapping in time to the beat, laughing and enjoying herself.

Someone caught Charlie's eye from the other side of the room and he stopped dancing, walking quickly to the edge of the circle as the others continued on without him. Jade stepped forward to follow him, skirting the edge of the circle of dancers. As Jade reached the doorway where Charlie was talking to Mr. Flannerly, the music stopped. Mr. Flannerly finished his sentence, still yelling to be heard in the now quiet room, " — move your ass!" All eyes turned to him. "I wasn't... oh never mind." He waved his hand as if batting them away and made a hasty exit. A wave of laughter flowed over the room.

Jade asked Charlie, "What was that all about?"

"He said there's someone at the door for me."

"But everyone's here. Literally. Well, except Willow and Crystal."

Charlie shrugged then led the way down the hall. "Which is why Mr. Flannerly left him on the front porch and told him not to move his ass." He chuckled and reached for the doorknob. Something stopped him and he removed his hand. He turned to Jade and grabbed her shoulders, gently moving her back a couple feet. "I've got a weird feeling about this. Wait here?"

She was about to argue when an eerie feeling overcame her. Charlie was right. There was something off. She nodded and Charlie turned back toward the door. He opened the door while Jade stood out of sight behind him.

"Good evening, sir. Are you Mr. Charlie Jordan?" The man's voice was deep and smooth, its resonance calming, like a lullaby.

"I might be. Who are you?"

The man's warm voice drifted around Charlie. "My apologies, sir. I forget my manners. My name is Benjamin Caldwell. May I ask you a few questions?"

Jade was intrigued by his sound, inexplicably drawn to it.

"What is this regarding?" Charlie sounded anything but intrigued, his voice harsh.

"You are Sugar Hill's mayor, correct?"

"You didn't answer my question. What is this about?"

Jade felt silly for hiding. He sounded charming, so she stepped to the side. The moment Jade saw him, she felt free of any compulsion. It wasn't magic, it was science. They were all in grave danger.

The man stood slightly taller than Charlie, and broad at the shoulders. His black trench coat reached all the way to the floor, nearly covering his silver-tipped boots. He wore a black leather fedora, which he tapped the brim of as Jade came into view. "Ma'am." He nodded to her.

His left eye looked normal, a pretty light brown shade with flecks of darker brown. But his right eye was unreal. A bright golden glow came from within the pupil and the area surrounding it, which should have been white, was gunmetal gray. The pupil contracted as he focused on her, the spiral in the yellow swirling as it closed. It wasn't his looks, but who he was that sent a shiver up her spine. His clothes were all black, except for the silver belt buckle on his wide leather belt. Its design matched the badge on his collar: a reaper's sickle and gavel, crossed on a shield, surrounded by a ring. A Sun City Lawkeeper.

Jade struggled to keep her breathing normal, but her heart was racing and she felt her skin grow cold. She sent a quick prayer to the Goddess for strength and pulled just slightly on Charlie's energy, leaning on his comforting presence. She stepped forward to stand next to him. There was no use hiding. Better to face it head-on. "Good evening, Lawkeeper Caldwell. With all due respect, you still haven't answered him."

Jade knew better than most what the Lawkeepers were capable of. Each had their own specific implants, this one apparently a visual. "Enhancements" they called them. But one they all shared was IDentity Verification. Whether the IDV was in the form of a fingerprint scanner embedded in their hand or the more obvious iris scanner like this one had depended on how much they wanted to blend in on assignments. Apparently, this Lawkeeper didn't care about being subtle, which meant he was probably one of the higher-ranking and more dangerous officers.

A polite smile crossed his face. "Oh. Miss Jade Cerridwen, am I right? I'm surprised to see you here, but I'm glad you are." His voice dripped with sugary sweetness. The softness in his tone was a stark contrast to his looks. "I'm here for . . . oh, wait." He reached inside his coat. "I believe you lost this." The Lawkeeper extended his hand and opened his palm. In it was a plain black bracelet.

All Citizens were assigned wristbands, simply called Bands, upon entering school. They served many purposes: phone; flash drive; internet connection; but most importantly, geolocation and identification. They could not be removed within the city limits, except at checkpoints or when instructed by a Lawkeeper. In fact, loyal Citizens would never consider taking them off. They were as much a part of them as their wrist or hand. Only criminals even tried to remove them.

They were linked to Sun City's transmit zone, so once outside its range, the Bands automatically unlocked. Jade had taken hers off when she came to Sugar Hill last year in order to stop the internal drive from recording her location. It was currently in the Cerridwen safe, shielded from magic and technology.

By giving her a new Band, and claiming it was hers, he was testing her reaction. He was also, most definitely, trying to track her.

He gave Jade that polite smile again. His lips spreading too wide, showing too many teeth. His eyes stayed rigid, fixated on her, as if watching for any sign of deception.

Jade stared at his hand and the Band that rested there, like bait in a trap. Electroshock, geotagging, and lie detection were only a few of the enhancements that could be hidden under synthetic skin. She reached forward and took the Band as calmly as she could. When nothing happened, she relaxed. "Thank you." If she were a Citizen, she would be expected to immediately put it back on, so she did, managing to keep the cringe she felt at the subtle click internal. "I'm so glad you found it." She kept her eyes on it a moment more, hoping to avoid her lie being read by the Lawkeeper's scanner. "I've been worried sick." She looked up at him. "Is this what brought you to Sugar Hill?"

"No, ma'am. Unfortunately, I have some rather troubling news. You may want to sit down." His brows pinched and mouth curled downward as he looked over her shoulder.

It was only then that Jade realized how quiet it had gotten. Sometime during their conversation, the music had stopped and the party-goers had gathered around them, watching from a short distance.

"Is there somewhere I may speak with you and Mayor Jordan in private?"

Charlie had kept his eyes laser focused on the Lawkeeper. "Please, speak freely," he said, obviously straining to be polite. "Whatever it is, I'm sure we can handle it."

The Lawkeeper opened his mouth to say something, then closed it again. After a sigh, he said, "I'm afraid I can't do that. I have a very strict code of conduct to follow. Please, somewhere private."

Jade cut Charlie off before he could speak. "Of course, Lawkeeper. We will comply. Won't we, Mr. Mayor?"

Charlie glared at her a moment before tilting his head at the Lawkeeper. "Of course. Please, have a seat in the library while I show our guests out." He waved at Aiden and Selene while Jade led the Lawkeeper into the room.

The front wall was framed by two floor-to-ceiling windows, between which was a large, antique, framed map of Sugar Hill Township. It hung over an ornate wood desk and comfortable leather chair. The wall opposite the foyer was covered in books, end to end. Many were ancient tomes, leather bound and dusty. The rest were the various sizes and shapes of modern volumes.

Jade waved the Lawkeeper to the comfortable leather couch directly in front of the bookcase. He placed himself in front of it, then waited until Jade took her seat in one of the two wingback upholstered chairs. Jade fiddled with her Band while they waited in silence for the last members to leave.

Once Charlie had closed the door and joined them, the Lawkeeper continued. "I'm investigating the disappearance of a Sun City Citizen, and am hoping you can help."

There were two people that could be. One was Richard Whetstone, her former boss and father figure. He had literally lost his mind last year when the ritual to bring his daughter back from the dead went horribly wrong. They had taken him to Siobhan Abbey in hopes the mystics could repair his shattered soul. Then Willow had helped Jade and Charlie do some damage control spells so he would not be missed anytime soon. It was more likely the inspector was looking for April.

She had a powerful family. They would have come looking for her sooner or later. Jade had hoped it would be later.

Jade continued to play the dutiful Citizen. "Oh no. That's horrible. Of course we'll be happy to help however we can. Isn't that right, Mr. Mayor?" She glanced at Charlie, hoping he'd get her hint and play nice.

Charlie hesitated only a moment before agreeing. "Of course we will. But we're quite a long way from Sun City. What does this missing person have to do with Sugar Hill?"

"Perhaps nothing, but I must follow all leads. May I ask a few questions?"

He wasn't really asking permission. The Accords gave Lawkeepers the right to search, detain, and question any suspects without warning or consent. But he was being too polite for a Lawkeeper. She needed to seem as close to a model Citizen as possible. She put on her best polite face and hoped it would be enough. "Of course, Lawkeeper. Anything we can do to help." Charlie opened his mouth but Jade cut him off. "Please, ask whatever you'd like."

"Thank you. And it's Inspector."

Jade felt her whole body flush. Inspectors were dangerous. They resorted to methods the lower-ranked Lawkeepers wouldn't dare, because they were immune. Any wrongdoings on their part were explained away or denied outright. They couldn't be touched.

Jade forced her breathing to slow. Quickly plastering a smile on her face, she said, "Oh. We're honored then. This person you're looking for must be quite important for them to send someone of your rank."

"Before we go further, I need to ask, do I have permission to begin my investigation?"

Jade knew it was a formality. If they said no, he'd simply do it anyway. "Yes, of course." She sat tall on the edge of her seat.

He fished into an inside pocket of his coat and took out a small black notebook and pen.

Charlie sneered. "Paper and pen? How quaint. And here I thought Citizens were all about the digital life."

"Charlie," Jade admonished.

"It's quite all right, Miss Cerridwen. It is an odd habit I picked up, but it has helped me catch countless criminals." He smiled pointedly at Charlie. "So I think I'll keep it. Besides, it's only supplementing my 'digital life.'" He tapped the badge on his chest. A shimmer formed at places over both shoulders and his head. Three small jet-black orbs appeared. Noiseless in their flight, the drones hovered motionlessly, one small red dot in the center of each, like the eyeball of some demon.

"What are those?" Charlie asked.

"Recording devices. To make sure I don't miss anything with my quaint methods," Caldwell replied while making notes in the book.

Jade knew they were much more than that, however. Recording video was secondary to their real purpose. "Say hello to Sun City, Mayor Jordan." She waved at them. "You're about to be famous. Isn't that right, Inspector?"

He gave her an odd look. "I suppose. This case has been one of the highest-rated live broadcasts this year so far. Understandably so, considering the victim. Before we begin, I must request Mr. Jordan leave this room. Only one interview at a time. You understand."

"No."

"It's all right, Charlie." It really wasn't, but the last thing she needed was to have him arrested for interfering. "It's Sun City procedure. And besides, I've nothing to hide, so nothing to fear. Isn't that right,

Inspector?" Reciting the familiar motto would be seen as compliance by the Citizens watching. She needed to appear a loyal Citizen. However his investigation turned out, Citizen opinion held a lot of sway.

"Indeed." He smiled at Charlie and waited.

"Fine." Charlie stood and walked around the coffee table. "I'll be in the other room." He glanced at Jade, then retreated into the living room, closing the wooden French doors behind him.

The inspector eyed her silently. It seemed he was weighing his options on how to proceed. He could have been scanning her though. She could now see scars on his forehead and jawline on his right side. There was no telling what other enhancements he had. "I have been sent by Sun City to investigate the disappearance of April Goodrich."

"April's missing?" She had known this day would come. After Richard had killed April and Raven took over her body, Charlie had helped Jade send messages from April's account to say she was taking an extended vacation and not to worry about her. It was a weak plan, but one they'd hoped to find a solution to before anyone started asking questions.

"I'm sorry to have to bring such sad news." His voice and expression seemed kind, but Jade had the distinct feeling he was watching her very carefully. A predator stalking his prey. "Her parents received a message from her saying she would be traveling for a while, but they've not been able to reach her, and her band is offline. These kinds of cases are rare, but they usually don't end well." He paused.

Jade did her best to appear fearful. She brought tears to her eyes, a trick she learned in childhood to get out of trouble. It hadn't always worked.

It seemed to serve her well now though, as the inspector was quick to add, "However, I'm hopeful I can find her, with your cooperation." He glanced at the drone over his shoulder, and a small green circle surrounded the red light on one of the drones. As he continued speaking, it slowly floated closer to her, stopping less than a foot from her face. "If you feel up to answering a few questions now."

"Of course. Anything I can do to help." She took the flutter of nerves in her stomach and tried to pretend it was concern for her friend's welfare. Tried to pretend that she hoped April was fine and back in Sun City.

He looked down at his notes. "You are Miss Goodrich's immediate supervisor, correct?" Jade nodded. "You're also listed as her emergency contact, and yet when her parents listed her missing, you did not respond to the summons. Why not?"

"Well, I didn't have my Band of course. I must have lost it before the summons, or I would have replied. Where did you say you found it?"

"Why didn't you return to Sun City for a new one when you noticed it was missing?"

"I didn't really need it. The Witches here have been taking such good care of me. I figured it would turn up eventually."

He marked in his book. "When was the last time you saw or spoke with Miss Goodrich?"

"Well, she came here with me at the end of October." His eyebrow rose slightly. "But she went back home soon after. I wasn't aware she'd not made it back. Do you have any leads?"

"What was the purpose of your visit?"

This was it. The story they'd come up with last month would be tested. She begged the Goddess it would pass. "Do you mean then, or now?" She cringed inwardly and scolded herself for giving him the idea to question why she was still here.

He stared straight into her eyes. "Let's start with then. When you arrived with Miss Goodrich in October."

"My boss, Mr. Whetstone, has history with this township. October is an important time for Witches and he had planned to visit, but something came up at the last minute and he asked me to come in his place." Easier to hide a partial truth.

"What came up?"

"He didn't tell me, only that he was unable to make it."

"I see." He marked his notebook. "I will ask you a second time, when was the last time you spoke with Miss Goodrich?"

Jade pretended to think about it. "Let's see . . . she stayed for All Hallow's Eve and left the next morning. So, November first."

"Do you have any idea what happened to her?" The gears in his right eye spun, the iris opening wider. The drone dipped slightly, the green ring glowing brighter. Jade knew what that meant. He was reading her reaction: breathing rate, sweat production, skin coloring. He was watching for a lie. He was also trying to intimidate her. Jade had seen both Witches and Citizens confess to crimes under Lawkeeper scrutiny.

She looked him dead in his digital eye. "I have no idea where April is." It was true, sort of. Raven was possessing April's body, but she didn't know where. A flash of April lying dead in her arms, covered in blood, went through her mind.

"And what about now? Why are you still here, in Sugar Hill?" The drone closest to Jade whirred slightly, its lens contracting, focusing on her face.

Jade focused on her intake of breath. Slowly. Calmly. "When I visited last year, I became close with Mayor Jordan. As friends. I decided to take some time off from work and stay in town for a while. There's something about the quiet out here. I sleep much better without all the city noise. Mr. Whetstone said I could take all the time I needed, so I stayed."

"You stayed because of your friendship with a township mayor?"

Jade wasn't sure how to answer. Citizens were never more than casual acquaintances with Witches, at least not publicly. "I'm not sure I like what you're inferring."

He raised one hand in protest. "I meant no disrespect." He leaned forward as if to speak only to her, though the drone over his shoulder moved in unison. "I personally don't care what your relationship with him is. It's just that, well, there are some people who say you're a Witch sympathizer."

"Well, they're wrong."

"Are they?" He waved his hand, and the second drone projected a holographic video in the space next to her. It was Jade, arguing with the cook in a food truck about Witches being charged more.

Jade had to tread lightly. In the eyes of the Lawkeepers, there was a very fine line between being a Witch sympathizer and being an actual Witch. It had been many years since anyone was falsely accused, but that was only because of how careful Witches were within city limits. She waited until the video stopped, then said in her most proper tone, "I know some of my actions may seem controversial. But I assure you, I have no wish for our races to be mingled. Yes, Mayor Jordan and I are friends, of a sort. But that friendship will surely come to an end when I go home to Sun City. My presence here is simply because I thought it would be a good opportunity to learn more about them." She was about to point out that it wasn't illegal for Citizens to stay in townships, just unusual. She stopped herself though and stared calmly at the inspector.

"I see." He wrote something in his notebook again. He looked up at her and was about to speak when there was a brief knock on the front door as it opened.

A woman in a dark blue pinstripe business suit entered swiftly. "My name is Ms. Scrivener. I am Miss

Cerridwen's legal counsel, and I officially request you cease this line of questioning immediately." She dropped her briefcase on the coffee table and stood next to Jade.

The inspector frowned, but did not move. "Citizen law does not allow representation during questioning."

"True, but you are on Witch property at the moment, and as I'm sure you know, the Accords are clear that the location of the accused designates the laws followed. Witch laws require a representative present during any official questioning."

"I see." As he marked in his notebook, he asked, "And what is your connection with or concern for a Citizen? You are a Witch, are you not?"

"Yes, I am. But I have been registered as legal representation in both Sugar Hill and Sun City." She handed him a small piece of paper with gilded edges. "You'll note my credentials are in order, and they allow for the representation of anyone I choose, Witch or Citizen."

She didn't wait for his response as he read. "Now, from my understanding of Citizen law, monitoring of physical reactions to questioning may only be conducted once an accusation has been filed. Am I remembering that correctly, Mr. Caldwell?"

He narrowed his eyes at her. "It's Inspector. I thought we weren't following Citizen law."

"We're not. But since we never monitor physical reactions during questioning, I'm deferring to your laws for this. As I said, an accusation must be filed before physical monitoring may commence, correct?"

"In most cases, yes."

"Most cases? From my understanding, the only case where it is allowed would be during a murder investigation. And so far, you are simply investigating a disappearance. In fact"—she turned to Jade—"Miss

Cerridwen, have you been informed you are being accused of any crime?"

"I . . . I don't believe so. I'm helping with an investigation. Aren't I?" She looked pleadingly at the inspector.

He closed his notebook. "Of course, Miss Cerridwen. I am merely gathering information. No accusation has been filed yet."

"Oh, well then, that certainly changes things." Ms. Scrivener strode to the living room door and opened it. "Mr. Jordan, would you please come here?"

The inspector rose quickly. "Ms. Scrivener—" He glanced at the drones, then toned down his voice. "Ms. Scrivener, this is highly irregular and I request—"

Charlie had entered and Ms. Scrivener turned back toward the inspector. She slowly walked toward him as she spoke. "Mr. Jordan, as Miss Cerridwen's legal representative, I officially request you politely ask Inspector Caldwell to leave Sugar Hill, in accordance with the Citizen/Witch Accords, Article 12, Section B."

Charlie didn't miss a beat. "Inspector, I'm officially requesting you leave Sugar Hill—"

"All right, all right. That's quite enough." The inspector stared down Ms. Scrivener.

"Do you require clarification? I could recite the article and section for you verbatim. Or print out a copy—"

"That won't be necessary. I will, of course, leave the township immediately. However, for the record, I don't appreciate your tone." His drones flew back to their places around him. Tipping his hat to Jade, he said, "Miss Cerridwen, I look forward to speaking with you again at another time."

Jade said, "Yes, that would be lovely. I'm so very sorry I couldn't help more. And I do hope you find her. I don't know what I'd do if she was hurt." She let the tears well up in her eyes, but didn't let them fall. Her concern needed to be palpable, but not too over the top.

He said, "Don't worry, I always close my cases." He turned and let Ms. Scrivener follow him out without another word.

The minute the door closed behind them, Jade stood and began pacing, trying to release some of the fearful energy she'd been holding down. That was close. He may have left, but it definitely wasn't over. They were going to need to come up with a plan as soon as possible.

"What's wrong, Jade? He left."

"And I'm grateful, but unfortunately it's not over. He said he's leaving Sugar Hill, but he didn't say for how long. Inspectors never give up on an investigation, especially one as experienced as this one seemed. I bet when he comes back, he'll be charging me with April's murder. Or at the very least kidnapping." She turned from him and plopped down on the couch, slouching down low, wishing she could fall in and disappear.

"Jade," he said gently as he sat next to her and took her hands, "we knew the spells we cast weren't a permanent solution. We're having to deal with it sooner than we thought, but I think we have time. The inspector can't exactly arrest you if there's no body."

Jade winced at the thought of April being referred to as a body. She still felt so alive sometimes. "Technically he can arrest me at any time, for any reason. But it's worse than that, Charlie. If I'm arrested for murder, it's just me. But if Sun City were to find out Witches can possess Citizens? That would bring about far more than a murder trial." She stood and began pacing again. "You don't know Citizens like I do, living in Sun City for all those years. Most of them are paranoid that Witches are out to get them. If they find out what really happened to April, it could mean war."

He considered this for a moment. "Don't worry, we'll figure something out."

"Like what? We don't have time." She looked down at the Band on her wrist, a lump forming in her throat. It was all such a complicated mess. She thought of how Willow always made everything feel so simple to her. Tonight she couldn't even stay until the end of the party. The strongest Witch in Sugar Hill was now weaker than she.

Just as she started to feel the burn of tears forming, Charlie was there, taking her hands and catching her gaze. "Breathe, Jade. Slowly, in and out."

She focused on his mouth. Closed as he breathed in deep, opened in an "O" as he pushed air out. She mimicked his breath and the fear subsided. She threw her arms around him and spoke into his shoulder, "Thank you." She couldn't imagine Charlie not being there to rescue her.

He rubbed her back as he spoke. "Anytime. Actually, I'm getting hungry. What do you say we go over to your house and have something to eat? Take our minds off it for a bit?"

Jade was sure they didn't have time for something so mundane as food, but the longer she stayed nestled in Charlie's arms, the safer she felt. Maybe they had time for a quick bite.

They drove to Jade's house, and after a light lunch, Jade was feeling marginally better. They'd heard from Ms. Scrivener by then. She'd gotten the inspector to promise, on camera, not to reenter Sugar Hill Township without a Writ of Inquiry. Those took time to get approved because of the intense level of detail required. In other words, she bought them at least a day or two before he could return to continue his interrogation.

Charlie seemed to breathe easier at the news, but Jade wasn't so sure. She'd lived in Sun City most of her life, always worried they'd find out she was a Witch. She knew what they were capable of, especially the inspectors. They were basically the right hands of politicians and men of power, able to twist the law as they saw fit. The live-streams of their investigations were supposed to hold them accountable, but the slight delay before broadcast allowed them to be manipulated before being streamed to the public.

Sunlight glittered off the lake behind her house. The old wooden dock beckoned, have a seat, think it through. But the idea of spending time in one of her favorite spots was tainted by the memory of losing April.

The hair on the back of Jade's neck stood up, and a shiver ran down her spine. She looked around the kitchen. Something wasn't right.

"Jade?" Charlie asked, worry coloring his tone.

"Something . . ." She felt eyes on her, and a dark, cool shadow at the edges of her senses. But she turned again and nothing was there. The same brightly lit kitchen, same island, yellow curtains over the sink. Nothing was out of place.

But she could feel it.

Charlie asked her, "What is it?"

"I don't know." Jade cautiously reached out with her senses. She could tell there was something just beyond, just out of reach. The sunlight sparked on the lake again. She slowly walked out the back door and onto the porch.

A whisper from behind her: "Jade."

She whirled around, bumping into Charlie. "Who's there?"

"Jade, what do you see?" He looked around, holding her shoulders protectively.

Birds chirped, a brief breeze rustled through the bare branched trees and swept fallen leaves across the path. There was no one there.

"Jade."

This time Charlie's head turned in the direction. Just off the porch. Toward the lake.

"You heard it that time, didn't you?"

He raised one finger in a shushing motion, then slowly pointed it outward, toward the dock.

After a moment the whisper echoed from one side of the path to the other. "Jade. Jade. Jade."

Jade's head spun and she reached out for Charlie, steadying herself against his arm. She knew it. Before she recognized the voice, before it said more than her name, she knew who it was.

A cheerful woman's voice greeted her, "Hello, lamby."

CHAPTER 3

April had been Jade's best friend long before Richard had used her body to bring Raven back from the dead. Hearing that voice brought back so many good memories, and at the same time, the heartbreak of losing her best friend.

Jade leaned into the pain and twisted it into the familiar fiery hatred Raven's name always inspired. She pushed away from Charlie and stepped partway down the path. "Where are you? Stop playing games, Raven. Show yourself."

"My little lamb not having fun?" Raven's voice came from directly behind them.

Jade spun, taking a couple of steps back. She felt relief to see Raven didn't look much like her old friend anymore. Her once sunny-blond hair was now jet black and cropped into a short asymmetrical bob. Her features were the same, but her bright blue eyes were warmed to a golden brown. Even her fair skin looked different. The faint freckles were gone, and a deathly pale replaced her once healthy peach glow. She was wearing a long black leather coat over black jeans and what could only be described as a red corset with black lace trim. She looked like April's dark, evil twin.

"What do you want?" Jade demanded. She gathered the hot anger within her, the familiar tingle of static pooling in her palms. She would probably only get one shot. She couldn't let her anger ruin her aim.

"Well, it's been a while since we girls chatted, and I thought I should drop by. You know, say 'Hi. How's it going? What's up?" She eyed Charlie briefly, then smirked at Jade.

He was slowly edging to the side, putting space between him and Jade so Raven couldn't see them both at once.

"That can't be all you want." Jade struggled not to shake as the power focused into a burning energy ball, just outside the visible spectrum. She wouldn't be able to hold herself back much longer, but she wanted to give Charlie time to get into position. With two of them firing from different directions, they'd have a better chance.

"No, but manners matter, don't th—?"

Jade threw the fireball and it burst against a large tree behind Raven, sending bits of flaming wood flying. She hadn't missed, she was certain. It had passed right through Raven, as if she wasn't even there.

"Rude!" Raven stretched her neck, the fringes of her jet-black bob swinging away from her face. She straightened the collar of her jacket. "I had a feeling you might try something like that, and if there's one thing I won't stand for, it's interruptions. Hence the astral form. Now, where were we? Oh yes. We were catching up. How do you like my new do?" She gestured to her hair.

"Are you serious?" Charlie clenched his fists.

Apparently, the Witch's flippant attitude was annoying him as much as Jade. While he talked, she scanned the woods around them, trying to feel how close Raven actually was.

"After everything you've done, you come here talking about fashion? We're not your friends." He glanced at Jade, who shook her head subtly.

Raven's face was like stone, but she seemed to read her mind. She looked down her nose at Jade. "Now, now, lamby. Don't try to ruin our nice chat. I'm somewhere you'll never find me. We'll have plenty of time for you to show off your training later. Let's just all have a civil conversation now, shall we?"

Charlie forced his fists open, and Raven nodded with a smile. "Better. And as a reward, I'll get straight to business. I've come to serve notice. I'm moving in. Not immediately of course, but before the sun returns at Yule, your coven will be mine."

"Over my dead body."

She pouted. "It may come to that, but let's hope not. Oh I have a whole process planned. After all, even I can't just walk into a full coven and say 'I'm here, let's start the party.'" She laughed. "No, it takes planning, torture, blood . . . oh wait, that's murder." She watched Jade closely, as if expecting a reaction.

Jade knew exactly what she was waiting for. The fact that Raven could do so much evil and joke about it infuriated her. She wanted nothing more than to put an end to Raven's existence, but since she was literally untouchable at the moment, Jade needed to focus on keeping her emotions in check. Getting upset wouldn't help anything and would only give Raven what she wanted. "What happened to you?"

Raven looked genuinely surprised. "What happened to me? Oh, you mean what happened to make me so mean and evil. Mwah ha ha ha." Raven took a step closer to her. The snarky smile vanished as she looked her straight in the eye. "My little lamb. You're under the mistaken impression that things happen to us in our lives, and we change because of them. Right? Cause . . . effect. What you don't understand is, it's all an illusion. Nobody and nothing ever makes you do anything." She stepped back and looked Charlie up and down. "Everything from what socks you put on in the morning to who you kill in the afternoon. You may not like your options, but it's always a choice. You choose who you are."

Jade clenched her fists, and Raven made note of it. "Hm, still struggling with that self-control I see. Here, let me help with that."

She flicked one finger toward her, and a moment later Jade couldn't move her arms. From the shoulders down, they felt like they'd fallen asleep. Jade's heart pounded in her chest. She strained to look over at Charlie. A Witch shouldn't be able to cast in astral form. Raven was more dangerous than they'd thought.

"We're not so different, you and I," Raven continued casually as Charlie raced to Jade's side. "Well, except I don't go running away from my problems like a little girl. But other than that, we both have power we haven't even tapped into yet. We both had our loved ones die on us."

"Yeah, but you killed mine. I had nothing to do with whoever you lost."

"That's not the point. The point is we've both suffered. The difference is that I'm doing something about it, and you're . . . well, you're trying, I'll give you that. You came back and your boyfriend here is teaching you what he knows. Of course, I know much more than him." She slinked up to him, and he stepped between her and Jade. A futile effort, but Jade's heart warmed at his quick protection of her.

Raven stood there, silent for once, and looked him over, head tilted to one side. After a moment her smile faded, replaced by a furrowed brow.

Charlie sneered at her. "What's the matter, Raven? Something not to your liking?"

She looked him in the eye and leaned close, her nose almost touching his. She closed her eyes, taking a deep breath. Suddenly, she backed up. "You know, I'm being quite rude. I believe you two kids were having a lovely moment together and I've interrupted." She walked back toward the edge of the path and waved her hand toward them.

Jade nearly fell forward, released from the spell. Charlie held her hand a moment and looked carefully into her eyes and whispered, "You okay?"

Jade nodded and stood tall next to him. She was shaking inside, but refused to let Raven see that. They watched as she drifted farther down the path.

"Besides, I have things to do, and you have people to see." She stopped and looked back. "Don't worry, we'll meet again soon." And then she was gone.

Jade reached out and grabbed Charlie's arm, partly to steady herself and partly to convince herself he was all right. "What the hell was that about? She cast at me? Have you ever heard of a Witch casting in astral form?"

"No, but Sophia said she was powerful. We should talk to her."

As they walked back into the house, Jade thought out loud. "We also need to gather the coven and work on a protection spell for the township—"

"And for you," he interjected.

"We can't wait around anymore, we have to find out where she's hiding. She couldn't be far to just appear like that. And what was with her sniffing you?"

Charlie held the door for her as she went into the kitchen. "No idea. Maybe she didn't like my cologne."

Jade appreciated his attempt at humor, but she could only shake her head at him. Raven was strange, to say the least, but the way she backed off so suddenly made her think there was something more to it than that.

Charlie crossed the kitchen floor to the space of wall between the hallway and the living room door. The wide planked doorframe was more than just a slab of rich brown wood. This was living wood, shaped by magic to be a useful part of the house. Its bottom edge extended below the floorboards, right down into the earth below. There, it became roots. And where there are roots, there is the mycelium network.

He waved his hand over a knot in the wood and said, "Surgere." Wake.

The wood doorframe began to hum. The knot in the wood shifted and stretched. It was a jerky motion, like watching a sped-up video of a seedling growing into a plant. A golden light spilled through the growing hole. A glowing amber sphere pushed through it, thin white filaments cradling it.

Charlie said, "Sophia," then turned back to Jade while he waited for the network to locate her and inform her of his call. "I agree we need to deal with Raven, but first priority should be protecting you."

Sophia's voice came from behind him. "Charlie? Is that you?" There was an odd vibration to her tone, as if her voice was sent through a filter of tinfoil and raindrops.

The orb had stretched out farther from the wood, curly black filaments woven through the white. Together they held the sphere at Charlie's head height. The sphere flickered brighter with each word spoken.

"Yes, and Jade's here too. We had a run-in with Raven just now, and we need your input."

They filled her in on everything, and she agreed to come over without hesitation.

The orb dimmed, and the black threads shrank back, signifying she'd disconnected on her end. Charlie waved his hand, and the orb retreated back into the knot, which closed up. Once again just another beautiful piece of the house's trim work.

While they waited, Charlie insisted on casting a circle of protection around the house. Jade tried to pass the time calmly by making some green tea. The familiar process of filling the kettle, retrieving the mugs, and waiting for the water to boil settled her. But then she had nothing to do but watch the bubbles form, and her mind began to spin.

Raven had mentioned Charlie teaching her, casually, as if she knew they were training. Jade wondered if that was a guess or if she'd been spying on them. If she was watching, she probably already knew about the inspector. But if so, why not show herself then and let Jade be arrested? Yule was less than a month away. The coven would raise a lot of power during the Holy-day ritual. Is that what she really wanted, to steal the coven's power?

Round and round the negative thoughts spun through her brain. She tried to counter each one with a positive thought, but it was getting harder as time when on. Finally, there was a knock at the door, and she raced to open it.

The moment she saw Sophia on her doorstep, she fell into her arms, hugging her tightly.

"Are you all right, dear?"

Jade reluctantly pulled away. The hug was a welcome respite, but there'd be time to deal with her emotions later. Right now she needed a plan. She dodged Sophia's concerned gaze and motioned into the house. "I'm fine. Thanks so much for coming. Charlie will be back in a minute."

Sophia led the way into the kitchen. Jade followed a few steps behind, breathing deep, trying to release the tension. She entered to find Charlie already there, putting the last of the spell ingredients away in the cupboard.

"I just finished the protection spell. We should be safe for now." He turned as Sophia reached the kitchen table.

"I've been thinking on the way over here, and I might have a solution. Covens are very self-sufficient. We have our own laws and justice system, we train ourselves using the ancient tomes passed down through the generations, we take care of our own. However, there is a place of higher learning. A place where the laws that we follow were first developed. This place is dedicated to the Goddess, and their connection to Her is even closer than that of a coven."

"You're talking about the abbey, right?" Charlie said. "That's where you and Crystal took Richard, to see if they could heal his mind."

"Yes. The abbey is more than just a place of healing. They are protectors of the entire region. It's possible, not likely mind you, but possible they can help. Of course, it will ultimately be up to Mother Abbess. We must first petition her for an audience. If she accepts, we can plead our case."

"I guess it's worth a try." Jade hated bringing in outsiders, but at least they were Witches. She'd share her failures with anyone if it meant putting a stop to Raven and protecting her township from Sun City's lawkeepers.

CHAPTER 4

Jade stood next to Sophia in the backyard, waiting patiently while the elder Witch cast a scrying fire. Charlie looked on from the porch. Sophia had insisted only she and Jade speak with the abbess. The afternoon sun's rays sparkled off the pond in the distance, competing with the yellow of the fire's flames.

The heat from the flames wasn't enough to burn, but Jade still felt the urge to step back. A vague sense of foreboding curled in her stomach. "Why don't we just call them?" She asked.

Sophia finished casting the scrying spell. The magic combined with the physical fire turned the flames gold and blue. "Because they always use scrying to communicate. I think they are able to read people better if they can see them. Now remember, let me do the talking. Unless she asks you a direct question, of course."

The fire flashed gold and the flames diminished, settling into a small ring of mini flames no more than a couple of inches tall. The space above them began to shimmer, like the air over pavement on a hot summer day. A face came into focus. A beautiful woman with naturally long lashes and full lips. She wore a cloak of thin beige linen, and the hood hid most of her hair. A couple of long blonde tendrils escaped over her collarbone.

"Sophia," her voice was soft, almost a whisper, "it's lovely to see you again. To what do I owe this pleasure?"

"Nice to see you too, Abbess Beatrix. I was hoping to speak with Mother. We have a dangerous situation here that could use her wisdom and support."

"I'm sorry, she's in seclusion for the next three days. Perhaps I can help?"

Sophia explained what had been going on, the Lawkeeper and the dark Witch. The abbess's face slowly became more serious as the story went on. When Sophia mentioned Raven had cast at Jade and Charlie while in astral form, the abbess simply raised an eyebrow.

"We are aware of the Lawkeeper's investigation. As long as he follows the Accords, there is nothing we can do to impede him. As for Raven, you were right to contact us. When she was young, we kept a close eye on her. She was always one of those Witches who rode the edge between dark and light. It's a shame she ultimately chose the path she did." After considering a moment, she continued. "Unfortunately, we are unable to interfere at this time."

Jade couldn't help herself. She leaned in next to Sophia. "What? You just said we were right to contact you." Sophia tried to gently push her back, but Jade held her ground. "No, I'm a High Priestess. I deserve an answer. Raven was able to cast while in astral form, something no Witch should be able to do. Don't you think that's a problem?"

The abbess looked calmly at Jade. "You heard me correctly. You were right to tell us about Raven. We need to be aware of possible threats, especially one as strong as her."

"Why, so you can watch her destroy us? Have a front row seat?" Jade's face flushed hot.

"We are unable to interfere because it is not our place. Just as each Witch is responsible for their own actions, each coven is responsible for their own Witches. As High Priestess, you do not punish Witches in your coven unless their actions negatively affect others who are unable to protect themselves. So too, we are only allowed to punish Raven if her power proves too much for you to protect against. So far, you have done a good job keeping her harmless."

"Harmless?" Jade felt she could dive right through the scrying fire and throttle this woman. Sophia placed a hand on Jade's arm. A calming warmth flowed through her. Jade took a breath and reminded herself of what Sophia had told them. The abbey was only concerned with Witches, and April and Richard were both born Citizens.

Sophia said, "May I ask a question?"

"Of course."

"You're keeping Richard Whetstone there for his own health and safety, correct?"

Jade was surprised she had brought it up. Apparently, so was the abbess. She hesitated a moment, then said with squinted eyes, "Why do you ask?"

"Because that shows your responsibility to help extends beyond Witches. You also give aid to Citizens, if their harm comes from a Witch."

"What are you getting at? Speak plainly."

"April Goodrich was a Citizen who was murdered as a direct result of Raven's manipulation of Richard.

Isn't that causing harm? Shouldn't she be held accountable for that?"

"Yes. And we have an entire legal system that prescribes exactly how to hold Witches accountable. So far, you and your coven have been more concerned with what she might do in the future. Maybe you should focus a little more on what your current responsibilities are. Have you had a trial yet? Do you even know what you would charge her with? Have you notified her of her rights?"

Jade struggled to keep her anger in check. She forced her hands to her sides and kept her voice low, but she couldn't keep her tone civil. "Raven is a manipulative, murdering bitch. She lost her rights when she killed my parents, aunt, and best friend." Jade slowed her breathing and used the positive talk Sophia had taught her to regain control of her thoughts. They needed the abbey on her side. She took a deep, cleansing breath and tried to think how she could convince the abbess that they truly needed their help.

"Abbess, please forgive me. My friend's death is still fresh and . . . and I'm not really sure if I'll ever get over her loss." Her voice warbled on the last word and her eyes warmed. Jade told herself she would not cry.

"Of course you won't ever get over it," the Abbess' voice was gentle, "My dear, the ones we love stay with us our whole lives. When we're frightened, but we find the strength to push through our fear, they're walking beside us. When we accomplish our goals, they're celebrating with us. As time goes by, we think of them less frequently, but out of mind isn't out of heart. There will always be times when you ache for them, but the pain will lessen over time. Faster if you accept it."

The pain of missing April mixed with anger, and her voice shook with power as she said, "It might be easier to accept if the person who caused her death were held accountable." The abbess's eyes widened for a moment. Jade took a deep breath and reined in her emotions. She needed to save her fury for Raven. "My coven will do its duty. I will call for a trial to judge her. But in order for her to defend herself, she must appear at the trial. How do you suggest we make that happen when she's in hiding and threatening to kill me and take over the coven?"

The abbess paused a moment. "I see your point, but our laws are clear. Until you have done everything in your power, we will not interfere. Merry meet."

Sophia said, "Merry meet."

The abbess's face disappeared, and the flames returned to normal. Sophia waved a hand over the weak flames and they blew out, leaving a small ring of black on the flagstone pathway.

She turned to Jade and pulled her into a tight hug. "My dear one, I know you're frustrated. I can feel your anger is bubbling inside you, ready to vent at the world." She pushed her away and looked into her eyes. "But have faith. They would not have said no if they didn't believe that we could handle it ourselves."

They turned and walked toward the back porch.

"And how exactly are we going to handle it? I'm supposed to hold a trial and inform Raven of her rights? Are they kidding? She's lurking in the shadows somewhere, able to cast magic while in astral form. That means she can get to me no matter where I am. And let's not forget Inspector Caldwell. He's gonna come back, and when he does, he could arrest me for anything he wants."

Charlie had come down from the porch and took her hand. "Jade, it's okay."

"No, it's not. You don't know lawkeepers like I do." The hint of panic breezed past her. Jade squeezed Charlie's hand, focusing on his presence. Her breathing slowed and she looked up at him. "What am I going to do?"

Sophia took her other hand gently. "You're going to stop trying to do everything on your own and lean on your coven. You are powerful, Jade, but calling on your coven expands your power tenfold. Let's call a meeting and talk it over with them. They deserve to know what's happening, and I'm certain that together we can figure out what to do."

Charlie nodded. "She's right, Jade. You're not alone." Jade smiled and he gave her hand one last squeeze. "Maybe you could help Sophia set up the chairs while I call everyone?"

"What, here? Why not go to the mayor's residence?"

"That's probably the first place the inspector will look. One of the few things we were able to get in the Accords in our favor was sealing coven members' records. Even if he looks specifically for it, he won't see the Cerridwen name on any Sugar Hill records, so he won't know this is your house. Combine that with the protection spell I cast and this is the safest place for you to be. At least for now."

"Okay, but I also need to do something about this." She lifted her left arm and pointed out the Band on her wrist. "It has GPS tracking. Unfortunately, I can't risk removing it. It's required to be worn by all Citizens, so if he happens to see me without it, it'll raise suspicions."

Sophia squinted at it for a moment, then waved her hands over it. "Interesting. I know a cloaking spell that should work, at least temporarily. He'd still know the signal was lost, but at least he wouldn't be able to track you."

She pulled a small vial of water from inside her cloak. She uncorked it, and as she mumbled something Jade couldn't make out, she slowly poured it over the Band on Jade's wrist. It was as cold as Jade expected, but there was something wrong about the texture. It seemed to move slower when it touched her skin. It felt like velvet, or satin. Incredibly soft and smooth.

Sophia muttered an incantation as the liquid seemed to soak into Jade's wrist and the Band itself. "There. That should cloak you for several days." She whispered, "I used to know a Witch who fought in the resistance." She raised a finger to her lips and winked at her.

Charlie went inside to call the coven members and Jade and Sophia followed him to set up chairs in the study.

CHAPTER 5

Jade's mind kept going back to Inspector Caldwell. As a Witch living illegally in Sun City, she had studied lawkeeper procedure closely. She knew they often used stealth drones to gather information when a physical presence was impossible or would draw too much attention.

Charlie entered from the kitchen. "They're on their way."

"Charlie, I was thinking. It's likely the inspector tried to leave a stealth drone in the township. Do you think the protection spell you cast will work against drones?"

"Well, technology is as susceptible to magic as anything else, but my intention was to protect you against Raven. Intention matters." He thought a moment. "I can recast it easily enough. Give me a few minutes."

Charlie went back out the back door to perform the spell. While he was gone, coven members began arriving and Jade met them on the front porch. Katie entered first with Mrs. Keepsake. Crystal and Willow were right behind them.

Crystal gave Jade a bittersweet smile. "Merry meet, Jade. Where's Charlie?"

"Merry meet. He's casting a privacy spell. Long story, but we'll explain once the meeting starts." Jade reached out and clasped Willow's outstretched hand. "Merry meet, Grandma Willow," she said, slightly louder than she'd intended.

Willow lifted her head. "Child, I am blind, not deaf. I thank you both to stop fretting over me." She sounded angrier than Jade could ever remember, her voice harsh and rough. She shrugged out of their grasp, wavering slightly before straightening up, head held high. "We have bigger things to worry about than me bumping into things." She spun her hands in a circle in front of her, then motioned as if tying a knot.

Crystal said, "Save your..."

Willow whispered low, but it immediately silenced her. "If you tell me to save my strength one more time." She paused a moment, then shuffled forward with her hand outstretched in a fist, as if holding a cane. As she approached the doorstep, Jade was relieved to see her step over it easily, as if she'd seen it. She continued slowly into the house, finding her way through the study on the right.

As Crystal passed her, Jade put her hand out, grabbing her arm gently. "How are you? Ready for Sophia to take over yet?"

Crystal chuckled. "I'm fine." She looked where Willow had gone, watching her with concern. "She has been snapping at me lately, but I think she's frustrated she's not back to her full power yet. I keep telling her she needs to take it slow and refrain from casting to build back her strength, but you know how stubborn Grandma Willow is. Don't worry about me though. I can assist as long as you need." She smiled broadly. "I'm just glad she's still here with us."

Jade nodded. "Me too." She couldn't help but feel a twinge of guilt.

Charlie came back inside. "All done. No worries about drones, at least for now." He touched her arm briefly, then turned and helped her welcome the rest of the coven.

Madame Belle entered and immediately was greeted by Sophia. Full of excited energy, she began telling Belle about a new spell she was developing. Mr. Flannerly followed at a distance, with Aiden and Selene behind him, arm in arm, as always. Last, but not least, Daisy snuck by. Jade almost didn't notice until she felt the wisp of her presence float past.

They were still missing one. Jade looked out across the handful of cars parked in front of the house. People usually rode their bikes to get around, but for coven meetings, they enjoyed the comradery of commuting together. She realized Ms. Scrivener was probably following the lawkeeper all the way to the township limit, just to make sure he complied. Jade sent her gratitude for the mayor's liaison and turned back into the house.

There was an official library at the front left side of the house, but the large room to the right of the front door was better stocked. Dark wood shelving ran from floor to ceiling and wall to wall. Many of the books were uniform in size and color, legal texts and bound contracts relating to the history and relationship between Sun City and Sugar Hill. Jade's father had been fascinated by history, and it showed in the variety of his collection. There were several shelves of older books, mostly cloth or leather bound and varying from thin journals to inches-thick tomes.

Charlie turned from the large chest on the windowsill and placed the most important book of all in the center of the desk: the Sugar Hill Book of Shadows. The sacred book was usually kept in the house safe, but Charlie had brought it out earlier in preparation for this meeting. The last of the sun's rays streamed through the window, bathing it in a warm glow. Jade took her place next to Charlie and held the thick tome on its spine. She closed her eyes for a moment to focus on what she needed. As she placed her hands on either side of the desk, the book slowly fell open, the pages fluttering and stopping on the exact ones she needed. Jade stood facing the book and her coven.

By the time everyone had found a seat, Mrs. Keepsake and Katie were entering from the kitchen, carrying trays of juice and shortbread cookies, holding them for each member to take their share.

Once everyone had their serving and was in their seat, Jade cleared her throat and said, "I call this meeting to order. Merry meet."

The coven members responded, "Merry part." And everyone finished, "Merry meet again." They all toasted with their juice.

Jade said, "First, I would like to officially welcome our newest coven member, Katie."

Gentle applause swept the room as every coven member honored her with smiles and nods.

"Our coven has many powerful Witches, with a wide variety of gifts. Each one of you lends something valuable, but I'm especially pleased to have gained, for the first time in our history, a Marrow. You demonstrated this ability well, Katie, and I'm looking forward to getting to know our local faeries through you.

"I'd like to thank you all for your patience. I'm sure seeing a lawkeeper show up to Katie's initiation party was troubling, to say the least. Instead of bombarding me or Charlie with questions, you've waited for us to tell you what's going on. We thank you for your patience.

"Unfortunately, the news is not good. What we feared happening has come to pass. Inspector Caldwell is investigating the disappearance of April Goodrich."

Jade immediately felt the wave of uncertainty as the coven members spoke to each other in hushed voices. She let it wash over her.

After a moment she raised her hand. "I know we said the spells we cast last month would keep us safe, but the inspector on the case is different. Somehow he's found his way here, and we need to be very careful. For one thing, he can't know that I'm High Priestess. As far as he knows, I was born and raised in Sun City. To him, I'm a Citizen."

Flannerly spoke up. "That's gonna be tricky, considering you're our High Priestess."

Katie asked quietly, "Right? What if someone in town needs your help?"

Murmurs floated around the room. Jade waited patiently for them to quiet down, head held high, sending calming energy. "He already thinks of me as a Witch sympathizer. My actions before I left Sun City confirmed that for him. So, we'll lean into that. I'm here to learn all I can about Witches. That explains Charlie inviting me to meetings and such. As far as my High Priestess duties go, I'm afraid you'll have to make do. You have before, I'm sure you'll be able to again. Luckily, the next holy day isn't for three weeks. We should have this all settled before we need both coven leaders for the Imbolc ritual." Hopefully, she thought.

Flannerly said, "That's all well and good, but what about when he comes knocking on our doors? You said he's investigating. Are we just gonna hope he doesn't find anything incriminating and goes away? What if he decides to fabricate evidence? I've heard those Sun City lawkeepers will do that when an investigation of theirs stalls." He crossed his arms and glowered at her.

"Mr. Flannerly, I can assure you, they don't fabricate evidence. You bring up a good point though. While Ms. Scrivener was able to persuade him to leave town, I'm sure it is temporary and I wouldn't be surprised if he tries to question others when he returns." She looked to Charlie. She was trying to keep a calm, confident appearance, but it was starting to slip.

"That's not a problem," he said. "Any questions the inspector has for the townsfolk can be redirected to me. All they have to do is state that the Accords specify the mayor is the first point of contact for any investigation within township limits."

This seemed to put them at ease. Another example of the closeness the coven members felt with Charlie. They trusted him.

Jade decided to use this lull in tension to her advantage. "There is one more thing. While we were walking back from the chapel this evening, Raven appeared. She was in astral form. We're guessing she's probably still weak from possessing April's body and didn't want to risk facing us in person. She did threaten us though. She said that before Yule she will claim the coven as her own." Jade felt a chill as she remembered how easily Raven had cast while in astral form. She almost told them, but then thought it might be better to wait until they had some kind of explanation or plan. No sense adding fear to the fire. At least, not until she understood the full ramifications. She waited for Charlie or Sophia to mention it, but they remained silent, watching the group.

Madame Belle, a tall older woman with white hair pinned up in a wreath around her head, chuckled. "Impossible." She scoffed, her French accent thick. "One cannot simply claim a coven."

Willow said, "That is usually true, but Jade is the last of her matriarchal line. If she were to die, any Witch may lay claim to the role of High Priestess. Of course, without the consent of every coven member, that claim can be rejected, but it does show how far she is willing to go if she's threatening Jade's life."

Charlie said, "Right. Which means two things. First, we need to perform a personal protection spell on Jade. Second, we need to make sure Raven and the inspector never cross paths. That means we need to locate her."

"And once we find her, then what? Ask her nicely to please not take over our coven?" Mr. Flannerly's sarcastic, gravelly voice grated on Jade's nerves.

She reminded herself that he was struggling and was understandably on edge. She knew her answer would be the exact opposite of a calming influence, but she felt she had to say it. Raven was the direct cause of her best friend's death. There was no forgiving that. It was time she let everyone know how she really felt so they could get behind her.

"We hunt Raven down and kill her."

Before she could say more, Charlie said, "With all due respect to our High Priestess, I disagree. That won't solve our inspector problem. He needs to find April alive and well. Finding a dead body means he continues his investigation until he finds who killed her and brings them to justice."

Jade couldn't believe her ears. Charlie was openly contradicting her. She stared at him, but he avoided her gaze.

Crystal drew her attention. "Could we spell the inspector into thinking that he found April, and she's safe but doesn't want to come home?"

Jade said, "That could work, but I know her parents well. They are distrusting and powerful, used to getting their own way. They'd want to speak to April themselves and try to persuade her to come home."

Selene suggested, "What if we find Raven and capture her, exorcise her out of April's body, and leave her body somewhere for the inspector to find?"

Jade's stomach turned at the thought. April deserved better than having her body left rotting in the woods somewhere, waiting to be found by a lawkeeper.

Crystal shook her head. "I bet it'd be even more difficult to capture Raven than kill her."

Jade said, "True. She seems to make it a point of avoiding capture at all costs. Also, we're left with the same problem as with killing her. The inspector will not stop until he dispenses justice, which means either finding April alive and well or finding whoever killed her."

Katie asked, "Could we enchant Raven into acting like April? Just long enough to fool the inspector and April's parents? Make her tell them she's moving somewhere far away. That would solve all our problems, wouldn't it?"

Jade was impressed by her ambitious thinking. "If we could accomplish it. It's a big if though. Enchantments are difficult spells, and Raven's magic is very strong."

"Not stronger than divine magic though, right? I mean, she's just one Witch against the whole coven channeling divine magic. Sounds like the odds would be on our side." Katie smiled sweetly.

Jade hated bursting her bubble, but it was necessary. They all needed to be clear how dangerous Raven was, not just to their own coven, but to the lopsided peace between Witches and Citizens. "Probably, but we need something foolproof. The enchantment would need to last a couple days at least. If anything goes wrong, Raven could break out of the spell and ruin everything. If Citizens found out a Witch possessed one of their own, not only would that shatter the Accords, but it would undoubtedly terrify them to the point of war."

Charlie said, "I don't think there's any such thing as foolproof when it comes to solving this crisis." He stood and began giving out orders. "We'll just have to do everything we can and pray to the Goddess it's enough. Katie, talk to your faeries and tell them it's imperative we find Raven. As soon as she's found, we'll meet and discuss strategy then. Crystal, gather whatever items you need for an enchantment spell in case we need it. Aiden, see if you can track the inspector and his drones."

Jade stood and tried to sound as confident as possible. "Everyone else make sure the townsfolk know not to talk to the inspector, and cast eavesdropping protection spells on all their homes and the businesses in town. Once you've finished, cast warning spells along the border. If Raven comes anywhere close to Sugar Hill, or the inspector, we need to know as soon as possible."

Charlie nodded. "Good idea. Since Ms. Scrivener's most familiar with lawkeeper procedure, when she returns, Jade and I will work with her on a spell to convince him his case is closed, as a last resort. The most important thing is that so far he has no idea what really happened to April. We need to keep it that way for as long as possible."

They wrapped up the meeting. Sophia agreed to stay and help Charlie cast a protection spell on Jade. Willow would usually do it, but she was looking pretty tired and excused herself, letting Crystal guide her out.

Jade stood next to Charlie as they said goodbye to each coven member as they left. He was good at that. She told herself it was because he'd spent more time with them, years when she wasn't there to help. But it was more than that. He had a gift. It was more than just charm or some magical power. Charlie was outgoing in a way that didn't push, didn't force others to interact with him. He was available. He was safe.

As the last member left and Charlie shut the door, Jade noticed Katie was standing by the fireplace, talking with Sophia in hushed tones. She glanced at Charlie and they both walked over to her. "Katie? Are you okay?"

The young Witch looked to Sophia. "Go ahead, dear," Sophia said.

After another moment of hesitation, she blurted out, "I think I know one place Raven might be."

Charlie asked, "Why didn't you say so during the meeting?"

Jade put a hand on his arm. "What matters is she's telling us now." Her actions during the initiation and the meeting told Jade that Katie was in a fragile transition. Jade could feel her energy shrinking and growing, wavering from confident to shy, as if she were arguing with herself. What she needed now was support and gentle guidance. Heavy-handed training could come later, if needed. "Any information you could give would be really helpful."

Katie met her eyes and straightened a bit. "You said you were near the chapel when you had your vision?" Jade nodded. "Sophia said there's a pretty powerful ley line that runs under the chapel, and it got me thinking: ley lines are mostly used for portaling and boosting power. What if she used them to astral project from a great distance? You said she's always finding a way to escape. What if she used the ley line's power to boost her own and astral project from somewhere you couldn't reach her easily?"

"That would be smart. And that gave you an idea where she might be now?"

"Maybe. Do you have a map of the town?"

Charlie pointed at the wall to her side, where the Township map hung.

Katie giggled through a grimace. "Oh." She slunk over to it and examined it for a moment. Glancing at Jade, she asked, "May I try something?"

When Jade nodded, she turned back to it and waved her hands over it in overlapping lines, top to bottom. Thin lines began to appear as if the paper was being lit on fire. They started at the chapel and spread southward through town. Each line branched, merged, and connected to other ley lines, some brighter than others. Soon the whole town was covered in a faintly glowing spiderweb.

Katie asked, "Do you happen to have a small crystal on you, one that was on your person when you saw Raven?"

Jade pulled one of her necklaces over her head and handed it to her. The small crystal pendant was mostly clear, but tiny fractures crisscrossed through it, giving it a frosted appearance at first glance.

Katie held it in her hands for a moment. "Perfect," she said, examining it closely. "Crystals are natural attractors of magical energy. And clear ones, like this, are great at catching dark energy." She closed her eyes and muttered something, then placed it gently over the map between the chapel and mayor's residence. As she slowly withdrew her hand, the chain dropped toward the floor, but the crystal remained, hovering in place against the map. After a moment it began to slide haltingly down the map. Katie remained close, keeping her hands nearby. The crystal continued in starts and stops, slowly following the ley lines. It turned east at one junction and stopped at the very edge of the map before free-falling. Katie reached out and caught it.

"Great," Jade said, disappointed. "She's out of town. Now what, larger map?"

Katie handed her necklace back. "No, this is good. It's exactly what I expected. The haunted mansion is that direction."

Jade looked at her, wide-eyed. "Haunted mansion?"

Charlie said, "I know the one you mean. There's an old mansion just outside the township limits. It's been abandoned since the North Devonshire battle, but every once in a while, you hear of some teenagers going out there on a dare and returning with stories of ghosts and demons. The coven discussed smudging the property once, but it was decided that it was too much land to bother with since none of the spirits had ever hurt anyone."

Jade was shocked. "You're saying there are possibly trapped spirits just outside our borders, and we are just going to leave them there to suffer?"

Sophia said, "You have to understand. After the battle, everyone was wounded in more ways than one. Even those who didn't fight were besieged with horrible nightmares for months. All anyone wanted to do was forget that place. It wasn't a decision we took lightly. We discussed it over many coven meetings, then we voted. Your aunt was the deciding vote. Her viewpoint was that if they were troubled by their position, they would be sending distress signals we would have experienced. Some spirits just want to be left alone."

"You don't think 'horrible nightmares for months' sounds a little like a ghostly distress signal?" Jade sighed and tried to calm herself. "I know what being wounded by a loved one's death is like." Her voice shook, and she took another deep breath. She still felt tense, but she needed to make them understand how serious she took this. The dead deserved peace.

"I spent over a decade trying to forget the image of my parents' burned bodies in my burned house. The problem is that kind of pain doesn't just go away on its own. You have to face it and deal with it." Jade could feel the anger and frustration burning within her. She reminded herself none of this was Katie's fault. "It's a tragedy what happened, and the fact that we've avoided dealing with it all these years is unacceptable." She began to feel more grounded, and her voice returned to its normal tone. "When this is over, we will take care of them at the first opportunity. Right now, we need to focus on the problems at hand."

She turned toward the map. "So, if Raven is there, why? Why not leave the area completely, or just attack? Why hide out there?"

Sophia said, "Maybe she's tapping into the residue of the magic used in the battle. That kind of power wouldn't dissipate easily. It would be stuck to the ground, trees, and building like sap."

Charlie said, "It would be a great place to recover from our fight last month and settle into April's body. There'd be lots of dark energy for her to draw from."

Jade turned to Katie. "You said you expected the spell would lead to the mansion. Why is that?"

"Well. A few years ago, I went there with some friends." She looked down.

Sophia told her, "Don't be shy now, Katie. We need your help, not your embarrassment. Head up." She gave her a smile.

Katie looked up, and seemed to gain confidence. "It was a stupid, childish dare, but I learned a lot about the grounds. I wouldn't go in the main house, but the challenge was just to remain on the property overnight. I explored a lot of the smaller buildings, and when I came to the west side of the property, I was going to keep walking, but something stopped me. I looked back and was drawn to what looked like a big boulder with a tree stump growing around it."

"That's not what it really was?" Jade asked.

"Nope. Well, I guess on the surface it was, but there was a small hole formed by the roots and rock near the ground. I was curious, so I sent one of my faeries in and she told me it was safe. I crawled in and it opened up into a study. At least it looked like a study. There were bookshelves and herbs in jars."

Charlie said, "I bet that's where Mr. Witherby hid during the Last Crusade. After I became High Priest, I studied a lot of the history of the area. Mr. Witherby owned the mansion for a short time around then, and there were rumors that he survived by hiding somewhere on the property."

Katie said, "I looked around and found a tunnel leading east. It must have gone straight to the main house, but I was too afraid to look any farther. My faerie said there were dark spirits about. I can deal with any faerie in existence, but spirits?" She shuddered. "Even the good ones freak me out."

"That's a good start, but we need more than that."

"No, I know. I mean, if any of us try to go see if she's there, she might find us. Even with a cloaking spell, if she's as powerful as everyone says, it's risky, right?"

"Yes . . ."

"But faeries are around us all the time and we never even know. Well, most of us don't." She smiled proudly. "Faeries could explore the entire property, and Raven wouldn't have a clue they were there."

Jade said, "They would do that for us?"

"Of course. They're pretty neutral when it comes to light or dark magic, but they've gotten used to the way this coven is and don't want to see Raven turn it dark any more than we do. What do you need them to find out? Besides if Raven's there, I mean."

Jade said, "Everything. They can sense magic, right?" At Katie's enthusiastic nod, she continued. "Then have them look for any magical traps, or warning spells. Whatever they can tell us about any spells on the property. Also the building. I doubt we'll be able to find any blueprints since it's in North Devonshire's territory, so whatever they can tell us about the layout would be great. Raven has had months to explore that place. If she really is there, like you say, we need to be as familiar with the place as possible."

"I'm sure they can help. I guess I should get going," she said cheerfully and picked up her cloak. Sophia walked her the short way to the door.

Finding Raven was only half the problem. In a fair fight they would have a chance, but Raven could do something no other Witch could. Neither Sophia or the Abbess seemed too concerned about Raven being able to cast while in astral form. Any being powerful enough to do that could be unstoppable. No matter what they did, Raven would win.

"Jade, dear. Are you all right?" Sophia asked while she put together a tea service for them all.

"No. Not really. I can't get over the fact that no one seems concerned that Raven can cast in astral form."

Sophia brought the full tray over to the kitchen table. "My dear, it's not that we're not concerned." She served Charlie and Jade, then poured her own cup and sat between them. "It's not possible," Sophia said matter-of-factly. "A Witch cannot cast while in astral form, no matter how powerful she is."

"I know what happened to me. I wasn't imagining it."

"I don't mean to suggest you were, dear. When a Witch is in astral form, her body is immobilized and her mind is separated from it. She is unable to cast. Period. It just simply could not have been Raven who did the casting."

Charlie tensed subtly. "You mean someone else was there. Someone we couldn't see, spelled Jade?"

"Most likely."

"So someone was hiding nearby and cast the spell for her? Raven has an accomplice. One she doesn't want us to know about." Jade shook. The very last thing they needed.

CHAPTER 6

Sophia stood. "There's nothing you can do about that now. Drink your tea, it will help calm you. The first thing we need to focus on is getting you protected from whoever may cast at you."

Charlie rose as well. "She's right. Jade has plenty of ingredients in the basement storage. I'll show you."

They left to supply up, and Jade sipped her tea as directed, but her mind kept spinning. She went into the living room, where the fire still burned brightly. She still felt tense and began pacing before the fireplace. It unnerved her, the idea that Raven could be so close and yet out of reach. That she had someone working with her. Someone powerful enough to cast easily, but remain hidden. Of course, Katie could be wrong about Raven's location, but Jade didn't think so. She'd done extensive research into possession in the time since April's body had been taken over by Raven. It took time for a spirit to fully possess a body, and it was a tricky thing to do. After the initial adrenaline faded, it became difficult to even move. Now would actually be the perfect time to take Raven out. She understood why capturing Raven was the better plan, but she hated it. Not only was it a great risk, but Raven had killed her best friend. She deserved to die.

Charlie said, "If you want a different carpet, just say so."

"Huh?"

"You're glaring at it like you want it dead." He smirked at her. His secret weapon.

She felt the grin tugging the corners of her mouth but she fought back. "Sophia's taking too long. Why isn't she back yet? How long does it take to pick some herbs for a spell?"

"She's probably struggling to find what she needs. Your storage is a bit messy right now. What's really bothering you? I mean, I know. There's plenty of issues to choose from. But I've seen that look before. What are you thinking?"

She turned and glared at the fireplace. She didn't want to admit what she'd been holding back all this time. She was supposed to be the calm, confident leader, setting an example of peaceful strength. But he'd been the one to teach her battle magic this morning. And he'd been there, saw what Raven did to April. He'd understand.

She turned to face him. "It's completely unfair." She threw her fury behind every word, twisting her energy as she spoke. "Raven murdered my best friend, and I have to pretend I'm okay with capturing her?" It felt so good to let that energy rage. The fiery tingle that Jade usually felt in her palms spread through her whole body. She leaned into the feeling, letting it burn. "She doesn't deserve that. She deserves to die!" The flames in the fireplace danced higher, their heat pressing against her back.

There was a gasp behind Charlie and he turned. Sophia was standing in the kitchen doorway, carrying a large basket filled with herbs, candles, and other spell tools. "Jade, ground and center now."

Jade did as she was asked, reluctantly letting go of the anger she'd unleashed. She closed her eyes and sent the rage and frustration down through the floor. The heat on her back from the fireplace lowered, and Jade took another breath, letting the last of her anger flow out with it. After the third breath, she opened her eyes. Sophia was standing next to Charlie, worry written on both their faces.

Jade said, "Thanks. I feel a little better." They continued staring at her. She gave a halfhearted smile and stepped toward Sophia, intending to take the basket and see what she brought. The elderly woman took a step back, then walked to the wall opposite the fireplace and set her basket down on a small table there.

"I appreciate that you're trying to calm down, Jade." She turned and looked at her seriously. "But if you allow yourself to get that upset again, I will be forced to spell you, for my protection."

Jade frowned. "Your protection?"

Her voice softened. "Yes, dear. One of the unfortunate side effects of being an empath, you are always at risk of catching others' moods." There was a breath of silence before Sophia continued. "Jade, please tell me you didn't mean what you said. Tell me you were just blowing off steam and would never seriously consider killing Raven without a trial."

Jade could feel the warning undertone, the tension behind her gentle voice. But she couldn't back down. Maybe if more coven members were present, she would have. "Of course I meant it. I—"

Charlie said, "I know you're upset, but we can't just kill someone. Not even after what she did. She must be brought before the coven and tried for her crimes. Then the coven, as a group, will decide what her punishment should be."

Jade was shocked. She gaped at Charlie. "What about all the training we've been doing?"

"I have to train you in battle magic, but the hope of every Witch is that they'll never have to use it."

Jade looked to Sophia and back to Charlie. Shock, sympathy, and disappointment were shown in equal measure on both their faces. They didn't understand. Trials and punishment were not what Raven deserved. She'd thought Charlie agreed with her, but apparently she'd been wrong. She sighed and prepared to tell the biggest lie of her life. "You're right. The laws of the coven are fair, and I was wrong to consider going against them. I just get so angry every time I think about what she did. It's not right."

Charlie put his arm across her shoulders. "Which is why we'll capture her and bring her to trial. Together we'll decide her punishment." He hugged her briefly.

"That's settled then." Sophia picked four white pillar candles out of the basket and handed them to Charlie. "Place these at the four cardinal directions. Jade and I have some work to do first." She picked a bundle of dried herbs and a large feather out of the basket. She pointed the feather at Jade as she spoke. "Before we protect you, we need to cleanse your aura. You're still very angry."

Jade kept quiet. Arguing that of course she was angry and why shouldn't she be would only make things worse. She kicked off her shoes and socks, the soft, worn rug filtering the Earth's grounding energy up through the soles of her feet. She closed her eyes and took several deep, cleansing breaths, trying to slow her breathing. Burning sage seared her nostrils as Sophia waved the smoke over her. It had the right effect though; the repetition of rituals and spells had conditioned her to relax at the smell. She felt the anger and frustration flow downwards, pushed out by the sacred herb.

"There we are." Jade opened her eyes to see Sophia smiling at her. "Much better. Though I think you might want to go back to daily breathing exercises until we have Raven well in hand."

"That's what I told her." Charlie handed her a crystal to hold during the protection spell.

"Yeah, well . . . maybe I will," Jade relented. She felt so useless during the short breathing practice, just sitting there, doing nothing, but somehow, she always felt better afterward. Charlie and Sophia took positions on either side of her and began the protection spell.

It felt weird just standing there while the spell wrapped itself around her. She was used to casting spells on others. It was like the first time she astral projected, looking back at herself. Like looking in an enchanted mirror, the reflection not quite moving the way she did.

The out-of-body experience faded away as the spell hugged her tight. It was made of Charlie's and Sophia's love for her. Their support manifested and combined with the power of the elements. When they finished, Jade marveled at the invisible armor surrounding her. During the spell casting, it had glowed slightly as it formed, like glass lit from below. Now it faded to just a feeling, light as a feather, but impenetrable.

Charlie put their candles and tools away as Sophia lectured Jade. "Now remember, this can only protect you against a surprise attack. Its effects are absolute for the first few minutes, but if you get into a full-on battle with Raven, it won't help much."

"I know. Don't worry, I'm not about to go charging after her on my own."

Sophia gave her a sidelong glance. "I certainly hope not." She picked up her cloak. "If you'll both excuse me, I need to go check on Willow."

Jade said, "I'll walk you out."

Charlie began cleaning up from the spell as Jade stepped out onto the porch with her. They walked down the steps toward Sophia's car. "I want to ask you about something, but I'm not sure how you'll take it."

Sophia took her hand. "Jade, dear, you know you can ask me anything."

"I was just wondering . . . how much do you know about dark magic?"

She dropped Jade's hand. "I certainly hope you're not considering dabbling in that." She stopped walking and pursed her lips. "I'm sorry. I said you could ask me anything, and I meant it." They began walking more slowly. "I know quite a bit about it since it's one of the required classes at the abbey. All theoretical, of course. What do you want to know?"

"That's just it. Everyone says dark magic is dangerous and I shouldn't try it, but those same people haven't ever used it, so how do they know?"

"They know, we know, because we've seen its effects. Dark magic draws its power from shadow, death, pain. It requires you to lean into all the emotions that are most destructive—anger, hatred, vengeance— and use them to force things to be as you wish." She rested her hand on Jade's shoulder. "This gets in the way of the greater good."

"And what is that? Who decides what's good?"

"Oh, you are wrestling with the deep questions, aren't you? My dear, balance is what's good. It's how nature works, and much as we humans like to pretend we're not, we are part of nature."

"Last year, Charlie said he had to kill someone in the battle with North Devonshire. He said that left a mark on his heart. I mean, he's fine now thanks to the Ascension ritual last month, but killing someone couldn't always do that, right? Otherwise every coven battle would result in both covens being dark."

They'd arrived at the car, and Sophia put her bag inside, then turned to Jade. "I can see you're struggling with this, but be at ease. As long as you don't practice dark magic, you're in no danger of going dark." She got in the car and smiled at Jade out the window. "My dear, we have a lot to prepare for, but I do want to answer all your questions. Why don't we meet at Bonfire Field tomorrow and we'll chat then, yes? Say around nine?" When Jade nodded, Sophia started up her car and drove off.

Jade wrapped her cloak around her tightly and watched the taillights vanish in the distance. It seemed like yesterday she'd arrived in Sugar Hill for the first time in years. She'd been so resistant toward anything having to do with magic then. Charlie had felt like a stranger, and all she'd wanted was to return to Sun City.

She turned toward the house. Her house, her home. Now, all she wanted was to protect it and everyone she loved. Charlie's shadow passed behind the living room curtains. There was nothing more to be done tonight. Whatever tomorrow brought, she would face it as bravely as she could. She shivered from the cold and chuckled. For now, she just wanted to get warm.

Jade went up the steps and into the house. In the living room there were candles everywhere, and a blanket was spread before the fireplace. On it were strawberries and champagne.

"Too much?" Charlie asked sheepishly from the other side of the room.

"No, it's . . . it's beautiful, Charlie."

He hurried over to her and took her cloak. She soaked in the warmth of the room.

He wrapped his arms around her and whispered in her ear, "The house is protected, you're protected, we're safe for now. It's just the two of us. We deserve a few minutes to ourselves, right?"

Her head was swimming, and while she normally wouldn't mind, worry skirted the edge of her thoughts. "We do." She pulled herself away from him. "But not right now. I'm sorry, but I wouldn't be able to relax." He looked so disappointed. "I promise, as soon as we take care of Raven, however that turns out, we'll take that break. For as long as you want."

He looked at her a moment more, then seemed to loosen up. "You're right. We need to focus on this fight and making sure the coven is safe. But then . . ." He turned her around and pulled her close, wrapping his arms around her again. He draped his head over her shoulder and nuzzled his face in her neck, breathing in deeply. "You're all mine," he growled and playfully nibbled at her.

She giggled and pushed him away. "As much as I'm enjoying this, we need to stay focused."

"Really? I thought I was focusing pretty well." He tried to pull her toward him, but she stopped him with a hand on his chest.

"Charlie," she warned gently.

His eyes hardened momentarily before they relaxed again. "Okay, boss." He sat on the rug and grabbed a strawberry. "But we wouldn't want these to go to waste now, would we? Get down here and help me get rid of them." He bit almost the whole thing, chewing joyfully.

Jade hesitated a moment. The brief darkness she'd seen pass through his eyes was gone and he seemed to be normal now. All couples got annoyed with each other sometimes. That must be what she was sensing.

She sat next to him and helped herself to the spread. The berries were a delightful combination of sweet and slightly sour. The champagne was drier than she'd expected, but it complimented the juicy berries nicely. The crackling fire sent Charlie's dark ringlets aglow and gave his eyes a sparkle as he caught her gaze. She felt herself start to relax.

She finished off the last of her glass. "Okay, let's talk strategy." Charlie offered her the last two berries, but she shook her head and continued. "I've been spelled for protection. We've got the town on lockdown, and Katie's faeries are on the hunt for Raven's hiding spot. I want to be prepared so that as soon as she finds her, we'll be ready to go. What else should we be doing?"

He moved to refill her glass, but she put her hand over it. He set the bottle down.

"There's nothing else we can do for now. We . . . oh, hang on." He gazed off in thought a moment, then downed the last of his glass. He leapt up and offered his hand. "I've got an idea.

She took his hand and he practically launched her up, off the blanket, and into his arms. She giggled at the rush. "Charlie! What are you doing?"

He grabbed their cloaks off the coat rack by the front door and threw hers at her, then pulled her after him as he led her to the kitchen. "Come on, you're gonna love this."

CHAPTER 7

Jade hurriedly threw on her cloak, rushing to catch up with Charlie at the back door. He held it open for her and she was hit with the frigid late-afternoon air. She slid past him and onto the porch. "I told you we need to be serious right now. I want every base covered with Raven. She's not slipping away next time we meet."

"And I heard you loud and clear. This will help with that, but it's also fun. We both get what we want." He smiled his lopsided grin as they went down the steps into the backyard. He stopped and turned to her. "Elementals."

His cheerful attitude couldn't stop the chill she felt at the name. She thought back to the Ascension ritual they'd had to go through to become High Priestess and High Priest. It had been an elaborate ritual with the whole coven and township attending. What stood out in her mind was confronting the Elementals. Earth, Air, Fire, and Water had each taken the form of a hooded figure that tested them in some way. It was an experience she didn't want to ever repeat. "Do we have to deal with them now? I mean, I already passed their tests once."

"What? Oh, different Elementals. Yeah, we really haven't had time to go over this yet, huh? The ones you faced at the Ascension were the raw power of the elements given human form in order to interact with us during a ritual. The Elementals you use in battle are elemental spirits, beings made solely of the energy of one element. They're able to inhabit any physical object, transmuting it into a creature of that element, an Elemental."

Jade raised an eyebrow. "How many times can you say 'elemental' in ten seconds?"

He chuckled. "Take the lion statues on either side of your property's gate. Most of the time, they're just marble statues. But every single thing, living or dead, has an energy vibration. Each of the elements vibrates in a specific range. Those lions vibrate at a frequency within the range for Fire, and that allows a Fire Elemental to inhabit it at will. When that happens, for all intents and purposes, that changes the very existence of the marble into a living thing."

"So, they could actually move? Like, get down and walk if they wanted?"

"Yes. In fact, the main use for Elementals is in battle. When a Witch goes to war, several things happen. The first is that they protect not only their body, but their spirit. Taking a life leaves a mark on a person's spirit. A Witch's ability to use magic links them to every living thing around them. When they take a life, a part of them dies too.

"One way they protect themselves against that is to channel an Elemental to fight with them. Use it as a buffer between their soul and the repercussions of the damage their magic inflicts. It can take the form of pretty much anything. Your aunt Joy's favorite

Elemental was a lion, her Fire Elemental." His eyes got misty. "She was magnificent. I wish you could have seen her. She walked through the fog that night with a lion on each side. They were larger than life and almost glowed with the essence flowing through them."

Jade tried to picture her aunt with a glowing lion on either side of her, but it seemed so comical. She nodded slowly but couldn't keep the smirk off her face.

"You think I'm joking? Here, I'll show you." He stepped back from her and looked around him as if checking the space. When he seemed satisfied, he continued. "I have to warn you though, Elementals are spirits in their own right and have their own will, just like you or I. They can't be commanded to do anything they don't want to do. In fact, if you even try, they are likely to make you regret it."

"Sounds dangerous."

"It's only dangerous for those who flaunt their power and misuse it. The first meeting is the most important though. It's when you introduce who you are to them. You have to dig deep. It's more than your name, or where you came from, it's about what drives you. What are your dreams and aspirations, and most importantly what do you value? What are you willing to fight and even die for?"

Jade smirked. "Oh, is that all?"

"There's the good and the bad of it. You don't have to tell them with words, they will sense it from you. You just have to be open to letting them figure you out. You can't want to hide anything. You remember at the Ascension? You had to face each Elemental and ask for passage into the sacred circle? Remember that feeling of letting go?"

Jade remembered the feeling had been as if she'd been stripped bare and pushed backward, free-falling into nothingness. It hadn't lasted long, thank goodness, but with each element, she'd experienced it again. "Yes."

"Well, it's kind of like that, or it can be."

"So what's first?"

"I'm going to call an Elemental I haven't used often, to give you an idea what it'll be like when you first meet yours. Just watch what I do." Charlie bowed his head and raised his hands outward to his sides, palms upward. After a moment, he lifted his head and spoke in a commanding voice. "Guardian of the South, I call thee. Element of Fire, I ask you to show yourself to me and meet me in perfect love and perfect trust. Come to me!" He tipped his head back and closed his eyes.

Time ticked by and nothing happened. Charlie opened his eyes. "Like I said, we don't know each other well yet. Why don't you try."

Jade followed his example, and called to the element of Fire. For a moment there was silence, then Jade heard something very faint. Like large footsteps on solid earth. Soon, it became a vibration under her feet. Something big was coming.

As the thudding came closer, she felt a presence approach from behind her. Heat radiated on her back, like an oven door was left open, rising in intensity. She resisted turning around, but she lowered her hands and opened her eyes, staring at the ground before her. The heat moved to her right, then its source entered her field of vision.

His huge paws padded silently on the grass. He was about her height, but his head was bigger than her torso. His fur radiated with a soft golden glow, as if every strand was lit from within.

She stared wide-eyed as the lion stalked between them, looking between Charlie and Jade. When he turned his head toward her, she noticed his form was absolutely perfect, except for his left ear. The tip was missing, leaving a ragged line as if it had been torn off.

It was the lion from the front gate. The one she'd thought she saw move the day she arrived in Sugar Hill.

He padded silently up to Charlie and stood perfectly still, staring at him. Charlie looked straight back into the eyes of the huge lion. His face became so calm and relaxed. A small smile tugged at the corners of his mouth. Jade realized he looked . . . blessed.

After a moment Charlie nodded once, and the lion turned to face Jade. She stared back at him, expecting Charlie to explain what was happening. Nothing happened. Seconds ticked by and she began to get impatient.

She sighed.

The lion tilted his head to the side. Jade got the impression that he wanted something specific from her. She couldn't guess what that would be though. She started to ask Charlie what to do, but the lion took a very slow step toward her and stopped. Then another. And another. He wasn't stalking exactly. His posture was completely upright, head tilted to the other direction than before. He seemed to be asking her something. Permission? Jade wondered.

He stopped inches from her and sat on his hindquarters. His head was still level with hers, and she could feel his hot breath in her face as he opened his mouth to pant. The hot air had no smell, which surprised Jade. She expected dog breath or something completely random like raspberries. She smiled at the thought of raspberry lion breath.

The lion stopped panting and slowly, but firmly, pressed his forehead into her face. His fur was the softest thing she'd ever felt in her life. Impossibly soft. She melted into it, leaving her body behind.

She was the lion.
The lion was her.

They ran through the forest, gracefully leaping over fallen logs and around boulders. They played with young Charlie in the stream, digging up crawdads and dropping them into a bucket.

They raced over the plains and roared from the top of a boulder. They jogged over the bridge with April into Sun City.

At night the moon lit up the grasslands like daylight as they stalked their prey. They shot arrows at an archery competition.

They lay in a cave with their family members, warm and safe in a jumbled pile of fur and paws. As they rolled over to stare up at the stars, Charlie held their hand.

Jade felt herself waking up, being pulled gently away from the comfort of a cat's nap. She opened her eyes and saw the golden-brown eyes of her new friend. The lion was that. She knew it without a word being spoken. He padded softly to stand next to her and face Charlie.

Jade looked from the lion to Charlie and back again. "What the heck was that?"

"You tell me. Everyone's experience with meeting an Elemental is different," Charlie said, sounding amused. "My first experience with one was pretty terrifying at first, but apparently yours is very different. What did you experience?"

"I don't know exactly. One minute I was looking at him, the next I was him. But, I was still myself at the same time." She frowned. "Is that even possible? Oh wait, did he give me a vision?" She had heard of people with the power of visions being able to gift their visions to others.

"Possibly. Visions are one of your natural talents. It makes sense that's how he'd communicate with you. You do look pretty magnificent together." He smiled broadly. "I'm glad this was your first experience."

"Well, it wasn't anywhere near as bad as I thought it might be. When I encountered the Fire element at the Ascension, it made me relive the night my parents died." She cautiously rested her hand on the back of the lion's head. He closed his eyes and repositioned his head so she could reach his ears. She scratched behind them, eliciting a deep, rumbling purr from his chest.

Jade smiled. "When he leaned his head into my face, I kind of, fell into him? It was like I left my body and became some combination of him and me." The lion lay down at her feet and rested his head on his paws.

Charlie said, "You went on a vision quest with him."

"I guess. I . . . we ran through fields, hunted a deer, even took a nap with what I can only guess was his family. But I also shared with him. We hunted crawdads in the stream, went to my archery competition. The whole time I felt more safe and loved than I can ever remember." She smiled down at the purring mass at her feet. "What was your first experience like?"

"Mine was a bit more forceful." The lion glanced up at him, then set his head back down. Charlie sighed. "I first called for the Earth Elemental. It rushed in and slammed me in the chest, sending me flying back on my ass."

The lion at Jade's feet huffed once in a way that she was sure was meant to be a chuckle. She struggled not to smile.

Charlie glared at her. "Yeah, real funny now. At the time I was just in shock."

Jade sat down and leaned against the lion's massive side. She was feeling more and more comfortable in his presence as time went on.

Charlie sat cross-legged and continued his story. "I sat up and realized that it had come in the form of a stag, antlers and all. And he was huge. I was surprised the hit hadn't injured me. He waited until I got to my feet, then he did this incredibly graceful bow, head all the way down to the ground, one front leg stretched out front, the other bent back. He rested on his knee like that for a moment, then stood and just stared at me.

"I tried to figure out what he wanted, but I had no ideas. That's the thing about meeting an Elemental— because it takes the form of an animal, you can't just talk to it. You have to find another way to communicate. Sometimes they take the initiative, like with you apparently, but sometimes they just wait to see what you'll do. So after what seemed like forever, I got the idea that since he was about the size of a horse . . . well, it was presumptuous of me, I know that now." He smirked and shook his head before continuing. "I climbed up on the tree stump next to where he was standing and managed to get halfway up before he bucked hard, throwing me back to the ground."

Jade couldn't help but laugh. "Wish I could have seen that. Sounds like he didn't want to make it easy for you at all."

"You ain't kidding. And it pissed me off. He knew what was at stake, with the battle against the North Devonshire coven looming. I was young and was starting to think I should give up. That's when he really tested me. He lifted his head high and let out the most eerie and terrifying sound. I've been told it was a bugle call, but it just sounded like a demon was laughing at me."

Jade laughed hard. "A bugle call? You know that's how they call for their mate, right?"

Charlie flushed. "I do now, but at the time I thought he was trying to scare me away. Like he didn't find me worthy and was dismissing me, hoping I'd run off. Well that got to me. I thought of all that was at stake and decided I wasn't giving up, no matter what.

"I reached up, grabbed his antlers, and stared right into his eyes. I said, 'Listen you, I know you're some all-powerful essence of the Earth, and I respect that. You're terrifying. I'm scared. The problem is I need you. I need you to help me save my coven. There's no way we're going to win this battle without you.'

"He tried to lift his head and shake me off, but I held on and used my body weight to keep his head facing me. I said, 'No! I'm not letting you go until you agree to help.'" Charlie paused, looking down at his right palm and rubbing it with his left thumb. "It was then that I found out just how dangerous Elementals could be. They can not only take the shape of any creature, but they can change that creature's shape however they want. He grew a new prong right under where my hand was, piercing it through the bone."

Jade winced and glanced sidelong at the sleeping beast beside her. Was he just waiting for a moment to do something similar to her?

Charlie saw her look. "Don't worry, I don't think he'll hurt you now."

"Why not?"

"Because he obviously has already accepted you. They aren't fickle creatures, Jade. They don't change their allegiance as it suits them, like we humans do. Besides, he wasn't really trying to hurt me. He was testing me. He wanted to see how committed I was to doing whatever it took. And I was committed. I held on and pulled even harder, letting the antler cut deeper into my hand. After what seemed like forever, he finally bowed and withdrew the antler from my hand. I cast a healing spell, and after a couple of days, it was almost like new." He rubbed the spot again, then stopped and chuckled. "Still weird to think about though."

He stood up and took a couple of steps back. "Let's do one more thing before you release him."

Jade stood. "Release? Is that why he's just lying here?"

"Pretty much. Like I said, we can't really control them, but they usually will follow our commands. You called him and you haven't said he could leave yet, so he's not." He smiled as the lion lifted his head and looked at Jade with what could only be described as devotion. "I'd like you to get the hang of giving commands a bit before you let him go."

Jade took a step forward. The lion had begun to rise when she'd moved. She turned to it and said sternly, "Stay." She felt a wave of disapproval, so she added, "Please?"

The lion took a proud sitting position, head high, chest out, his front legs two strong pillars. She continued walking over to stand next to Charlie. "So, now what?"

"You need to find your tone. It may change over time as you get to know each other, but, as you could see, he didn't like how you commanded him just now. I'm guessing he would rather you ask him for what you want until you know each other better. Some Elementals do better with strength from their humans, some kindness, some even bribery. It also depends on what you want them to do. For training, it's less imperative, so they often feel you shouldn't be so bossy. Of course in a battle with life and death at risk, they can get pretty focused on the task at hand and often won't even hear you unless you're firm with them."

"So it's about your tone of voice?"

"Not just your tone, also your intent. You can speak if you want, but after you've been working with him for a while, you shouldn't need words. Your thoughts and intent should guide your energy in a way he understands."

Charlie closed his eyes for a moment, then turned his head up to his left. A spotted black-and-white eagle swooped down and landed precisely on his left shoulder. "Martial here was the second Elemental I called, but I'm closer to him than the others." Martial pecked at his cheek and Charlie smiled. "We just click." He nodded to the eagle, and Martial took to the air, circling them from high above.

"When you're being attacked and you're full of fear and helplessness, it can either heighten your connection to your Elemental or disrupt it." He made a slight movement with his index finger and Martial began a dive straight toward Jade.

She reflexively raised her arm while dropping to the ground. When nothing hit her after a moment, she peeked out from under her arm. The lion sat facing her proudly with Martial clenched in his massive jaws. Martial wasn't struggling, and Jade feared the worst. Just as she thought that, the lion released Martial, who flew up to Charlie's shoulder.

He stared at Jade. "That was amazing. You didn't even use a vocal command."

"Well, I wish I knew how I did it." Jade looked Martial over. "Is he okay?"

Charlie dismissed her concern. "Yeah, Elementals can't really hurt each other. Their physical forms can take damage, but the Elemental is a spirit, which can simply leave the form and eventually take on another. Let's try that again." The lion growled at Charlie and lowered his head. Charlie eyed him warily. "Or not. It's up to you, Jade. He's your Elemental."

She smiled at the implication. She had the power. If she said yes, then he'd get to see another amazing show, but it was ultimately her decision. She looked at her lion and patted his head, silently asking what he wanted. He purred for a moment, then stood and shook from head to tail.

"There's your answer. Let's stop for now." She nodded to her lion, and after one last look at her, he trotted off. Jade watched him lumber away, amazed such creatures existed.

"Definitely my favorite kind of Elemental." She turned back to Charlie. There was a darkness shadowing Charlie's eyes.

"Yeah," he said, looking at the eagle perched on his arm, "they are pretty great." His voice was tinged by a hardness Jade rarely heard. He dismissed Martial and the eagle flew away over the trees into the sunset. Charlie turned toward her, all traces of shadow gone, his face relaxed and cheerful once again.

"Charlie, are you all right?"

"What do you mean?"

"For a moment you looked . . . dark."

"Dark?"

"Yeah, I've seen it before a few times. It's like a shadow passes over you or something." His silence tightened her chest. He was looking away from her. "Charlie, are you sure your shadowed heart is cured?"

He turned back to her, same lopsided smile, no hint of shadow anywhere. "Of course it is." He walked up onto the porch and she followed.

She reached out and took his hand, stopping him. "Charlie, I'm serious. It has something to do with that Witch you killed during the North Devonshire battle, doesn't it?"

"I'm fine."

"Please, just tell me what happened."

He hesitated a moment, then sat on the porch swing and motioned for her to sit next to him. Once she sat, he said, "When we went to battle with North Devonshire, we were fairly well matched at first. Surprisingly so. I'd been so worried in the days leading up to it.

"Anyway, we were doing well, but then something happened. Our spells started backfiring, or not working at all. And they were overtaking us. We were going to lose, so... I cast dark magic. Several spells in a row. It worked, I was able to push them back and fix what was going wrong with our magic, but it came at a cost. One of my spells drew the power from a nearby Witch." He looked down at his hands, as if noticing for the first time he'd been rubbing his palm. "I took all her power. I killed her." His voice broke.

She took his hands and squeezed tight. He looked up at her and sighed. "I didn't mean to, but you're right. I still have a shadowed heart. The Ascension ritual didn't completely fix me. But there's really nothing to worry about. Turns out dark magic isn't as big a deal as we thought."

Jade released his hands and stood. "How can you say that?"

"I can feel the darkness in me, but it doesn't control me. Everyone gets dark impulses sometimes—it's human nature. The point is to not act on them. And I don't. I don't even want to. It's just that . . . well, I guess with your abilities you're able to see those impulses as a shadow. Really, I don't feel all that different than I used to. I'm just more aware of my feelings than before."

"Are you trying to convince me, or yourself?"

He sat back. A slight frown creased his forehead. Apparently, he didn't have an answer for her. After a moment he said, "Do you remember last month when I talked to you about dark magic?"

"Yeah, I also remember you scolding me for using it just a little bit."

Charlie smirked. "Yes, well, using dark magic without the proper training is forbidden for a reason."

"You mean using it at all. That's what you told me. You said other covens might use dark magic, but in ours it was forbidden. Period."

"It's actually a good thing I used dark magic. If I hadn't, we would have lost the battle with North Devonshire and never have learned about dark magic's true nature."

"What do you mean, true nature?"

He stood and began pacing. "When we fought the North Devonshire coven, we found out their coven mixed dark and light magic. We were not prepared for that. We talked a lot about it afterward. Dark and light magic have different . . . I guess you would say flavors. It's like mixing sweet and sour. Do it right and you get a delicious new dish. Do it wrong and you'll make yourself sick."

"And North Devonshire?"

"Oh, they were master chefs." He chuckled. "They blended dark and light magic in a way that surprised even Willow."

"Okay, but what does that have to do with your shadowed heart?"

He stopped pacing and took her hands. "What I'm trying to say is, dark magic is not the absolute bad evil toxin that we've been taught. I've been living with it now for years and I'm perfectly normal."

"I wouldn't go that far." She smirked at him. The joke was a little forced, but she needed it. He was right. He'd been acting normal, for the most part. And they'd been working together since she came back last month. She looked at their intertwined hands. He was definitely not the dark Witch she'd been taught you'd become when practicing dark magic. Even she'd used dark magic last month when she cast the blood spell against Raven, and there hadn't been any side effects from it.

He stepped closer and murmured, "Besides, dark magic is just another form of magic, and all magic comes from the divine, right?"

She nodded. It was a contradiction that no one seemed to have an explanation for. "One of the Great Mysteries."

"Right. Under normal circumstances I'd say stay away from dark magic. You don't need it. But we're dealing with the abnormal here. A powerful Witch returned from the dead, intent on killing you so she can take over our coven." He looked pained for moment, then determination set his jaw. "I think we're allowed to try something a little risky to prevent that."

It made sense. She felt so close to him right now. They'd always worked so well together. She thought back to the coven meeting when he had contradicted her suggestion they kill Raven. The shadow and darkness she'd been feeling didn't bother her as much as that did. "Why did you shut me down in the meeting? Killing Raven could be a viable option if we have the whole coven behind us. You didn't even give them a chance to react to that idea."

"Because I knew what their reaction would be. Look, we're the coven leaders, and our coven will do what we say in the end. But we're in a dangerous place right now, with the inspector and Raven. They don't understand dark magic. It's forbidden. We can't let them think we'd be willing to kill a Witch without trial. They'd start questioning us, and one hesitation from any of them in battle could be disastrous."

She took a moment to think about what he said, turning away from him. He wasn't wrong. Their situation was fragile. It wouldn't take much for the inspector to find out what really happened, then it would all come crashing down. Their partnership had to appear seamless to the coven, and nothing more than an acquaintance to the inspector. She needed to figure out why dark magic was so feared, and if it was as bad as she'd always been taught. If not, it seemed to be their best chance of defeating Raven, and Charlie seemed her best chance to learn it. "Teach me dark magic."

Charlie blinked. "Did I just hear you right?"

"I'm not saying I want to go completely dark, I'm just saying I need to understand how dark magic works if I'm gonna have a chance against a dark Witch like Raven. And the best way to really understand something is to experience it. However," she cautioned him, "we need to take it slow. And the moment I feel anything going wrong, I'm calling a stop to it. In fact, I'm not even saying I'll really use it at all. I just need to practice. Just a couple of spells." She could feel herself backpedaling, the fear over what she was committing too inching up inside her. She stamped it down. "Just show me the basics, and I'll make my decision then." She sounded stronger than she felt.

"Of course." He took her hands and looked deep into her eyes. "I would never do anything to jeopardize you, Jade. I love you."

He rarely said it, and it sent a warmth racing through her body, melting away the fear. "I love you too." She leaned in and they kissed. Just a short one, but the connection was strong. Charlie was her home.

When they parted, he looked at her lips for a second before shaking his head. "Right. We need to practice this somewhere we won't be disturbed." He thought a moment, then said, "The mayor's mansion." He turned and Jade followed him through the house, toward his car in the front drive.

"Why there?"

"Last weekend I warded the basement. It's basically been soundproofed, but for magic. We'll be safe there."

When they reached his car, he let her in and sped off the property. Jade felt the butterflies in her stomach from what they were about to do. It was like being a kid again, sneaking off to try out some new spell she'd found. Back then she'd been powerful, and Charlie had tagged along to help. Now it felt like the roles were reversed. As he sped down the winding forested road, the headlight only illuminated a few feet ahead. She felt that was her life now, uncertain but ever racing toward her.

CHAPTER 8

It didn't take Charlie long to drive Jade the short distance to the mayor's mansion, but the uncertainty creeping into the edges of Jade's mind made time feel slowed down. She decided to counteract with knowledge. Focus on what she could control. "Is dark magic stronger?"

"No, but it is easier. Dark magic taps into the emotional energy of yourself and sometimes your enemy, especially fear and anger. And there's the catch. Fear is one of the hardest emotions to control, and it often stems from hatred. If you hold those emotions in your heart too long, then they can overpower you."

"So is love the emotion that counters it?"

"It can be, but a better defense is acceptance. Acceptance of the situation, the person wielding the dark magic, and acceptance of the outcome before it happens."

"Well, that's not going to work for me. I will never

accept Raven or any outcome where she's not dead at my feet. And yes, I know that's hatred, but I don't care. She killed my best friend."

"Technically, Richard did that."

Jade did a double take. Richard had been Jade's boss, mentor, and surrogate father figure for most of her life. Even though he'd betrayed Jade, Raven had been the one to manipulate him into doing it. She couldn't believe Charlie was blaming him. Could he really be putting this all on Richard? "What?"

"It doesn't matter that Raven was manipulating him from the other side. It was still Richard who did the ritual. He was the one who drove the knife into April's back. Raven only gave him the idea. He was the one to follow through with it of his own free will."

Jade found her voice, and it was harsher than she'd expected. "How dare you defend her? How dare you!" As much as she'd hated Richard for what he'd done, she couldn't help feeling Charlie was protecting Raven, trying to shift the blame away from her. She wished she could get out of the car, but they were just exiting Main Street. The front drive of the mansion loomed in front of them.

His eyes went wide. "Jade, I'm sorry." He reached out for her hand, but she pulled away. "I didn't mean it like that. If it wasn't for Raven, Richard wouldn't have killed April. I just meant that you need to keep clear in your mind who's responsible for what. Yes, Raven needs to pay for putting the wheels in motion. And we will make her pay. But part of the reason you've struggled to control your magic is your inability to keep your emotions in check. When you're facing Raven, you can't afford to let your anger blind you. You have to keep a clear head. The best way to do that is to separate your feelings for Raven and your need to avenge April's death. Raven didn't kill April. Richard killed April. Raven was the mind behind it."

Jade considered this as they came to a stop in front of the mansion. He was right, logically. The anger toward Raven was so strong though, tied to pain as it was. Charlie may be right that she needed to distance herself, but she wasn't ready to. Not yet.

"You're probably right," Jade said, defeated. She got out of the car and leaned her back against it with arms crossed. When she'd found out Richard had been lying to her all her life about who he was, she'd been outraged. But Raven was the one who had manipulated him into doing the ritual that killed April. She could be furious at two people at once.

Charlie had come around the car and stood in front of her, trying to catch her gaze as she glared at the ground. "Of course I'm right, but I appreciate the torture it took for you to say that out loud." He winked at her, and she couldn't help but smirk. "Now, let's get inside before someone sees us."

The sun was long gone, but the lights from Main Street cast a dim glow on the mansion. They had no idea when or if the inspector and his drones would return. Even with her Band spelled, there was no guarantee they wouldn't find her.

They entered the mansion and left their cloaks by the door. Charlie led her to the basement door and strode down the steps without hesitation, even though it turned pitch-black two feet inside the doorway.

Jade watched him disappear down into the darkness. She turned instinctively to look around.

There was no one there, and she scolded herself for being silly. There was a wood handrail against the wall on the right side, which vanished into the darkness below. Grabbing it, she could feel a cold undercurrent, like it should have been made of steel. She took a deep breath and slowly started down the steps, the door swung shut behind her.

Plunged into darkness, she clung to the railing, feeling her way down each step, unable to shake the eerie feeling of being watched. When she reached the bottom step and the railing ended, she stood frozen in the black. She couldn't even tell if her eyes were open or shut. "Charlie?" she asked the darkness.

She was startled by his voice much too close to her left ear. "I'm here."

Jade jumped. "Was that necessary," she glared at Charlie. It took a moment for her to realize she could see him. There was a soft light growing in front of her.

"Sorry. But look."

She couldn't see any details other than his face. The light in front of her might have been a lantern or a sconce. She couldn't tell; it was just a light.

Charlie stepped forward, blocking the light. His silhouette allowed Jade to see the other items directly next to the light. There was a long table stretching the length of the wall in front of her. On it were various items: a coffee mug, several glass jars and bottles with various herbs and liquids, and a stack of books. Charlie took one step to the side, and Jade was blinded by the light. Although it wasn't very bright, her eyes had gotten used to the pitch-black around her. It hurt to look at, so she tried to focus on the half silhouette of Charlie standing next to it.

He stepped once more in front of the light, revealing the items again. "Do you see? You can't just have light, it will blind you. You need to have the darkness to be able to see clearly."

"So . . . dark magic is the absence of light magic?" She was so confused.

"Not the absence of it . . . I'm not explaining it very well. Let's try something else. Luminaria," *Lights* he commanded, waiving a hand to the dark space. Instantly, lights flickered awake.

The basement was minimally finished. A bare cement floor with a couple of large throw rugs and wood-paneled walls. He took her hand and guided her into the room, over to the small altar on the east wall. It was just a simple table with a cabinet underneath. He opened one of the doors and took out a singing bowl with a small wooden dowel with felt covering one end, and two crystals; one smoky and the other clear. He set them down in the middle of the room and went back to the altar. Jade sat cross-legged in front of the bowl and crystals.

Charlie came back with a wand and four black candles. "I think it would be better if you help me set up the sacred space. That will set both our intentions better than only one of us doing it. The process is the same as with light magic."

She rose and took two of the candles from him. She followed him around the circle, placing a candle at the West and North compass points while he did the East and South. He walked the circle a second time, using the wand to direct the formation of the circle.

When they arrived back at the beginning, they both sat on the floor across from each other, and Jade said,

"So with dark magic you still set up a sacred circle? I wasn't expecting that."

"Dark magic isn't evil, Jade. It's just different." Charlie held a crystal in each open palm. "The most basic we can get is for you to get familiar with the feel of dark energy. Just like with light magic, dark magic has its own feel, and it may be completely different from what you're used to. For instance, if you usually smell magic, with dark magic you might hear it."

He placed the crystals on either side of the singing bowl. He picked up the hammer and began dragging the felt wrapped end along the outer edge of the rim. Soon it began to hum with a low tone. He placed the hammer down next to him, and the bowl continued singing.

He pointed to the clear crystal. "Sense the magic in this crystal."

She didn't feel anything strange from it. Just the usual sensation all magical tools had. A kind of baseline energy humming in the background. "Okay. Now what?"

He pointed to the smoky crystal. "This crystal has a small amount of dark magic within it. Reach out and sense it."

She did as he said. At first, there was only the instinct that it was magic. But then, something eerie. A void, a hollow, darkness made material. It was cold. She snapped her attention back from the uncomfortable item. Charlie looked expectantly at her. All the times she'd felt Charlie was cold, she'd been sensing the dark magic within his heart.

"Okay. And now?" she asked.

"Now you need to move the dark magic from one

crystal into the other."

She didn't want to touch it again. Now that she realized what it meant, the darkness wasn't just cold, it felt wrong. But she needed to know how to deal with it. Raven wouldn't use light magic to make her comfortable. She reached out with her senses slowly. When she felt the cool of the magic within the crystal, she tried to grab it, but it slipped out of her grasp. She tried again, but the same thing happened. "I can't get a grip on it."

"Don't try to grip it. Invite it."

"Invite?"

"Yeah. Reach out and ask it to enter your grasp." His eyes had a spark to them. A cold excitement.

Jade shook her head and tried again. She didn't like the feeling of any of this. It was wrong. Not morally, but it felt dangerous. She couldn't stop now though. She needed something more than her usual spells to defeat Raven. And if it meant she could understand what Charlie was going through and help him out of it, that was a welcome bonus. Besides, she could still feel the protection spell around her, like a lightweight spring sweater. She was safe.

She reached out toward the dark crystal again and felt the edge of the cold. She had an idea then. Instead of moving the darkness directly, she could use the energy in the clear crystal to direct it. Like using a napkin to pick up a bug.

She redirected her focus and gently pulled the energy from the clear crystal. It stretched and flowed toward the darkness. Soon it had enveloped it, and Jade let it go. The light energy snapped back into the crystal, pulling the darkness with it.

The crystals now seemed reversed, with the dark one where the light one had been, and vice versa.

"See? I told you, you could do it." He was smiling so big, the way he used to when they were little.

"Now what?"

"That depends. How do you feel?"

"Not tired. I feel pretty good. About the same as I would doing any magic of that level."

"That's good. Let's try something else." He lifted the box next to him and placed it between them. "When I lift the lid, you're gonna be surprised, maybe even frightened. Don't let that stop you. Immediately reach out and find the darkness, then take that darkness and place it into the clear crystal."

Jade squinted at him. "What's in the box?"

"You'll see." He placed his hand on the lid. "Ready?"

"No."

"Jade, you have to trust me. I know you can do this, so believe in yourself and just do it."

She gazed into his pleading eyes for a moment. She did trust him. She always would. "Okay, fine." She focused on the box and pulled the clear crystal's energy toward it, holding it steady, directly in front of the edge of the lid, a shield against whatever was inside. "Ready."

She barely had finished the word when Charlie lifted the lid. A black snake was coiled tightly in the box. As the lid lifted, the snake sprang upward. Jade wrapped the energy tightly around it so it couldn't move.

She could see now that it was over a foot long, the end quarter of it still in the box, the rest hovering in the air, trapped in the magical energy she'd wrapped around it.

She reached out with her feelings, searching for the dark energy within it. But there wasn't one area of darkness; the entire thing was dark. From head to tail, every scale was seething with a cold energy. Jade shivered and refocused her attention. She stretched the crystal's energy further around the snake, but it wasn't enough. She sent some of her own energy to it, merging into a force big enough to envelop the whole snake.

After a moment she felt it was attached enough to the darkness and she let go, sending a small amount of force toward the crystal. This time the energy moved only partway, then slowed, like a rubber band reaching its limit.

Jade reached out and pushed the darkness with her mind. She quickly felt the dark energy envelop her, the cool mustiness of a swamp. It was danger and sorrow. She wanted to stop, but she kept going. Soon the darkness in the snake broke free and flew into the crystal. As it did, Jade heard a loud snap, and several cracks appeared on the crystal's now glossy black surface.

Jade shook her hands, trying to release the cold pins-and-needles feeling that was trying to creep up her forearms. She felt antsy, impatient to get up and do something.

The snake had lowered back into the box, and Jade had the impression that it was frightened, trying to hide itself within its own coils.

Charlie closed the lid gently. "Perfect! See, I knew you could do it."

The dark was still touching her; she could feel it slowly sliding over her skin, up toward her shoulders.

She needed to get rid of it. "Okay. I get the feel of dark magic. Now let's try a spell. Something I can use against Raven." She felt if she could cast, she could get rid of this eerie feeling.

"You already have. Jade, dark magic isn't just about a certain pattern of words or a specific element. It's more holistic than that. It's a combination of your intent and the energy you draw from. The blood magic spell you used on Raven was dark magic not just because you drew on the energy of blood, but also because you were feeling vengeful."

"Damn right I was." Her throat tightened. "April was dead and that bitch was in her body."

"Right. But you could have used the same spell without the vengeful intentions and it wouldn't have been dark magic."

She glared at him and he backpedaled. "I'm not judging," he said. "I was upset you used it then, but I was just worried you'd get carried away with it. Once you start using dark magic, it's easy to lose your control and let it consume you. That's what happened to Raven. I didn't want that to happen to you."

She didn't care whether he judged her or not. The realization surprised her. She couldn't remember a time when she didn't care what he thought of her. It was the darkness. It had to be. The cold was starting to feel slimy. It crept down her spine and up the back of her neck. Jade jumped up and began cutting a doorway in the sacred circle. As her finger traced the outline, she could hear Charlie behind her, but he sounded distant.

"Jade, where are you going? Jade?"

She finished and stepped through. She had to get out of there. Had to get this creepy coldness off her before it found a way in. She had to get away.

Charlie grabbed her arm. "Jade!"

She turned and focused on him. The cold slid toward him, down her arm and onto him. The minute it left her, she felt better. Calmer. She looked him over carefully, reaching out with her senses. She half expected to find the shadow consuming him or growing in some way. But he seemed the same. He'd shown no reaction when the darkness had reached him.

"Charlie? Are you all right?"

"Am I all right?" He released her. "I was about to ask you the same thing. What happened?"

"The darkness." She stretched her back, rubbed her arm, tried to clear her mind of the impulse to run. "Give me a minute." She closed her eyes. She breathed deep and slow, pushing the desire to run down into the ground with her out breath, and pulled up calm, stable energy from the Earth with each in breath.

She'd spent years running from her past, from confrontation, from anything that she wasn't comfortable with. Over time it had become a habit, an impulse she had to work to counteract. Over the past month, Sophia had been working with her on it, teaching her breathing techniques and letting her talk out whatever was bothering her when she needed to. She'd made progress, but the moment the darkness had touched her, it had returned. That same desperate need to be elsewhere.

Feeling calmer, she opened her eyes. Charlie was watching her, but he looked bored. His expression changed to one of concern. "You okay now?"

"Yeah. I just really didn't like the feeling of that dark energy. I had to touch it to get it to leave the snake, and for a moment it didn't want to leave me." She looked down at his hand. "Did you feel anything when you touched me?"

He raised an eyebrow. "Like what?"

She tried to sense the shadow on him, but there was nothing there. Just Charlie. The same old Charlie. "Never mind." She looked at the Band on her wrist, the reflex for checking time from when she lived in Sun City. "Wow, it's getting late. Let's call it a night."

Charlie drove her home. Most nights they slept together at her house, but occasionally they'd sleep at their own places. Jade always slept better with Charlie next to her, but tonight she felt the need for space.

"I don't like the idea of you being along right now." Charlie glanced out at the darkened drive.

"I'll be fine. The protection spell will keep me safe from any attacks, and the Accords shield owners names from property records, so Inspector Caldwell won't have any reason to come snooping here. I'm just going to go up to bed and crash. I promise to call you if anything happens."

"All right, but I'm coming back first thing tomorrow." He gave her a kiss and left.

Jade watched him drive off, then turned to go inside.

The vision hit her hard.

The whole world spun around her. Dizzy and disoriented, she reached out and found herself falling into darkness, the porch and house left far above. She landed on bare earth that was blackened from fire.

She attempted to rise, but a cold presence pressed her down, whispering in her ear, words she couldn't understand. The smell of dust and gear grease stung her nose.

The whisper became the buzz of a drone. She swatted at it.

Her fingertips brushed grass. She was lying in Bonfire Field. The sunrise blinded her. A deep, rough voice at her ear said, "Go back."

CHAPTER 9

Morning light streamed through the window. Jade sat up in bed and lifted her face to the sunlight, drinking in the warming rays with closed eyes. She knew she should be worried. She hadn't been able to decipher last night's vision, but she found herself feeling hopeful. There was a lot of work to do, but she had everything she needed.

She rose to start her day and think about what she wanted. Charlie would help her learn how to control dark magic, putting her on an even level with Raven. At least she hoped. She hadn't been able to figure out exactly what had happened with the dark magic after it had left her body, but she didn't feel comfortable talking to Charlie about it. He seemed too close to it. Sophia had promised to answer her questions. It was time she did just that.

After a quick breakfast, Jade still had plenty of time before meeting Sophia. She decided to call Katie and see if she'd heard anything from her faeries yet. She hadn't. She sounded pretty disappointed, so Jade invited her over for a chat, which she excitedly accepted.

As they sat drinking tea in the eat-in kitchen, Jade said, "I'm glad you accepted my invite, Katie. I'm very interested to learn more about your gift."

"Thank you so much for inviting me." She glanced at the kitchen door. "Will the High Priest be joining us?"

Jade smiled at her. "You can call him Charlie when we're not in circle, but no, I wanted to get to know you personally. You can meet with him later if you want."

"So, what do you want to know about faeries?"

"Well, in the Book of Shadows there are spells that are categorized as faerie magic, but I've never been able to speak with a faerie before. I used to see them when I was little, but rarely. Most often over the lake behind my house. And of course meeting Boon at your initiation, but I've never really communicated in depth with one. I guess what I'm trying to say is, based on your demonstration at your initiation, you are the expert in faerie magic, and I'd just like to learn all I can."

Her eyes widened. "The expert? Huh, I never thought of it like that. Pretty cool."

"So, if you were to teach someone who knew nothing about faeries, where would you start? What's most important to know?"

She seemed to think about this a minute. "Well . . ." She looked out the window to the backyard. "Is it all right if we go outside? Faeries are much more comfortable in nature, unless they're house faeries of course. They'll come to me wherever I am, but since they don't know you very well yet, it might help encourage them to appear."

"Of course." She stood and placed both their teacups in the sink, then they grabbed their cloaks and went out the back door.

Jade's property had been in the family for generations. It held a mansion, rolling fields, a creek and pond on the northern side, and on the western side of the house, an expansive garden that once supplied enough fruits and veggies for a large family. On the East side was a long-untended apple orchard, with several rows of trees that had been neglected for some time, growing wild. There were a lot of underbrush and vines hanging everywhere. It looked more like a forest. That was the direction Katie led them.

As they walked, she explained, "I don't think there's any one thing that's most important to know about faeries. I've been working with them my whole life, and each thing I know seems tied to other things. One of the cool things about faerie magic, it often has a healing effect on your aura. It's also the easiest kind of magic to practice, at least in terms of energy use. They really do most of the work. You just have to know what to say and do to get their attention. The best part is you don't even need any special tools like candles or herbs. Once you establish a relationship with a faerie, they are all you need to work faerie magic."

Jade smiled at Katie's enthusiasm. "That sounds pretty easy."

"Oh, I'm babbling, aren't I? I'm sorry, I'm just so excited to be able to contribute to the coven . . . finally." She rolled her eyes.

They had reached the small gate into the orchard, and Jade opened it for her. "What do you mean 'finally'?"

"Well, my cousin Harmony had been in the coven since I was nine when my family came to town." She ducked under some vines and Jade followed. "But I haven't ever really been good at magic, so I've always just been there, you know. During holy day rites, I'd repeat the ritual words with the rest of the township, but never felt anything magical. Which is fine, there's nothing wrong with that, but I always looked up to Harmony. I wanted to be more like her, you know, like call the quarters, or raise the circle, something that contributed. Of course, I'd have to have been in the coven for that." She looked down sadly, then brightened as they reached a small circle of bare earth. "Oh, here. This will work perfectly. It's the beginnings of a faerie ring. You know, when mushrooms grow up in a circle in a yard?"

"Yes, I've always wondered about those. The books say they're sacred to faeries and crossing them is risking their wrath."

Katie laughed. "Yeah, there are all kinds of scary tales about them. And if you were to intentionally mess with them, dig up the ground or whatever, I'm sure the faeries would retaliate. But as long as you treat them with respect, there's nothing to worry about. In fact, this is a perfect place for you to meet them."

She stood facing the circle with head bowed and began mumbling something under her breath. As they had walked through the orchard, it had become darker as the overgrowth cast thicker and thicker shadows. Here in the space around the faerie ring, it was darker still, dim as twilight. It had also become warmer. Not to the point that Jade wanted to remove her cloak, but it wasn't so cold that they could see their breath anymore.

Katie said, "Okay," and calmly stepped into the circle and sat cross-legged on one side, her cloak splayed out around her. She pointed in front of her. "Have a seat."

Jade cautiously stepped into the circle and sat, looking around her. The quiet stillness was comforting. Like being in a blanket fort. She could feel the tension draining down into the earth without her even trying. "Before we start I want to clear something up. You seemed a bit down about not helping as much as you thought you should. It may seem like repeating ritual words isn't doing much, but you should remember that every person at a ritual is offering their energy and focus to the circle. If even one person isn't participating correctly, it drags down the energy. Usually, it won't cause harm, but sometimes one person can disrupt an entire ritual, and the participants can actually get hurt. Trust me, every person is important, coven member or not." Katie seemed to take heart at this. "So, I'm guessing you were trained in faerie magic by your mom?"

Katie looked uncertain. "Sort of. I've had training, but I've always been able to see faeries. I mean, they're pretty much everywhere, at least in this town. Or they are now. When we first moved here, I only saw a handful. Over the last month they've been showing up more and more. I think it has to do with how much untamed land there is here. Mom and I moved here from Boston. It was all concrete and steel." She made a face and stuck out her tongue. "Not conducive to faerie magic, or any kind of magic in my opinion. Anyway, I could always see them, but I didn't have the natural talent of being able to use them in spells, or rather request their help, as I've come to realize." She leaned over and whispered to Jade, "It's not just Boon, they can all be a little oversensitive."

"You weren't born in Sugar Hill?"

"No. My dad was a Citizen in Mayfair, and my mom was a Witch in Springfield Township. Her family was from here though, so when they decided to get married, they moved back here. After we moved here, my mom started officially training me in faerie magic. It took a while to get the hang of it because she used all these ancient Latin texts. I struggled to understand the words, but I was good at repeating what my mom said, so I did that. Eventually, the faeries agreed to help me, and I could do some spells. It never really felt natural though." She smirked. "I mean it wasn't effortless like it seemed to be with my mom." She looked up at Jade excitedly. "Then, one night when I was twelve, it changed.

"I had cast a circle and was sitting there waiting for the faeries to show up. I thought back to when I was little and they would dance around me, or hide my socks. I can even remember when I was really young and they would play peekaboo with me in my crib. They were friends to me then, not some mysterious spirit that I should control. So I sat there wishing they would come talk with me like when I was younger, and they did. Boy did they ever. I didn't speak a word out loud, but we talked for hours. They told me that I'd been doing it all wrong. They said they had missed me. That confused me because I'd been seeing them for my whole life." She smiled affectionately.

"What they were trying to tell me is that when I started using my mom's text to communicate, it cut off the natural connection we had built all the years before." She sighed. "I'm not explaining this very well." She paused, thinking. "Oh! Okay, it's like this. When you first learn to write, you have to concentrate on each letter and word, drawing the lines just right so people can read them. Over time it becomes so easy you don't have to think about it, you just write. Communicating with faeries through the ancient text is like when you were little and had to concentrate — you get the words out, but it's hard and takes forever. The way I communicate, and how I'll teach you, it's like once you're older, you just do. Does that make sense?" She looked hopefully at Jade.

Jade smiled at Katie. She wondered how she managed to breathe. "Yeah I get it. It's actually the way I do magic. I learned all the spell text when I was little, but never really used it. My mom would tell me what to say, and I would think it over and then speak whatever words came to mind. It goes much faster and smoother that way."

"Exactly!" Katie exclaimed. "So you ready to try it?" She practically beamed at Jade.

"Sure."

"Close your eyes and ground and center."

Jade closed her eyes and took several deep breaths. She calmed her mind and grounded her nervous energy into the Earth beneath her.

Katie's voice was almost a whisper, calm and gentle. "First, you should smile. Be happy. Remember the joy of your youth, when life was full of fun and adventure. Those are the feelings and energies that faeries are drawn to."

Jade followed Katie's direction. Almost immediately, a faint glow appeared outside her closed eyelids.

Katie let go of Jade's hands. "Open your eyes."

The area around them was lit up with hundreds of tiny glowing lights. Jade focused on one of the lights directly in front of her, hovering in the air. The flickering green orb slowly changed shape. Details came into focus and Jade realized it was a tiny person. A little girl no taller than an inch. She was mostly green, but had a pink dress that looked a lot like a ballerina tutu. She wore sparkling bracelets, and her neckline was covered with tiny dots that looked like a necklace of stars. She had a tall hat that looked like it was made of the most delicate down feathers. Then Jade saw her wings. They were sheer like a dragonfly's wings, and they glowed with their own green light.

Jade had only ever seen one faerie this close before, and this was completely different than the one at Katie's initiation. Now here they were, hundreds of them surrounding her. She looked around, trying to see the details of each light. Some she made out easily. They were different sizes and colors but none bigger than a tennis ball. A few hovered in front and around her, and others bounced lightly on the grass next to them. There were several decidedly round ones that did not glow, forming a ring around them. They were about the size of a softball and frowned constantly, glancing over their shoulders into the darkness behind them. They reminded her of toadstools brought to life.

Jade pointed to them and asked, "Those bigger ones. Are they acting as sentries?"

"Those are Ballybogs. My mom's great grandma brought them from Ireland. Or rather they stowed away with them." One of the Ballybogs stuck his tongue out at Katie. She laughed and continued. "They're always hanging around our house. They're kind of the self-appointed guardians of our family. A few of them have watched over us for generations."

One of the larger Ballybog faeries took a deep bow toward Jade.

"So not all faeries glow?" Jade loved the gentle light that surrounded them. It felt like another layer of protection surrounding her.

"No, there are some that definitely do not glow, like the Ballybogs, and some can choose if they want to glow or not based on the situation. In fact, most of these don't normally glow, but I asked for you to be able to see better out here and not be afraid or worried."

Jade smiled. "Well, tell them that's very thoughtful and I appreciate it."

Katie laughed again. "I don't have to tell them anything, they can hear you. They understand every language of humans and the animal kingdom too."

"Impressive. Can they all grow and manipulate wood, like the one at your initiation?"

Katie smiled mischievously at Jade. "Nope. They all have different skills, just like Witches. We'll show you." She stood and walked several feet away, the faeries moving to keep her within their circle of light. She picked up a fallen branch and stuck it into the ground a couple feet in front of Jade. "Okay, this stick is Jade's enemy, my enemy too, actually." She looked at one of the larger faeries that had sat between her and Jade. "Kiker, you know what to do."

Kiker got to his feet and smiled sweetly at the "enemy stick" in the ground. He walked slowly up to it with his hands behind his back, weaving one foot in front of the other. He chirped a high-pitched run of sounds. When he got right in front of it, he stopped and tilted his head to one side, making another high-pitched sound like a question. He looked completely innocent and really cute.

Suddenly, he stopped glowing. His head grew to the size of a basketball. He opened a mouth full of razorlike teeth and screamed a loud screech unlike anything Jade had heard before. Kiker raised his hands, now covered with sharp talons, and he attacked. He scratched and clawed, bit and tore at the stick, until there was nothing left but sawdust.

As quickly as Kiker had escalated into this shredding machine, he morphed back into the cute, tiny faerie that glowed with the comforting blue light. He turned and smiled sweetly at Jade and took a graceful bow.

All the faeries around them clapped and cheered and hollered in their high-pitched, twittering voices. Katie smiled proudly at Jade. "And that's just the start. Some faeries can shield you, some can heal you. They can't cast spells like Witches can, but their talents are just as powerful. Like Nyra here." She pointed to the faerie that had hovered in front of Jade earlier. "She can create an illusion so real that not even the most powerful Witch would be able to tell the difference."

Jade was impressed. "Well, I'm sorry I underestimated you."

A few more showed their powers, seeming to compete for attention.

"Thank you all so much for sharing your gifts. I'm sure you'll be very useful when it comes time to fight, or those who want to will be." She turned to Katie. "I need to get going now. You'll let me know as soon as the faeries return with news of Raven?"

"Of course."

Katie dismissed her faeries and walked with Jade back to the house. When they reached the porch steps, Jade realized one faerie had followed them home, her pale pink light floating along with them. "That's Indora. She's a luck faerie. I told her about what happened to you and what you're trying to do to Raven, and she asked if she could be your house faerie." Katie looked hopefully at Jade, as did Indora.

"Sure. What's a house faerie?"

"It just means that she'll live here, protect your property, and help you when you need it."

"Thank you, Indora," Jade said to the tiny ball hovering between them. "That would be lovely."

Katie frowned at the faerie a moment, then stepped close to Jade. "Indora says we're being watched." She looked out toward the orchard they'd just come from.

Jade followed her gaze, just in time to see a flash of sunlight reflected off metal. The lawkeeper's drone. It disappeared, leaving several branches shaking in its wake as it hid in the greenery.

"Great," she mumbled under her breath, then said quietly to Katie, "I think we'd better get out of here."

They rushed back to the house and in the side door. As soon as the door was shut, Jade waved her hand and said, "Sigillum." *Seal.* Every curtain and shade flew shut. Jade peeked out the door's window and watched the shadows of the orchard. Katie was pacing behind her, nervously babbling in a low voice.

Jade replaced the curtain and turned to her, taking her writhing hands firmly. "Katie. It's okay, we're safe. He can't come inside without cause, and even if he could, we've done nothing wrong."

"But you said, if he finds out you're a Witch—"

"He won't. Even if the drone saw everything, he didn't see me cast any spells, did he?" She shook her head. "Then we've nothing to worry about. Now, take a nice deep breath and let it out slowly."

The young Witch did as she was told, and her hands stopped trembling. "Sorry. I—sorry." She looked sheepishly at Jade.

Jade let her go. "No worries."

The front door opened with a bang, and Charlie hollered through the house, "Jade! Are you all right?"

"We're in here," Jade yelled back as she hurried to look down the hall.

Charlie was closing the door behind him. "You locked the house so tight, I almost couldn't get in. What's going on, why the extra security? Hi, Katie."

Katie grinned and looked to the side.

"Katie and I were walking back from the orchard when we caught a drone spying on us. We made it back into the house as fast as we could, but I think it's still out there." Charlie peeked out the curtains as Jade continued, "I spelled the house. Well, it was a fear response I guess. I know they can't enter, but I felt like they could. I guess I was just startled."

"Understandable. Inspector Caldwell doesn't know you own this property, so I'm guessing he sent his drones to do a township-wide search for you. Now that he's seen you, he'll be looking closer."

"So what do we do? I don't want him hanging around my house, trying to catch me casting."

Charlie thought a moment, then focused on Katie. "For all he knows, this is Katie's house."

"My house? I wish." She giggled nervously.

"What are you thinking?" Jade asked.

Charlie said, "If the drones were to clearly see us leave and Katie stay behind, it might be enough to avoid suspicion, at least for a while."

"It's worth a try. You don't mind hanging out here, do you? At least for a few hours."

"Not at all," Katie said. "Your house is beautiful. But is that all?"

Jade said, "No, you should probably be outside for at least a little. Gather some herbs, sweep the porch, something to show you're caring for the property. It doesn't have to be a long task, but do it shortly after we leave so there's a better chance they'll see you."

Charlie said, "And while you're outside, try not to look around to see them. They should think you don't even know they're there."

She grinned mischievously. "I feel like I'm a spy or something, on a secret mission to fake out the Big City."

"Well, I'm glad you're having fun," Charlie said. "Walk Jade and me out? You should act like this is your house starting now."

CHAPTER 10

It took Jade and Charlie almost an hour to find a way to ditch the drone that was shadowing them. They stopped in at Mrs. Keepsake's and told her what was going on. She brought them downstairs and let Jade pass through a portal, much like the one they'd used to get to Hidden Lake. This one led to the end of River Bridge. It was a short walk from there to Bonfire Field, but the road passed Jade's property, so she cut east along the creek's bank.

Charlie stayed behind to keep an eye on the inspector's drone, still hovering near the edge of Mrs. Keepsake's property. He would follow Jade and warn her if it suddenly left, signaling it was going after her.

When she finally arrived at Bonfire Field, Sophia was waiting beside her car. "I checked in with the rest of the coven, and they managed to get all households and businesses spelled last night."

"That's fast," Jade said.

"Well, that's because we didn't do full properties, just the buildings on them. I would have preferred to spell the people as well, but Willow pointed out that since we were uncertain where Raven was, we needed the fastest solution. Better than nothing I guess. What we really need is our township border spell reset, but that's just not possible right now. I still can't believe she managed to break through it."

"It'll be fine, I'm sure. So what I was asking yesterday, about how killing with dark magic—"

"Right. We'll get to all that, but first we need you to pick out some trinkets."

Jade sighed at being put off again. Charlie seemed to be the only one willing to talk about dark magic. She decided to try being patient. "Trinkets? I thought those were just used to amplify and focus spells for Witches still in training."

"That's their main purpose, true, but even as an experienced Witch, they can improve your spell casting. Especially for focus. You can't have too much help in dealing with Raven."

"It's worth a try I guess."

"Lovely. Let's get started." She led Jade to the edge of the woods. Sitting on a large tree stump was a wooden chest. "I took the liberty of choosing several potentials for you, just odds and ends I had lying around. You can always change them out at any time, but these will get you started. They've already been charged to their respective elements. Just pick whichever ones speak to you."

Sophia opened the chest, revealing a shallow tray full of feathers, leaves, and pressed flowers. She lifted the tray out and placed it next to the chest. There was another tray under it, this time filled with half-burnt sticks and nuggets of various metals. Under that was a tray of sea shells, driftwood, and sea glass. The bottom of the chest was full of various stones and crystals.

She stood back and motioned to the assortment of items. Jade looked over each tray and picked out the four items that caught her eye: a golden sun stone the size of a quarter that glittered as she picked it up, a small white downy feather, a small misshapen blob of silver, and a piece of smooth turquoise sea glass.

As Jade turned the items over in her hands, she had a feeling of being watched. She looked up at Sophia and realized it wasn't her. She turned slowly, following her gaze across the wide expanse of barren ground.

She whispered to Sophia, "Someone's watching us."

"Yes, I feel it too." After a moment she seemed to decide something. "It's actually quite rude." She pulled a crystal out of the folds of her dress and waved it in the air before them. "Revelare." *Reveal.*

One of the Lawkeeper's drones shimmered into view near the tree line. Jade wondered how much of their conversation it had caught, and whether it was the same drone at the Keepsake's or a different one. It glided toward them and stopped several feet away. It projected a beam of light at a spot eye level with Jade and a couple feet away from her. A holographic image of Inspector Caldwell appeared.

Jade said, "Inspector Caldwell, what a pleasant surprise."

Sophia brightened. "I heard you had to return to Sun City." She gave him a huge smile. "What a shame."

The inspector smiled back stiffly. "I did, but I've concluded my business and will be returning tomorrow morning."

"Is that so?" Sophia glanced at Jade.

"Yes. I have been given temporary jurisdiction over the township in order to complete my investigation." He tapped his left arm, and a holographic document appeared next to him.

Sophia stepped forward and skimmed through it. "You've sent a copy of this to the mayor, I assume?"

"I have. I will be staying in town until this case is closed. So, Miss Cerridwen, it seems you will be seeing much more of me in the coming weeks."

Jade struggled to keep a smile. "Lovely."

The inspector opened his notebook. "Since I have you here, I have a few questions for you. Were you aware that in his will Mr. Whetstone left his entire company, including a sizable fortune in stocks, bonds, and properties . . . to you?" He looked at her intently, pen poised, ready to make notes.

Jade replied casually, "No, but I'm not surprised." She steeled herself against what she needed to say next. Something the old Jade, before she'd been betrayed, would have had no trouble saying. "He was like a father to me, and I was an indispensable part of his company. His right-hand woman, people have said."

"Hm . . ." the inspector muttered and made a note.

While his head was down, Sophia waved her hand and his image disappeared, immediately followed by several sparks and smoke emanating from the drone. It swayed and bobbed before dropping to the grass at their feet.

"Oh dear. Looks like his technological contraption is broken. Too bad I don't know how to fix something like that." She winked at Jade.

Jade looked nervously around. "Lawkeepers usually have three drones."

"Don't worry, dear, my spell works in a radius much bigger than this field. If his other drones didn't leave town with him, either they are too far to see us, or they're also broken." She motioned for Jade to follow her.

"Wait. First, we need to deal with this." She pointed at the lump of metal. "Tampering with lawkeeper drones is a pretty serious offense. He'll come looking for it, then he'll be looking for you."

"Don't worry, dear. I've dealt with his kind before. He's all about the evidence, and he has none proving I touched his drone. It'll take him a while to get here, and we'll be done and long gone by then."

She turned toward the dark forest and walked through the trees. Jade followed her into the woods. Just on the other side of the thick tree line, the space opened up again. It was a small area of grass and trees in a wide shallow gully. In the middle of that was a stone structure. The main wall was about two stories tall with an arched opening in the top half.

The bottom half of the main wall had an alcove fitted into it. Two other stone walls extended out from the main wall, like open arms. Where they connected to the main wall, they were almost the same height. But as they reached out from it, they shrank in height until at about twelve feet out there was nothing left. It reminded Jade of some old forgotten ruin of a church.

There were moss and vines everywhere. Trees had grown up through the rubble, their canopy dense enough to obscure the ruins from above, but there were hardly any branches on the trunks below. It gave the space a sheltered feeling.

Sophia turned toward the remnants of a crumbling wall. "This place was so beautiful once. Let me show you." She turned toward the main wall and raised her hands over her head. She moved her hands outward and down. As they went, the world before Jade's eyes changed. As if time were reversing, the vines were retreating, the cracked walls were un-crumbling, replacing their own stones by some unseen hand. As the high-ceilinged roof filled in with its huge beams, Jade noticed the most amazing piece.

The late morning light shone through a huge stained-glass window. It was a multi-scene artwork. The large arch continued around to form a full circle. Along its edge were thirteen coven members, each practicing their unique gifts. In the center was a single face, that of the Goddess Brigit.

She smiled down on the bottom two panels. The left side showed Jade's father, Lee. He was dressed in black robes with a gold rope belt. In one hand he held an athame, in the other a wand. On the right panel was Jade's mother, Rose. She was also dressed in ritual garb with a silver belt. She held a chalice and pentacle disk. Most of the window was constructed of large panes of glass, but their faces were built out of tiny shards, giving them a more realistic appearance.

She missed them terribly some days, more so since she had returned to town last month for her aunt's crossing over. The light that shone through the window was a warm, colorful light that soothed your soul. She looked around and marveled at the complete structure surrounding them. She knew it was an illusion, but it seemed so real.

Jade didn't need illusions now. She needed power, enough to capture or kill Raven and maybe even stop the inspector. "Look, I've tried to be patient. You said you'd talk to me about dark magic, but you keep putting me off. Wouldn't you rather I learn about it from you? I don't have to use it in battle, I just need to understand how it works so I can defend against Raven. Please?" She felt so helpless. If Sophia wouldn't teach her about it, she'd have to keep working with Charlie. The last thing she wanted was to expose him to even more darkness than she already had.

Sophia gently took both Jade's hands in hers. "Jade." She paused, frowning slightly as if trying to find the words. "You are the High Priestess. You don't need anyone's permission to choose what magic you practice. All I can do is guide you as wisely and honestly as I can. However, if you insist on using dark magic to battle Raven"—she withdrew her hands—"you will do it alone."

The warmth she always felt in Sophia's presence withdrew. Jade shivered, head to toe. She did not like the feeling. "You would abandon me?"

"No. Never," Sophia responded quickly, and Jade felt a small amount of the warmth return. "What I mean is, the other coven members and I will stand by your side no matter where you lead. But you alone will choose the path we take. I will not guide you into darkness. And neither will Willow."

Jade considered that a moment. She had always relied on the two senior Witches for guidance. The idea they would refuse to council her hurt. She signed and sat down on a large, weathered stone. "I know you don't want me using dark magic, but Raven uses it. How am I supposed to compete with that?"

Sophia sat next to her. "You obviously won't let this go easily. You're frustrated and disappointed. You feel you're out of your depth and unable to beat Raven without the edge you think dark magic can provide. I'm sorry if I led you to believe I had the answers, if you thought I would give my blessing. I won't. You haven't seen what dark magic can do, not really. You haven't seen it infect an entire township, little babies slaughtered or left to starve because they didn't fit in with a dark Witch's plans. It's not evil, Jade, but it is a sickness."

Jade felt sick. The warmth she'd felt moments before had twisted into a scalding, sour taste in her mouth. She wanted to run, to escape the feeling and the images Sophia was describing. She couldn't take it anymore. "Please, stop." As soon as she spoke, the feelings were gone. She breathed deep, relief flowing through her. It was almost as if it had never happened, but when she looked in Sophia's troubled eyes, she remembered. Like a nightmare, the faded memory of the sickening images remained.

"I don't like to hurt you, Jade, but words alone haven't dissuaded you. Sometimes the harsh truth is the only cure. Do you see now why I can't help you with this? Do you see why dark magic is not to be messed with?"

Jade had never experienced the full force of an empath's active power. She'd heard it was possible for a truly powerful empath to make others feel what they felt, but she'd never dreamed Sophia would do that to her. Certainly not with such painful memories. "I understand now. And I'm so sorry you had to endure that." Sophia was such a gentle soul, Jade couldn't imagine her being in the middle of such darkness.

"Good." She sniffed and shook her head. "We should ground and center. We don't want to carry such energy into your training."

Jade stood with Sophia, and they closed their eyes. After a few moments, Jade asked, "Training?"

"More like practice. I heard Charlie worked with you to call your first Elemental."

"Yes, the Fire Elemental. Aren't the rest the same?"

"Yes, but the first time you call one, you need to be focused. Better to do it now than in the heat of battle." She walked to the center of the ruins and pointed down. "Stand here and call your Fire Elemental. Since you've called it before, it will be a nice little warm-up to calling the rest."

As she moved away, Jade took her place. She looked up at the cathedral ceiling stretching over two stories above her. She could tell she was in the exact center because all the beams converged at a point directly over her head.

She closed her eyes and raised her hands outward to her sides, palms facing up. "Guardian of the South, I call on you. Element of Fire, I ask you to show yourself to me. In perfect love and perfect trust I ask, come to me!" She waited, frozen in place.

It took a little longer for her lion to appear this time. Jade guessed it was because she was farther from the house and he had to run the distance. He was just as she remembered though, glowing gold and larger than life. As he passed through the barrier into the sacred space, a thought occurred to Jade. "Is he able to see through the cloaking because he's an Elemental?'

Sophia was staring wide-eyed at the magnificent creature sitting regally beside Jade. "Um . . . Yeah . . . Wow." She continued looking him over for a moment, then looked at Jade's quizzical expression. "You have no idea what you have there, do you?"

"I think so. Leo is my Fire Elemental." She smiled at him and patted his mane gently, reveling in the luxurious, warm softness.

Sophia shook her head, amazed. "There are many forms an Elemental can take based on several factors: your status in the coven and amount of power you control, and the level of the Elemental itself. Even though in essence there is only one element of Fire, an Elemental is a manifestation. Therefore, the form it can take is limited by the Witch."

She waved her hand in the air over her head in an arch, then left it stretched out. After a moment a flaming bird swept down and landed on her arm. He was a literal phoenix. He stretched his beak up and screeched. The flaming feathers glowed brighter for a moment.

Sophia said, "This is my Fire Elemental, Freddie." The phoenix bowed his head gracefully. "I believe he came to me in this form because of my close association to the element of Air. The element you associate most closely with, the one that's easiest for you to control, is your primary element. It informs the shape of all your Elementals. Rose and Joy both had lions for Fire. Theirs were more silvery-looking than gold, though." She admired Jade's lion. "Yours is much larger I think. The point is, the fact that you received a lion tells me that you are a natural born leader." She smiled at Leo.

"I guess it runs in the family." Jade felt a moment of doubt speaking words so bold, but when she looked at the majestic beast sitting proudly next to her, the doubt quickly passed and she felt they were true.

Sophia released her phoenix, and he flew up into the sky, leaving a trail of glowing smoke in his wake. "Now. Let's see about finding your other Elementals. You're going to make the same call to each of the elements in turn and see what comes to you."

Jade sighed and tried to clear her mind. When she felt ready, she began the call for Water. She opened her eyes but nothing had changed. She and Sophia both looked around for several moments. Just as she was about to ask Sophia if she should try again, there was a crunching sound, like leaves underfoot. It was coming from behind her.

They both turned to look in that direction. The Plants shook as something small but strong pushed through the undergrowth. It slowly drew closer and passed through the sacred barrier and into the open space. It was a turtle. It had a blue and green shell about three inches wide by four inches long. It climbed awkwardly over the pebbles toward Jade.

"Really? A friggin turtle? It's not even big enough to hurt anything." Jade was disappointed she didn't get a cooler animal, but even more concerned about the time she felt she was wasting. Leo could obviously do some real damage, but this? This wasn't going to help anyone. Unless they wanted to get Raven to laugh herself to death.

Sophia broke through her thoughts. "Jade dear, don't you remember what I told you about Elementals being able to change their shape? This is just how Water chose to greet you. She's probably testing you."

"She?"

"Yes, dear. Remember the Element's correspondences: Water and Earth are feminine energies, Air and Fire are masculine.

"Well, wish me luck." Jade looked down at the tiny turtle in front of her. She sighed and bent down on one knee and placed her hand on the ground in front of the Elemental, palm up. The turtle immediately crawled onto her hand. Jade lifted her and rose to her feet, holding her at eye level. "Hi. Um . . ." She had to admit the creature was cute if nothing else. The turtle looked at her, blinking her big black eyes slowly. "Okay, you're cute, but what I really need now is ferocious." She remembered the story Charlie had told her about the stag growing new antlers at will. The turtle just kept looking at her as if waiting for something. Jade thought about how Sophia had said she was testing her. "I have no idea what you want from me so . . . how about you just show me what you can do? Please?" Jade knelt down and placed her hand on the ground again.

The turtle stepped awkwardly off her palm and walked in a slow circle until she was facing Jade again. She began to grow, very slowly at first, then faster. As she grew, she changed the shape of her shell. Ridges formed in rows from front to back, then spikes grew out of the rows. The edge of the shell became thinner until it looked razor sharp. The legs became scalier, and small spikes grew all over the feet. The toes began to look more like talons. As her head grew, a type of helmet began to form, covering everything except her eyes and nostrils. Spikes around her eyes made her look like she was frowning and angry.

The Water Elemental continued to grow, forcing Jade to take a step back. She stopped when she was the size of what Jade could only compare to a tank. The turtle slowly bowed her head low. Jade stepped forward and gently placed her hand on the flat part of her head between her eyes. She bumped into her hand gently several times. Jade could feel the weight behind her massive head.

Jade smiled. "Now this is what I'm talking about. I'll call you Tank." The turtle made a low gurgling sound and bowed her head. Jade looked at Sophia. "Quick question, have I just been lucky or what? Charlie told me about how the stag greeted him, and neither of my elements have caused me any pain like that."

Sophia shrugged. "Sometimes they challenge you, sometimes they don't. They may be elementals, but they do have opinions and free will. They aren't forced to follow your commands, they choose to. It may be that the elementals know why you're calling them now and have already decided to submit to your will for the cause. Why don't you give her a command and see how it goes?"

Jade looked around. "You said these walls are just an illusion?"

"Of sorts. Although, if you're thinking what I think you are, it might be better in this setting if you tried defensive instead of offensive. We can find something for you to knock down later."

"Fine." She wanted to see some bricks fly, but Sophia was probably right. An idea occurred to her. "Can one of your own Elementals attack you?" Both Tank and Leo looked up at her. "I mean if I commanded them to just for training, would they?"

"No. Once they bond to you, they bond for life."

"But what about Raven? Does she still have Elementals that follow her commands even though what she's doing is wrong?"

Sophia considered this. "Magic is neither good nor evil. The person using it could do evil things, but the magic itself has no intent. It's even truer for Elementals. They are neutral. While they do have opinions and can disagree with what you are using them for, they bind to the person, not the person's intent." She paused, her eyes seeming to hunt for some distant memory. Her smile was bittersweet when she looked at Jade. "You should know, Raven wasn't always so dark. She and your mother were close when they were little, and it's only since they grew up that Raven lost her way."

Jade frowned. "You talk about her like she used to be a good person and just made a mistake. She killed my parents, killed my aunt, and even killed my best friend. Those aren't the actions of someone who is lost. She's just evil."

Sophia shook her head. "You need to be clear about one thing. Like magic, people are neither good nor evil. It is only their actions that can be categorized. Even the worst serial killer was not born with hate in their heart, and the most passive person can be driven to violence under the right circumstances."

Jade crossed her arms and turned away. She didn't agree, but didn't want to argue either. "I got it, judge the actions not the person. Can we call my next Elemental now please?"

Sophia sighed. "Yes. Why don't you try Earth."

Jade dismissed Tank in her mind. She shrank down to the more manageable size of a Labrador and slowly trod over to take her place to Jade's left.

Jade sighed and closed her eyes, trying to put her anger away. The way Sophia talked reminded her of her mother's talks about morality. She'd told Jade pretty much the same thing, and Jade had agreed with her mother then. She'd had no idea at that age, of course, that there would be someone who would gladly destroy a person's family. Now she knew better.

She took another deep breath, and another until she felt calm enough. She called for the Earth Elemental to show itself. Again she heard something coming from the darkness beyond the borders, but this time it sounded like a gallop. Suddenly, the trees beyond the border seemed to draw back like a curtain, and a gigantic horse burst through the clearing. It continued running at full speed until it was just before Jade, where it skidded to a stop. It reared up on its hind legs and let out a loud neigh. As it dropped down to its front legs, Jade noticed it was covered in vines and leaves, woven together and forming an armor over the horse's cherrywood-colored coat. This was undoubtedly a war horse.

It glared at Jade with green eyes that sparkled like jewels catching the light. Jade expected Earth to bow as the others had, but it remained standing, its eyes boring into Jade like it was able to see right through her. After a moment it began to make Jade uncomfortable.

She looked away, but the horse whinnied. Jade looked back at it. She wondered if she was meant to go on a vision quest like with Leo. She took a step forward, but the horse took an equal step back. Jade frowned and tilted her head to one side, trying to figure out what to do next. The horse mirrored her movements. It suddenly dawned on Jade: "You don't want me to do anything. I'm supposed to just stand here with you. But for how long?"

Earth made no reply but stayed still as stone, only its tail swishing. Jade sighed and thought to herself, *As long as needed I guess.* She could swear Earth smiled. It wasn't that its mouth changed exactly, it was something about the expression in its eyes. They were still fiery but more relaxed somehow. Jade settled into her stance and resigned herself to staring back into the deep green eyes of Earth.

After a few moments, she noticed she was feeling much more relaxed and stronger at the same time. She felt rooted, like not even Leo could push her over. She smiled at the feeling of security that washed over her. It was a kind of connection like she had experienced with Leo but not as visual or even physical. It was a connection of mind and spirit.

Earth bowed its head once briefly, then pranced over to stand behind Jade. It positioned its head just behind Jade's left shoulder. Jade turned her head slightly and felt the horse's breath as it snorted. Jade looked to Sophia, content and ready to move on.

"Are you naming this one too?" Sophia asked, amused.

Jade looked in her horse's eyes as it stood guardian over her left shoulder. "Ace."

"Ace?' Sophia frowned. "That's not very Earthy, or feminine. You know she's a girl," Sophia whispered in jest.

Jade considered her a moment. "Ace. She's the primal Earth element, the Ace of Pentacles in the tarot deck. I like it." Ace let out a playful whinny and nodded her head. "See, she likes it too."

"One left," Sophia responded. "My favorite, in fact."

Jade smiled. One more and she'd feel she had a whole army behind her. She closed her eyes and raised her hands, calling the element of Air. Nothing happened. She waited and waited but there was no sound, no movement beyond the barrier. She frowned at Sophia.

Sophia walked over to her and rested her hand on Jade's forehead. After a moment she withdrew her hand and said calmly, "You're not ready."

"What? How could I not be ready? Look, I have three elements; they all think I'm ready. I thought you said the element would appear in whatever form I was able to handle. What's going on?"

Sophia replied, "I'm not sure, but I would guess Air wants to appear in a specific form, but it feels you're not ready yet." Jade pouted like a child. "Be patient, dear. The Elementals are wiser than we are. Have faith."

She turned and looked at her three Elementals: the lion, the horse, and the turtle. She thought there must be a joke there somewhere. She mentally thanked each one for coming and released them. They each trotted off toward their respective directions.

Jade's stomach growled loud enough for Sophia to hear it. They both laughed. "Guess we should stop for lunch." Jade began walking back to the car and Sophia followed.

"We're pretty much done working with Elementals until your Air Elemental decides to make an appearance. But I think you should have a talk with Charlie."

"About what?"

"I know you think Raven is the more important problem, but you've got your protection spell on, and the whole township is keeping their eye out for Raven. I think you and Charlie should figure out how to deal with the inspector first. His drones found you at home and now here? That sounds like too much coincidence. And what's stopping him from deciding you're guilty and arresting you?"

"Nothing really." They'd reached the clearing, and she looked around before stepping into the open space. No inspector and no drones. It appeared they were safe for now. She shook her head as she placed the supplies in the back of Sophia's car. She saw the Band on her wrist, and she knew.

"Sophia, is there any chance your cloaking spell didn't work on my Band?"

"No. Well, most likely not."

"Most likely?"

"The spell never failed the Witch I learned it from. Problem is, they're always coming up with ways around our magic and the last time we used that spell successfully was about… twenty years ago?"

"So it might not be working? Why didn't you tell me this when you cast it?"

"I'm sorry, dear. I was so certain it would work."

Jade leaned against the back of the car and scanned the surrounding underbrush. Was a drone hiding out there now, watching from the shadows, recording everything?

Sophia stepped close to Jade and whispered, "Why don't you take it off? I could carry it with me and lead them away from you."

"You don't understand. If I'm caught without it, he could add charges." She'd been able to keep their conversations short, avoiding the possibility his cyborg sensors would detect her deception, but it was only a matter of time until he demanded she be questioned fully. If he got even a moment of drone footage with her not wearing the Band, he'd have cause to do just that. Alone with him in an environment controlled by him, she would be at the mercy of the highest technology Sun City could offer. If there was one thing they'd perfected over the years, it was discovering Witches.

"So? Not to be defeatist, but if you're already facing a death penalty, what else could they do, kill you twice?"

She'd said it as a joke, but as Jade lowered her serious gaze on her, it sank in. Sophia's expression went from a nervous smile to shocked worry. "Oh."

"Yeah, oh." Jade stood and gave Sophia a big hug. "Don't worry about me. I'll go talk with Charlie and we'll figure something out. In the meantime, I have to make it seem like I'm just a curious Citizen."

CHAPTER 11

When Jade arrived at the mayor's mansion, Charlie wasn't home, but Selene's husband, Aiden, was waiting on the front porch. He was about Selene's height, with black curls cut close to his scalp, dark brown skin, and a muscular build.

"Hello, Aiden. Have you seen the mayor?" She hoped he would catch the official title and know what it meant. She hadn't seen any sign of a drone for a while, but that didn't mean they weren't hiding just out of sight, but within earshot.

Aiden nodded and led Jade into the house as he spoke. "Actually, that's why I'm here. He asked me to meet you and offer his apologies for not greeting you himself."

They passed the threshold, and Jade felt a distinct change in the air. It wasn't just the warmth of being indoors; she'd crossed an invisible barrier of some sort.

As soon as Aiden shut the door, he spun and spoke quickly. "We just had a visit from the inspector. He barged into Mary's Tavern, all upset that someone broke his toy. Charlie stayed behind to try to placate him a bit, and I came here to let you know."

Jade rolled her eyes. "Great. I had a feeling that wasn't going to be forgiven easily."

"I also have an update. The border spell is complete. Raven won't be able to cross into Sugar Hill without us knowing. Or rather, you knowing." He pulled out a dark crystal bangle from his cloak and handed it to Jade. "If she enters the township limits, this will glow."

Jade glared at the dim quartz beads. "I could use one of these for the inspector," she quipped. "Any luck tracking his drones?"

"I'm not sure. I cast several different spells, but got no results. Then while I was waiting for you, I tried again. They should have shown up as being in or near Mary's Tavern since I just left them there, but for some reason they didn't show up then either. I'll keep checking in case they actually did leave while I was on my way here, but I would feel better if I knew where they were now."

"Me too. But you did your best. Keep me or Charlie informed if anything changes."

There was a crunch of gravel from the driveway. She peeked out the door. The inspector's silent electric vehicle pulled in the drive. The lawkeeper got out and slammed the door, then stormed toward the front door with two of his drones directly behind him.

"Well, we know there's drones here now," Jade whispered.

Aiden took a crystal out of his cloak pocket. "This should be red if they're within a hundred feet."

The inspector banged loudly on the door. Aiden held up the crystal; it was snow white.

There was no time to figure out why they weren't triggering the spell. As Aiden hid the crystal back in his cloak, Jade put on a smile and opened the front door.

"Ah, Inspector Caldwell, nice to see you again. The mayor's not here at the moment."

"I didn't come for him." He glared at Jade. "Jade Cerridwen, I'm hereby charging you with destruction of Sun City property."

Jade raised her eyebrows at him. "What are you referring to?"

"Don't play games with me. You broke one of my drones," he fumed. The iris of his robotic eye spun, and a blue laser shot out, scanning her. He was looking for deception and not being subtle about it.

As calmly as possible, Jade said, "I did not break your drone." It was the truth. She'd not even known it was about to happen.

He squinted at her. "That may be true. We'll know soon enough. They're inspecting it as we speak, and I should have the results by the end of day. Either way, I can tell you are hiding something from me. That is not wise."

She looked up into his eyes as they stared each other down, and Jade could feel the anger flowing off him. She glanced at the drone hovering next to him, its red eye signaling it was transmitting to Sun City.

She realized then, this wasn't about one broken drone. He was getting nowhere finding out what happened to April. He had no case. There was no proof that she'd done anything to April. They came to town at the same time, Jade stayed, April didn't. With only that to go on, there was nothing he could do and it was making him look bad.

Unless Raven decided to make an appearance, of course. All she'd have to do was glamor her clothes and hair, then she could make a scene as April and claim she was kidnapped, causing Jade to be arrested. Worse yet, she could show him that she was no longer April. Then all bets were off. Jade needed him out of there. A car was approaching, the familiar rumble of Charlie's muscle car. She'd have backup soon.

"Inspector Caldwell, this is exactly the kind of rude, invasive behavior that has made me question whether I wish to live in Sun City. Here in Sugar Hill, people are not accosted on private property. If you wish to officially question me, I will be happy to accompany you to the town hall. Otherwise, I politely request that you step back."

Caldwell waited only a moment before he took a step back. "My apologies," he said tensely. He turned and looked directly at the camera. "I certainly meant no disrespect. However, it is my job to protect and serve the Citizens of Sun City." Charlie had parked and was walking up as Caldwell turned back to Jade and continued. "And one of them is missing. Damaging my equipment hinders my investigation. I'm sure you want me to have every tool at my disposal to find Miss Goodrich. You will forgive my overzealousness."

Jade said, "Of course. She is my friend, and I want to know she's safe. But as far as I know, she went back to Sun City."

Charlie had reached them and stood next to Jade. "Are we having a problem, Inspector? I thought I'd made it clear—"

"No. No problem at all. Miss Cerridwen was just being kind enough to answer a few questions." He smiled at her. "I'm curious about one more thing. Why didn't you go with Miss Goodrich when she left for Sun City?"

"Since you are being civil, I will answer your question. Why wouldn't I stay here?" She waved her arms at the expansive yard and trees at the edge of the woods. "Look at all this nature. I love the technology in Sun City, but there are only so many places you can go to see greenery like this."

He took a step toward her. "So it has nothing to do with your Witch sympathies? You're not planning on staying here and converting?"

She laughed, sharp and sudden. "Convert? Look, I sympathize with the Witches. I sometimes feel they are treated unfairly. But I have no intention of becoming one. No offense, Mr. Mayor."

"None taken." He played along.

"I was raised as a proud Citizen, graduated with honor from the most prestigious university, and became vice president of Whetstone Enterprises. My life is one many can only dream of. Why would I ever give that up?" She stared him down, trying to stay relaxed. She reminded herself she hadn't lied.

Caldwell said, "I will return when the drone's findings are complete. Do not leave this township." He turned and strode away.

He was almost back to his car when a small golden light whizzed past him and stopped right in front of Jade. It was Indora, and she was frantic. She zipped this way and that, sounding like a hummingbird whistle.

The inspector had stopped walking and was staring at them. Jade whispered to Charlie, "He's watching. Do you understand what she's saying?"

He whispered back, "Not a clue. You?"

The inspector slowly walked toward them. Jade was able to sense the faerie's frantic emotions, but they needed to understand what was behind it. Jade glanced from the inspector to Charlie.

He took her clue and spoke to the sparkling light. "Indora, shhh, calm down. I can't understand you. Take a breath."

The tiny faerie began to slow down. Soon she stopped her pacing and hovered in front of Charlie and Jade. Jade still couldn't understand her high-pitched twittering, but she was able to feel more than panic from her. Fear, anger, and worry washed over her. She still had no idea what to make of it, other than there was trouble. Katie had said she'd eventually find a way to communicate with her. They needed that time to be now.

Fully aware of the inspector's eyes on her, Jade had no choice but to interact. This was her faerie, and her instinct was telling her she'd only communicate with her. "Listen very carefully." She held out her hand, and the tickle of tiny feet and wingtips brushed her palm. "We don't understand you. How can we fix that?"

She only had to wait a moment before the vision came. Most of her visions were invasions of her psyche, a message delivered with a hammer. This time it felt so easy. A message that floated in on a breeze. There was trouble, Jade needed to go home, something was growing. Growing?

Jade dropped her hand, returning Indora to a fluttering sparkle. She turned toward Charlie. "We need to go now."

Charlie muttered through clenched teeth, "What about you-know-who?"

Jade turned to find the inspector standing there, staring at her with his arms crossed. She smiled. "Inspector. Was there something else?"

He nodded at Indora, his face and voice unreadable. "That's a faerie?"

Charlie said, "Yes. What of it?"

"I thought they were myth." He smiled pointedly at Jade.

"Apparently not." Jade tried to sound surprised. She really wanted to make a snide comment about how even inspectors don't know everything, but she was hanging on to the illusion of being a Citizen by a thread. Citizens never questioned the lawkeepers. At least not outwardly.

***

The drive from the mansion to Jade's house was a tense one. The inspector would eventually figure out she was a Witch, but she didn't need to rush it or make him think she was "one of the dangerous ones." Charlie had insisted she and Aiden go with him, and the inspector followed in his own car. Indora had flitted ahead of them the whole way.

There was no sign of danger as they entered the open gates. Indora rushed around the side of the house as they all parked in front. Jade got out quickly and ran after Indora as the others followed.

When they finally rounded the corner to the backyard, the path between the back porch and the lake was consumed by the strangest bonfire she'd ever seen. It hurt her eyes to look directly at it. The typical yellow orange was blindingly bright, but it was more than that. There were black flames, hauntingly dark, but no less painful to look at.

She'd heard about cursed scrying fires, but they were a rare occurrence. If it truly was one, there was something very wrong with her protection spell, and the spells protecting every Witch in the township.

Next to the path in her backyard was a small garden surrounded by a white picket fence along the border. Even in the cold months there were perennial herbs that kept their green, but although it was several feet from the flames, the plants on the side nearest the bonfire were burnt and decaying, the vines withered and bare branches in a tangled mess. One last row of flowers remained within the garden, and even those proud crocus were beginning to droop. The curse was slowly spreading.

As she approached the bonfire, she realized someone in a red Sugar Hill cloak was standing between the fire and the back porch. They were waving their hands at the fire, casting sigils: a binding X, a pentacle, and another Jade couldn't quite picture.

Before she could recognize who it was, a strange mixture of heat and cold pushed back against her skin and she raised her arm to protect her face.

A chill shot through her body as she remembered the last time she'd been in this position. She'd been a child then, but the emotions that memory caused felt very present. She stopped dead as a wave of fear washed over her.

Not again, she thought.

The pain of panic gripped her torso, and her legs twitched as if trying to run of their own accord. She'd dealt with her traumatic past months ago. She'd faced the pain and sorrow of losing both parents to a house fire. But if she'd truly moved on, why did she feel that old familiar urge to flee? She looked back toward Charlie, desperately wanting to run to him for safety.

The inspector and Aiden stood behind him, shock on one face, determination on the other. Aiden charged forward, drawing something from his pocket as he went.

Jade knew that the moment she began casting in front of the inspector, she would lose what little advantage she had.

She looked pointedly at Charlie. He nodded. "I've got this." He spoke louder. "Stay back, I don't want either of you getting hurt."

Jade retreated to stand next to the inspector, and Charlie rushed up to join Crystal and Aiden around the fire.

"I've never seen a fire quite like this. This should be interesting. Don't you think, Miss Cerridwen?"

She smiled and batted her eyes at him. "Why yes. Very." Jade was itching to help them, but she had to keep up the pretense of being a Citizen.

The three Witches were spread out around the fire, each doing their best to beat the strange flames back with incantations and gestures. Their success was minimal. The flames slowed, then advanced several feet, then slowed again. It wasn't working. They needed help. They needed her.

Jade focused on the present. She wasn't a child, she was a grown Witch and a High Priestess, with all the power that entailed. She would deal with the inspector after she had done her duty to her coven. She drew from her strength and forced herself to turn toward the inspector, head held high. "Put away your drones." Her tone left no room for argument.

He seemed about to protest, but after a tilt of his head, he sent the drones back to their places in his coat.

"I'm a Witch. In fact, I am High Priestess of the Sugar Hill coven. This fire is more dangerous than you realize, and if you don't let me stop it, there will be severe consequences."

The inspector narrowed his eyes. "First of all, I never bought your 'I'm interested in their culture' story, so your being a Witch doesn't surprise me." He shied away from the flames and took a slight step back, apparently feeling their heat rise. "Second, that Band is Sun City property." He held out his hand, and Jade felt relief at being able to finally remove the device. She placed it in his hand. "Lastly, I will allow you to do what you can to stop this strange fire, but then you will answer all my questions."

Jade faced the fire and lifted her arm, but this time she pushed through the initial fear and moved with purpose. Drawing from the Earth and sky, she pulled on the cool quiet of evening, sending it before her as a shield. The temperature normalized, and she was able to approach without cringing.

She stepped to Crystal's side, expanding the shield to protect her as well. "What do you need?"

Crystal looked at her with relief, her arms continuing to cast the signs, but beginning to falter. "I'm trying to cast a binding spell, but it's only slowing it down. This fire is magical, but it's also physical. We have to put out the flames as well, but it's already taking all of us to keep it from spreading."

Jade said, "You and Charlie keep working on binding it to slow down the spread. Aiden, use a water spell to put the physical fire out. I'll see if I can syphon away the magical energy."

Charlie yelled back, "It's too dangerous. I'm better at syphoning, let me."

"No! There's no time to argue. Just do as I say." There was no way she was going to let Charlie handle dark energy with his heart already shadowed.

She began walking toward where Charlie was standing to keep them spread out. She nearly tripped over the inspector. He'd been bent down, reaching out toward the line of dead grass. "No!" Jade yelled.

He stood to face her, a questioning look on his face. She tried pushing him toward the house, but he didn't move more than an inch.

"Go inside the house. You'll be safe there."

"I assure you, I am safe anywhere." He tapped his Lawkeeper badge, and Jade could feel the energy of the force field that surrounded him.

She really didn't have time for him. "Suit yourself."

Aiden had cast a water spell to drown the fire. Rain was pouring down on it in a localized column from the clear sky. As the normal yellow-and-orange flames began to dissipate, the strange black flames grew.

Jade turned toward the fire and began casting. The cold of the dark flames reminded her of the snake in the box. She drew energy up from the Earth, stretching it forward, trying to use it to capture the flames. They were moving too fast though. She couldn't catch them.

The fire's base was spreading steadily, rising from the line of black, which killed the greenery as it went. They needed to get a grip on the dark flames before they caused any more damage.

Jade reached into her cloak pocket and grabbed the blob of silver. She switched to a binding spell and, keeping the cool Earth trinket snugly in her palm, twirled her hands in circles then pulled them out as if tying a knot. She held still for a moment, urging the slow-moving energy of Earth from her palm into the spell.

Once it felt secure, she gathered with Charlie, Aiden, and Crystal next to the path. The darkness had nearly reached the porch. It was still spreading, though not as fast as before. "It's not working."

"Yes, it is. It takes time for binding spells to work on something like this," Charlie said. They waited in tense silence, the flames slowed, then died back, taking their eerie cold light with them as the sun's warm light replaced it.

Jade asked Crystal, "That was a scrying fire, wasn't it?"

"Yes, but it was contaminated. I came by to let you know I had everything for the enchantment spell, but you didn't answer the door. I came back here and cast a scrying fire to try to get a sense of where Raven was. Unfortunately, she's so powerful it seems she countered the spell at the source."

"So you sent my house faerie to find me?"

"No. I didn't even know you had one."

Jade looked around for Indora. "Anyone seen her?"

Charlie said, "She's fine. I saw her on the porch."

As the flames shrank to almost nothing, the inspector strode toward them, a drone following on either side, his right hand tucked under his left arm. "Jade Cerridwen, you are under arrest"—he winced, slowing his pace, then continued—"under arrest for impersonating a Citizen of Sun City." He gave a curt nod, and one of his drones sped past him and encased her in a confinement field.

She'd seen the glowing energy surrounding people who were being arrested only a handful of times, usually at the end of a foot chase. She never realized those captured within it were in pain. Not the severe kind from being cut or crushed, but the needle-sharp shock of electricity. She jerked back from the first shock and was hit again from behind. Each move seemed to come with a new stab. She pulled her arms in and made herself as small as she could. The painful jabs stopped, and an overall tingling surrounded her, warning her not to cross it.

Aiden confronted the inspector. "You can't do this! We are on township property, you have no jurisdiction here."

"Unfortunately, he can," Charlie said. "I received notice earlier this morning."

The inspector groaned softly, then reached out with his left hand, and the field around Jade opened for him. He quickly snapped the cuff around her neck. As the cold black metal clicked together and touched her skin, she shivered. Having her magic bound was an eerie sensation, but his movement had given her a glimpse of his right arm. He was injured.

Charlie said, "We have every right to practice magic in Sugar Hill."

The inspector took a step back, a grimace clear on his face as he stood slightly hunched over. The drone beside Jade beeped once and he looked up. He straightened stiffly and soon looked just as imposing as when she'd first seen him. Except for his half-hidden arm.

"The Accords allow you to practice magic . . . as long as it causes no h-harm." The stutter was subtle, but even with her magic cut off, she could tell. He was hurting much more than he showed.

"You touched the grass, didn't you?" Jade asked him.

He spoke as though he hadn't heard her. "Article 12 of the Accords states . . . you will be transferred to Sun City pending . . . pen—" He crumpled to his knees, clutching his arm tightly to his chest, a guttural groan escaping him.

Crystal tried to approach him, but the drone not holding Jade blocked her. "I'm only trying to help."

The inspector's voice was strained. "I don't need—" He looked up at the drone. "My shield should have worked."

Charlie crossed his arms. "Well it obviously didn't. Let us help you."

The inspector looked at each of them and said, "Fine," his voice rough.

Charlie glanced at Jade. "First, release her."

"No. She's under arr—" The word turned into an agonized groan.

"She's the only one of us who can heal."

The lie worked. The inspector groaned a moment more, then tapped his left temple. The drone containing Jade released the field, then both drones took their positions on either side of him. "What are you going to do?"

"Are they streaming?" She was referring to the drones' live feed. If he was only recording, she'd have a chance to persuade him to delete the footage later. If he was live-streaming, there were mere seconds between transition and when the public saw it.

When he shook his head, Jade quickly pulled an amethyst out of her pocket. Each crystal has a different vibration. That vibration decides what energies the crystal projects. Amethysts give out healing energies. I'll pull that energy from the crystal and transfer it to your injuries." She looked down at the grass. The darkness had stopped spreading, but there was a lot of damage in its wake.

Jade glanced at the inspector. He was hunched over again and rocking as if he was trying to fold into himself. She focused on the amethyst in her hand. She felt a warm calmness from it and pulled that energy into herself. She knelt down in front of him. "Give me your hand."

The inspector hesitated, then held out a shaky, blackened claw. His coat sleeve had been burned away to the elbow. His dark olive skin looked almost normal there, but the darkness was slowly traveling up from his hand. It had encompassed his wrist and was halfway up his forearm. He groaned slightly then and his breath started coming in gasps.

She held his arm at the elbow, the amethyst in her other hand. She reached out with her feelings for the energy that was hurting him. It hit her hard. A darkness similar to what she'd felt with Charlie, but different somehow. It was burning and painful; it was death.

She recovered and focused on the healing energy of the stone. She pulled on it and pushed it forward over his hand. He groaned loudly and the energy rebounded. Jade tried again, more gently this time. Again it bounced back.

"You're making it worse," he cried out.

Something was keeping the healing energy from being absorbed. For a moment she thought it was too far gone to help. Then she noticed the burnt areas looked more like tar than ash. There was a shine to them. His hand needed to be cleaned first.

"If you're gonna help me, do it already," he grumbled, staring wide-eyed as the dark line slowly crept up his arm.

Jade let go of him. "You want to travel all the way back to Sun City and hope you get there before it consumes you, or do you want to shut up and let me do my job?"

He tilted his head at her, then nearly doubled over as another wave of pain hit him. The line was only an inch from his elbow now.

Jade quickly grabbed his arm and stretched her hand out over it. There was a palpable barrier. She tried pushing it away but it bounced back. Deciding to try a different tactic, she held the crystal in her right hand, and with her left, she pulled on the darkness. Gently, carefully, she directed the energy into the crystal. She was careful not to let the dark energy pass through her. It moved straight from one hand to the other. Soon the crystal began to darken, its light purple areas becoming more opaque and its darker purple areas turning black. Within minutes the entire crystal was black as a night without stars. There was no reflection on its surface. Looking at it you would think it was a void of some kind. It was containing the darkness, but she didn't feel safe holding it with her bare hands. It tingled in her palm, a burning cold, like holding ice that didn't melt.

Jade asked Crystal, "Do you have a cloth or handkerchief, something to wrap this in?" Crystal pulled a black neckerchief out of her cloak pocket and handed it to her. Jade quickly wrapped the amethyst and handed it back. "Go to where the stream enters our pond and bury it in the water, under some rocks." Water would cleanse the dark magic over time, like most other spells that needed to be released.

Crystal took the dark amethyst and left quickly. While she was gone, Jade pulled living energy up from the green-covered Earth at her feet and directed it through herself, toward his hand. Now that it wasn't encased in the dark energy, it was soaking up the healing energy. She passed her hand back and forth over his wounds, stitching together the skin, bringing forth new cells, and repelling the dead, corrupt ones.

The inspector groaned and mumbled something about, "Backwoods excuse for medicine."

Jade said, "I know this hurts, but it's necessary if you want to heal properly and not get an infection."

The inspector tried to pull his hand away. "If that's all you're doing, I have my own antibiotics."

Jade held fast, pulling him even closer. She stared into his cyborg eye. "Magical infections aren't the same as physical ones. Only magic can heal this." She paused, watching the iris spin. "Tell me I'm lying."

After staring back at her for a moment, he grumbled and stopped pulling his hand. "Make it quick."

Jade resumed healing him. "Think about something else. Tell me how you managed to track me down at Bonfire Field. I know it wasn't from my Band."

He hesitated, probably not wanting to give away too much, but after a sharp intake of breath, he said, "Something wasn't adding up, so I decided to trust my instinct that you're actually one of them, despite the lack of hard evidence. I'd say it worked out in my favor. My drone's scanner is capable of tracking magical energy signatures. I simply had it follow your trail from the last place I knew you were."

The black burnt scales had smoothed, and his natural color returned. There was still a rough texture to his skin, as if it were scarred from a decades-old wound, but that would fade in time. He was healed.

She sat back on the grass, feeling drained but relieved. She was already in a huge mess. The last thing she needed was to add a dead Sun City Lawkeeper to the mix.

The inspector stared at his hand in disbelief, then shook his head and looked at the burnt remnants of the fire. After a moment he looked up at her. "That . . . was unexpected."

Jade smirked. "You have a gift for understatement."

His face softened for a moment. Not quite a smile, but Jade took it as such. She stood, then held a hand out for him to take. "I don't suppose you could let the whole impersonating-a-Citizen charge slide, could you?"

He took her hand and stood stiffly. He winced and looked down at his hand, flexing it. "Are you sure it's safe now?"

"It'll probably still ache for a while, but it shouldn't get any worse. The magic is out of you. It will heal naturally." She watched him expectantly. She couldn't tell if his dodging her question was a good or bad sign. She couldn't read him at all.

Crystal returned to Jade's side. "It's done. Buried it under that big center steppingstone."

Jade thanked her then looked at the inspector. He was frowning at her as if considering his options.

He waved a hand, and the drone that had been hovering nearby went dark and returned to its docking place on his shoulder. "I will have to charge you. However, I have the authority to delay judgment in order to pursue a higher crime. I know you had something to do with whatever happened to Miss Goodrich, and I suspect she's in grave danger. What I don't know is why, if you are as guilty as I think, you would even bother to help save me from what would surely have been a gruesome end."

"It's simple, Inspector. We value all life. Even the lives of those who would see us dead." The words rang in her heart. It was easy to say in relation to a lawkeeper just trying to do his job. When it came to the dark Witch responsible for her best friend's death, that was much more difficult.

He looked her in the eye steadily. "I can't make any promises, but you did save my life, so I'll do what I can to return the favor. At the very least, I can give you twenty-four hours. My drones and I won't return before then." He turned and strode off.

Once he was out of sight, Aiden turned on Crystal. "What were you doing casting a scrying fire on Jade's property?"

"I was trying to help locate Raven. How was I supposed to know she would backdraft it?"

"Maybe because she's a powerful Witch and—"

"Enough!" Jade stepped between them. "Crystal made a mistake, we handled it. He was going to find out about me eventually. The last thing we need is to start fighting among ourselves." They both shrank back slightly, their anger ebbing for now.

"I'm sorry about the fire. I should have asked before casting it here," Crystal said dejectedly.

Aiden crossed his arms. "It was thoughtless of you. But I recognize you were trying to help."

Jade asked them both, "We good?" They nodded reluctantly. "Good. Because we have our work cut out for us if Raven is capable of pushing her magic through my property defense." She looked around at the scar left by the fire. A wound cut the line between her home and her pond. At least it hadn't happened on her property's ley line. If it had been much closer to the house, it could have spread down her ley line to the whole township.

"Crystal, you said you had the enchantment spell ingredients?" She nodded, so Jade continued. "Aiden, would you please work with her to make sure everything's ready? If you could make it into something we could quickly deploy, that would be great. Since we're keeping it for last minute, I don't want to waste time setting up candles or anything."

Aiden brightened noticeably. "Oh, I have just the thing. It's a grenade-style casting that Belle and Sophia have been working on. They have a prototype they want me to test out."

"Good. You two stay together until it's done. I don't want anyone alone until Raven's dealt with."

Aiden nodded to the younger Witch and they both left.

Jade told Charlie, "Let's spread the word among the coven and townspeople that it's not safe being alone."

He looked at her funny. "Um . . . how long has that been lit up?" He pointed at her wrist. Sure enough, the bracelet was glowing faintly.

"Great." Jade looked around but didn't see anything out of place. "Next time someone makes an early warning system, let's make sure they include a way to locate where the warning is coming from."

"Right. In the meantime, we should do a sweep of the township limits."

"Are you serious? Searching all those miles will take too much time. We need to know where she is now."

"So, we get help along the way."

CHAPTER 12

Jade and Charlie had contacted every coven member and told them to search the outlying properties, but Raven was nowhere to be found. They reinforced the protection spells on all homes and businesses as they went. It was past sunset when they finally made it back to Jade's house. After checking the property's protection spell one last time, they went to sleep.

Jade woke around 4:30 a.m., the echoes of the inspector's voice in her head. One arm was draped over Charlie's chest, the other snuggled up between them, as asleep as she had just been. He was snoring lightly in a steady rhythm as he breathed. She listened for a minute, finding a calm comfort in the sound. She slowly pulled back from him, the pins and needles protesting as her arm straightened. Charlie mumbled something in his sleep and rolled over away from her. She sat up slowly, flexing her arm as the blood rushed back into its proper place. After a moment Charlie's breathing resumed its steady pace, without the snoring this time. She threw on a robe and her slippers and snuck out of the bedroom.

The house was quiet. The black patch of dead earth faintly visible from the kitchen window, just a darker spot within a dark world. Jade thought about everything she'd been through the last two days, dealing with the impending fight with Raven, never knowing when the inspector would show up, and her uncertainty about Charlie's heart, were all vying for her attention. She needed space to think. She couldn't face the ruin of her backyard, so she headed back into the living room and out the side door.

The predawn chill sent her immediately back inside to grab her cloak. She tried again, closing the side door quietly behind her. A high-pitched chime, like the tinkling of a tiny bell, sounded briefly from the bushes next to her. She scanned the greenery in the dim moonlight, but there was nothing there.

She turned and strolled down the path, hugging her cloak around her and watching the trail of smooth pebbles pass beneath her feet. The frosty air nibbled at her nose and clawed at her ankles, but otherwise she was toasty warm. Her cloak still smelled of lavender and vanilla from the decades her aunt had had it. She used to love that combination, but now it was bittersweet, bringing the memory of when she'd first heard her aunt had died.

At the time, that call from Willow had felt like a shock. Looking back, she realized she'd known. Her nightmare the night before had warned her. Even when she'd moved to a city that denied magic's ability to do anything more than parlor tricks, that magical connection had followed her. It was part of the reason she'd done so well in her job. She could sense things others couldn't. Some called it luck, but she knew better; it was clairvoyance.

The bell sounded again, and Jade spun just in time to catch the briefest glimpse of a golden glow ducking behind some foliage. Most of the garden was dead or dormant, but a few hardy perennials survived. They peppered the terraced beds with pops of green.

Jade smiled as she turned and continued slowly down the dimly lit footpath. It was comforting to know at least one of the faeries was considering showing themselves to her. It meant they were beginning to trust her.

She sat on a stone bench at the juncture of several paths. When no faeries appeared after a few minutes, Jade closed her eyes and took a deep breath. Ground and center. Clear your mind. She tried to release her fear and worry and replace them with curiosity for the tiny being who was watching her.

A rustling of leaves in the bed directly in front of Jade. She opened her eyes. Again, the flash of gold as the faerie hid.

"It's okay," she said gently, "you can come out. I don't mind your company, and I won't hurt you." After a few moments, Indora peeked out from behind a stem.

"Well, hello there. Indora, right?"

The small orb floated up to hover in front of Jade's face. She bobbed up and down a couple of times, which Jade took to mean yes.

"It's nice to see you again. I wanted to thank you for warning us about the contaminated fire earlier."

The light dipped slowly, giving Jade the impression she was bowing.

"I don't mind you being here, but I'm afraid I'm not very good company right now." She missed April. She could always talk to her about anything. With her gone, she felt alone.

Indora floated over to the bench beside her and plopped down on its surface, as if to say, *I'm here.*

"I appreciate you. And I know I'm not really alone, it just feels that way sometimes. I'd known April—she was my very best friend—since I was twelve. We grew up together, went to school together, even worked at the same company. I can barely remember a time before she was in my life."

Jade stood and Indora followed, floating along next to her. Her golden glow was comforting, a warm light escorting her through the darkness.

"That first week back home, after my aunt's funeral, it was hard, but I made it through because of April. I could feel the magic growing stronger inside me. At first, I fought it because it frightened me. I wondered where it would lead, and if I went back to practicing magic like I used to, would someone else I loved . . . end up dead?"

The image of April's bloodied body flashed through Jade's mind. She closed her eyes tight against it. "April didn't die because of magic. She died because of Raven."

She played with the four trinkets in her pocket. Jade had been so eager to take on Raven from the beginning, but now she saw she hadn't been ready. Part of her said to wait until she was, but she had a feeling that time might never come. The most she could do was prepare, do her best, and hope it would be enough.

She looked up to find herself at the pond behind her home. Without meaning to, she had walked around the contaminated ground and found her way here. The dock on her left pointed toward her home and the wounded spot mere inches from it. She turned and walked the other way, along the edge of the water, avoiding the mark left by the cursed fire. In time her coven could heal it, and there'd be nothing left to show where it had been.

The sun was nearing the horizon, and the blue twilight it cast made everything look frozen. This hour before dawn was a magical time, as much as midnight or dusk. The barrier between night and day. Anything was possible.

She stopped and looked back at the end of the dock. She'd sat there once with April. The pain of her loss rose up again, making her chest tighten. She was tempted to run back to the house, take shelter in Charlie's arms, and let him make her forget, at least for a little while. That's what she'd been doing for a month now, but the pain was still there, waiting for quiet moments like this.

Sophia had told her time and again that the only way to get rid of the pain would be to face it. Jade knew that was true. She'd thought the pain of her parents' and aunt's deaths would overwhelm her when she returned to Sugar Hill, but she'd faced it and survived. She still missed them, but she didn't ache for them. She did ache for April. In some ways more than she ever had for her family.

Jade walked along the lake's shoreline. She wished she hadn't seen that dock. Why couldn't she have walked a different way?

April's face came unbidden to her mind.

Smiling.

Happy.

Her voice, laughing. The way April's hand slipped into hers, comforting and empowering her every time. She'd never feel that again. Not with Charlie, not with anyone.

She was alone.

Jade's throat tightened and her eyes stung. "No." Indora zipped into view, and Jade felt she was asking what was wrong.

"I can't do this now. I don't want to." She swallowed the lump in her throat and looked to the heavens. The sun had turned the sky the most pastel pink.

April's favorite color.

The tears came in a rush, and Jade collapsed to the ground. Sobs wracked her body as she let her sorrow pour out of her.

April was gone. She'd never see her again. Jade didn't even get to say goodbye, it was over so fast.

She screamed, guttural and raw. Her throat hurt, but she kept going until her breath was used up. Again and again, she screamed out all her sorrow and rage at losing April, at losing her heart.

She curled up in a ball, her cloak draped around her. It was so unfair. If she could just see her one more time, tell her how she loved her, how she made such a difference in her life.

Only Jade's own memories whispered back. Snatches of conversations they'd had. And one moment, one precious moment when April seemed to heal her with just her words.

It was the night of her aunt's Crossing Over ceremony. Jade had fled to the dock and sat staring out at the lake. April had sat next to her and they'd talked. Jade had confessed she'd not felt her aunt's presence at the ceremony. She should have felt her.

April had replied, "I'm sorry you couldn't feel her presence like you thought you would, but that's what every one of us goes through when we lose someone we love."

Then April draped her arm across Jade's shoulder and pulled her close. "It's cold, and harsh, and it hurts like hell, but you will get through it. Just like everyone does. You're not alone, Jade. It may feel like it now, but you're not."

April knew Jade's fears, though she'd never spoken them aloud. She knew in that moment what Jade needed to hear.

Jade curled up tightly, imagining April's arms around her, her voice whispering, "You're not alone. You will get through it."

Jade sat up and released a big shaky breath while she wiped the tears away. Indora was still there, watching over her. She gave the small faerie a brief smile. "Thank you, Indora. I appreciate you being here." It really was sweet of her to hang out while Jade cried. If April were here, she'd have done the same.

She stood and took another deep breath. "April's gone. I'll always miss her, but I have to move on. April would want me to. I have a coven to protect and a dark Witch to bring to justice. I've just got to figure out how."

Indora spun in place and twittered a long string of sounds. Jade thought she was asking a question, but she wasn't sure. "We really need to figure out how to communicate better. I'll have to ask Katie about that next time I see her."

Indora chirped and this time a clear thought came to mind. Similar to Jade's visions, she just knew, it was time Jade called the Air Elemental.

She thought about all she'd learned. Ground and center. Feel the energy around her. Release all doubt and worry, accepting what would be. Recognize the duality, each element contained in its opposite. She thought of Air and all it represented, and then she called out, "Element of Air, power of the east. You are knowledge, awakenings, newness, and beginnings. I call you now in this hour of dawn. Come to me. Begin this new day with me. In perfect love and perfect trust, I humbly ask." She stood with arms outstretched, waiting, anticipating nothing, being open.

There was no sound and no movement of air. She felt caught in a vacuum. Her breath stilled, and while she felt a momentary panic, she simply acknowledged it and it passed quickly. She settled back into waiting. The world held its breath. There was only now.

A slight breeze caressed her face. She opened her eyes and saw nothing had changed except the sky was brighter and the top crest of the sun had just crossed the treetops. She squinted into the light for a moment before realizing it didn't hurt. There was something between her and the sun. There had to be. She was looking straight at the rising sun, in all its brilliance, yet she could see clearly.

She looked down, and just as her eyes moved, she caught a ripple in the air. There was something in front of her, but it was invisible. She looked back up and realized there was no warmth on her face, as there should be in the sunlight. She looked down at the grass in front of her. There were several large depressions in the grass. She tilted her head, trying to make out their shape, to translate it into a form she could recognize.

A gust of wind blew on her face, warm and moist. Jade had a thought it might be breath, which made her frightened and curious at the same time. Whatever it was, it was huge. Bigger than Leo even. She remembered the turtle changing shape.

"Whatever you are, I appreciate you being here for me at this time." She bowed her head slightly, then looked up proudly. She raised her two hands, palms up in front of her. "You are powerful in many ways, and one of them is transmutation. I ask that you show yourself to me. Please."

She lifted her hands slightly. There was a very low rumble, then a gust of wind hit the ground in front of her, blasting into her from the ankles upward, sending her cloak flying out behind her. After a few seconds, the weight of a small watermelon fell into her palms. She looked carefully, seeing the same shimmer as before. Slowly, it grew visible.

Claws pricked her skin like the spines of a cactus. Though they didn't puncture, she knew they easily could. Feathery wings, tipped in gold at the ends, had a metallic shimmer of yellow and orange, with red along the front edge. The same feathers covered its whole body, shining in the sunlight like flames. The feathers over its eyes were more like horns, curving back as they swooped over its head. It was pure fire and sunlight, but it didn't burn her. She stared in wonder as it coalesced into a bird of fiery splendor.

It let out a high-pitched screech and suddenly changed color. From its beak to its tail, the color rolled like a wave. The gold, orange, and red shifted, fading through different colors. Finally, it settled on blood red that shifted lighter or darker depending on the angle viewed. She smiled and threw her hands upward quickly. It took to the sky, growing as it climbed until it was big enough to dwarf her house.

She smiled as she watched it circling effortlessly for a few moments. It flew toward the sunrise, fading away until Jade could no longer look at the sun's brilliance. Jade turned and stared wide-eyed at Indora. "Did you see that? I can't wait to tell Charlie." She turned and ran toward the house, shouting as she went, "We have a phoenix!"

CHAPTER 13

Jade ran up the stairs and to her bedroom. Calling her last Elemental felt like the final piece falling into place. She flung open the door and paused just inside to catch her breath. The heavy curtains were drawn, but an eerie green light shone from a large oval ring in the corner of the room, faintly illuminating a dark shape.

Charlie stood next to the bed . . . No, not Charlie, he was lying where Jade had left him. She focused on the hooded figure leaning over the bed, one hand hovering over Charlie's chest, the other over his forehead. Raven turned her head toward Jade, a huge grin spreading. "Lamby."

"Repellere!" *Repel.* Jade shouted to cast the spell.

Raven flew backward, crashing into Jade's altar, a pained grunt escaping her. She tried to recover and advance on Jade, but she cast the spell again. This time she maintained the pressure with one hand out, pressing the spell into Raven's chest, holding her against the wall. This was her chance to end Raven.

She'd attacked Charlie; Jade had every right to defend him.

A golden streak of glitter flew toward Raven and began flitting left, right, up, and down in front of her. Mere inches from Raven, glowing threads began to appear in the glitter's wake. Indora wove a web around the dark Witch, pinning her arms to her sides and her back to the wall.

Raven struggled against the web, but Indora made quick work of her hands, immobilizing them within moments. She stopped struggling and smiled at Jade. "My little lamb. Did you miss me?"

Raven could wait. Jade turned to Charlie. His eyes remained closed, but he groaned softly and moved restlessly, as if having a bad dream. "Charlie. Charlie, wake up." He didn't respond. She whirled on Raven. "What did you do to him?" Static rushed to her palms, her whole body tensed. She spoke through gritted teeth. "I should kill you now and be done with it."

Raven laughed, loud and hard. "Kill me? That's a good one." She stopped laughing and stared Jade down. "You don't have the guts."

Jade pulled fire into her hand, building it until it burned. "Wanna bet?" She lifted her hand, but a groan from behind her made her stop.

"Ugh. Jade?" Charlie looked past her and his eyes grew wide. "Raven." He scrambled out of bed to stand next to Jade. "What are you doing here?"

Raven was squinting at Indora as she hovered in front of her. "Ah, I see you've got the pests on your side. No matter. I have—"

Jade reached toward the pale, lacy curtains that hung over her window and stretched their energy until strips of black fabric grew from them. She wrapped them over Raven's mouth, cutting her off. "Shut up."

Jade dropped the fireball she'd been building. It landed in a puddle of flames and quickly went out. She turned toward Charlie. "I can't listen to any more of her smug bull. Are you okay?"

Charlie nodded. "I think so. I thought I was having a nightmare, but I guess not." His eyes went wide at something behind Jade. "Look out!"

She spun and raised her arm at the same time, pulling an energy barrier up against whatever was attacking her. The air in front of her exploded with a million multicolored shards of glass as her bedroom window crashed into her spell.

As the last of it fell to the ground, she heard a high-pitched whistle as Indora slammed against the wall below the now shattered window. She lay slumped and unmoving.

Charlie reached his hand out, pinning Raven to the wall, the web Indora had built hanging slack and fading.

Jade let him deal with Raven and rushed to Indora and crouched down next to her. "Indora, can you hear me?" She didn't move, but her light was still bright. She must be unconscious.

A strange scraping sound caused Jade to turn. Raven was dragging Charlie toward her, his arms and legs dangling helplessly, his bare feet trailing across the floor.

Jade cried out, "No!" She leaped up and pulled the room's heat again.

Raven caught Jade's eyes and smiled. She placed Charlie between them, only her head visible behind his limp form. Raven whispered something in Charlie's ear as she held him close.

Jade couldn't cast without risking hitting Charlie. Or could she? As Raven continued whispering to Charlie, Jade decided it was worth the risk. Closing her eyes, she pushed down her anxious feelings and pictured Raven's face as clearly as she could, just past Charlie's shoulder. She focused in closer. That smirk, her eyes squinting slightly and sparkling with delight. She focused on that spark, a bright white speck in Raven's eye.

Water and Fire.

She set it ablaze.

Raven's scream sent a chill down Jade's spine. She opened her eyes just as Charlie flew into her arms. She caught him and they stumbled to the floor. Raven disappeared into the glowing green portal, and it slammed shut, cutting off her scream.

Charlie was coughing and holding his throat. Jade held his shoulders and tried to look into his eyes. "Are you all right?"

"I'm fine," he croaked. "Go after her."

She scrambled up and dove for the spot where the portal had been. She reached out, trying to sense the energy, get some idea of where it was going. But there was nothing. There was just her altar, its items knocked over and strewn on the floor around it.

She couldn't believe it had happened again. Raven always managed to slip away from Jade, just when she almost had her beat.

She faced Charlie. "Why does she do that? Every time we get close to beating her, she portals out. Is she a coward?" She wished Raven was a simple Witch with a wicked reputation, and without the stones to back it up. It would make everything so much easier.

Charlie got to his feet. "She's no coward. I think she's just overly cautious. She knows how strong you've gotten. She knows that you're close to being able to beat her, and she values survival more than anything. What I'm more concerned with is how she got into your house."

She heard a small squeak and looked toward the window. Indora was moving slowly, trying to sit up. Jade knelt down and placed her hand next to her, letting the tiny faerie lean on her and climb up into her palm. She lifted her to eye height. "Are you all right?" she asked quietly.

Indora nodded and pulled something out of the tiny pouch that hung at her waist. She opened the stopper on a tiny bottle and tipped it up, downing the entire thing in one go. Capping it back up and placing it in her pouch, she slowly stretched, and after a moment, was able to float up hesitantly and hover between Charlie and Jade. She let out a series of whistles and tweets, her hands pointing to and fro.

Jade tried to understand, but it was no use. "I'm sorry, Indora. I can feel your urgency, but I just don't get it."

"Maybe we should call Katie here and let her translate."

Indora squeaked something at Charlie, then shot out the window, leaving a faint trail of sparkles behind.

"Well, I guess she agrees," Jade said. "When we get a minute of downtime, I need to really work on communication with her."

"We should talk to Willow. See if she has any idea how Raven could have managed to get past the protection spell."

Jade looked him over carefully. "What was she trying to do to you anyway? You don't seem any different to me. How do you feel?"

"Fine. I mean I'm a little freaked out a dark Witch was trying to spell me in my sleep, but I think whatever she was trying to do, you interrupted her before she could complete it."

"Well, that's a lucky break. Still, I'd like Sophia to check you over."

"That's not necessary. I said I'm fine."

"We can't afford to take chances, Charlie. We're going to see her. Now."

Charlie sighed and rolled his eyes. "Fine. But let me do one thing first." He positioned himself in front of the ragged hole that had once been a beautiful mosaic of leaded glass. He circled his hand above the shards on the floor around them. "Redi." *Return.*

Slowly, one by one the glass and lead pieces began to wiggle upward, floating back to their places. Soon the window looked as it had before. The sun was fully up now, and the rays shone through the various panels.

The colors swirl and combine, a kaleidoscope of patternless colors. They began to fade, growing less saturated until Jade is standing in a dark field, all shades of gray.

Black feathers falling like ashes, bloodied and broken, torn out by the root.

Cold emptiness, hollow and dark.

A battlefield, covered in blood. Jade rises to stand triumphant. She looks down at Raven, lying broken at her feet.

It was just a flash, over before she realized she was having a vision, but it told her all she needed to know. This was the last time Raven would leave Jade's life a mess in her wake. Raven would fall. They would win.

CHAPTER 14

When Jade told Sophia what had happened, she said she'd meet them at the mayor's house. She didn't seem too concerned about Charlie, but agreed it would be best if she had a look at him, just in case. On the drive over, Jade distracted her worry over Charlie by thinking over her other problems. Raven had escaped again, but Jade had everything she needed to finally beat her next time. Faeries, Elementals, and her growing power, which had become very precise. Add in the whole coven backing her and she felt she couldn't lose.

But first, she needed to come up with an attack plan. If they could just find Raven and attack without her being warned, the surprise could be a huge advantage and maybe be enough to keep her from portaling away again. Portals could travel quite a long way, but Jade had a feeling she was close. After all, she'd said she wanted Sugar Hill, she seemed to want Jade, and for some reason she couldn't understand, she definitely wanted Charlie. Badly enough to find a way through her protection spell and right into Jade's bedroom. She shivered at the memory of her standing over Charlie's sleeping form. She could only hope Sophia didn't find anything wrong with him.

When they arrived, Sophia was waiting for them on the front landing. They all went inside, and Charlie took a minute to refresh the protection spell on the building. Without fear of the inspector eavesdropping, they filled Sophia in on what happened.

"Oh dear. Well, let's have a look at you, shall we?" She motioned Charlie to follow and led them into the study. As she pulled the shutters closed over the windows, the room dimmed considerably. With a wave of her hand, she lit several candles. She pointed to the large desk. "That will do. Make yourself as comfortable as you can. This will take a couple of minutes."

Charlie slid onto the desktop easily, but fidgeted as he tried to find a place to rest his hands. After a moment he stilled and closed his eyes. Sophia began walking around him, muttering incantations and occasionally looking at him through her Holy Stone.

Jade was just about to ask how much longer it would be, when Sophia said, "Jade, would you please get Charlie a cup of tea? I had to drain his energy a bit, and he could probably use a sip. Green, if you have it." She extinguished the candles and opened the shutters, then turned and helped Charlie slowly sit up.

"Is he okay?"

"Jade. Please do as I asked."

Her stern tone surprised Jade, and she hurried toward the kitchen. She made the tea as quickly as she could, giving the water a magical nudge to get it to boil faster. She placed the pot and three teacups on a tray and headed back. As she passed the front entryway, a knock at the door startled her.

Balancing the tray in one arm, she opened the door. "Katie. What are you doing here?"

She stepped past Jade and looked around. "Are you alone?" She seemed slightly out of breath.

"Charlie and Sophia are here. What's wrong?"

"Well, my faeries returned. Good news is, Raven is at the mansion. Bad news is, she's raising an army. Like, literally raising from the dead. She's using necromancy!"

"Okay, okay. Take a breath. We're going to handle this. Come with me." She led her to the study.

Katie followed. "Handle it? The risen can't be killed. They can't be enchanted, they don't even feel pain, so wounding them doesn't even slow them down!"

They had entered the study and Sophia intercepted her. "Katie!" She placed her hands on the young Witch's shoulders. In a calm voice, she murmured, "Just breathe."

While Sophia helped Katie calm down, Jade placed the tray down on the desk next to Charlie and served him a cup. "How you feeling?"

"I'm fine. A bit tired, but not bad." He took the cup and sipped. "What's going on?" He nodded to Katie.

She seemed calmer, but still her words tumbled out without resistance. "All those souls that were trapped on the mansion's property, Raven's animated them. Basically, she's raising an army of the dead."

Charlie groaned. "Oh great. Fighting the risen is such a pain. They're basically reanimated corpses, so they have no magical abilities themselves, but the only way to stop them is to stop whoever raised them."

"Okay, so we take care of Raven first." Jade took a sip of her tea, hoping it would soothe her tightening throat.

Katie mumbled dejectedly, "See, that's the point. She'll have them surrounding her, protecting her. We have to get through them to take her out."

Sophia said, "We will find a way. We need to call a coven meeting right now."

They called the coven meeting, and while they waited for everyone to arrive, Sophia continued working Katie through her anxiety, while Jade helped Charlie prepare the tea and cakes.

Charlie brewed a second pot, while Jade portioned out shortbread cookies onto tiny paper plates. She eyed Charlie. He seemed okay, but the silence was grating on her nerves. She stopped and turned to face him. "Are you gonna tell me what Sophia said or what?"

The pot wasn't quite boiling yet. He raised his eyebrows at her. "Maybe," he drawled, stretching out the word far too long

"Charlie!" Jade snapped.

He chuckled. "Okay, okay. She checked my aura, energy signature, everything she could. There's nothing wrong."

"Everything? What about your shadowed heart? Did she check that?"

He frowned and turned away from her, focusing on the tiny bubbles that refused to float. "It's still shadowed. But she says it hasn't grown at all since last time she checked." He turned back to her, his voice calm and low. "I'm fine, Jade. Please stop worrying. Sophia said whatever spell Raven was trying to do must have been interrupted before it could latch on. No harm done."

Jade wasn't so sure, but she let the subject go. For now.

***

The meeting room was full of friendly chatter, but there was an undercurrent of tense energy. The whole coven was seated, finishing the last of their cakes and tea. Jade stood next to Charlie as Sophia helped Willow to her seat next to him, then took her own in the front row.

Jade turned to the coven members and waited while everyone quieted down and looked to her. She told them about her fight with Raven and how she almost beat her, but Raven portaled away at the last minute. "And there's more bad news. Katie's faeries have returned with news of Raven's fortress." She turned, making room for Katie, who stepped forward shyly.

Katie waved her hand over the township map as she had before. The lights designating ley lines on the map glowed a little brighter, then split so there was kind of a double image, a second web glowing just above the first. The second image lifted, and the lights twisted and morphed before settling in a pattern. Before long Jade could recognize the town map glowing in the air before them.

The ley line under Jade's house glowed brighter than the rest. It pulsed from the house eastward along the line and right off the edge of the map. A few inches out, it stopped and formed the outline of a house and property.

The front gate was in a wall to the north. The wall extended around the whole house, several hundred yards out from the building itself. The property went on much farther than that, but it was mostly left wild with woodland, fields, and a small stream. In the field to the east, several small spots began to glow red.

"Raven is raising an army of the dead, using the Witches buried on the property. If she raises everyone who was killed there, when we attack Raven, we'll also be facing close to a hundred risen."

The expected surprise and worry flowed around the room, but Jade continued studying the map. There had to be a weakness. Some point of entry that would allow them to sneak in under cover, or at least get close before being noticed.

The building itself had four wings and a large empty circle in its center. Jade pointed and asked, "What's that circle?"

Katie replied, "The mansion is several stories tall. In the center of the building is a grand spiral staircase, which travels through each floor. The center is open, and on the roof is a large glass dome." She paused to glance at the glowing map. "It really is quite beautiful. Or so I've heard."

"So what about the rest of the building? One that size must have blueprints on record somewhere."

"Oh, we don't need a blueprint. The faeries gave me a very detailed description." Katie waved her hands over the map. The lights brightened and dimmed on each section of the map as she described them. "There are four entrances to the building itself, at the end of each wing. The north wing faces the main gate. There is another gate in the property wall to the southeast, but it is much smaller, only large enough for one person to go through at a time really.

"Since the mansion is built on the side of a hill, the north wing has a large stone staircase built into the ground. That door enters onto the main floor. The east wing entrance is located behind a meditation garden and enters onto the second floor. The south wing is behind a firepit and enters onto the ground floor as well. Finally, the west wing entrance is located behind a duck pond. That entrance is below the ground floor." She paused and pointed to that part of the map. "They said there's something odd about this entrance. They think it's cloaked."

"Cloaked?" Jade asked. "How can they tell?"

"It's a feeling. Faeries are pretty sensitive to magical energy." The lights were flickering at that end of the building like a light bulb with a loose wire.

Sophia said, "It must be a very old cloak. They can degrade over time, especially if the caster has passed on and no one claims and recharges it."

Jade thought on it, then asked Katie, "Where exactly is the hiding space you told us about the other day?"

Katie pointed just west of the cloaked area. "There."

Jade saw a small circle glow brighter. "It can't be a coincidence that the one space we can't see clearly is so close to it." Jade looked over the property.

Charlie asked, "What are you thinking? Try to surprise her though that entrance? If it even is an entrance. I'm sure she has wards up."

"I'm sure she does too. So, what if we make it look obvious that we're trying to catch her by surprise? What's Raven's one obvious weakness?"

There was silence until Katie said, "She has none."

"Wrong. That's what she wants you to think. Her weakness is her superiority complex. She always thinks she has the upper hand."

Mr. Flannerly muttered, "Maybe because she does."

"Yes, but if we know that going in, we have the advantage. Play right into her hand and she'll never realize that we are doing it on purpose."

Katie said, "I still don't get it."

"What would you do if you thought you had won?"

Katie shrugged. "Be happy, I guess. I'd probably throw a party . . . Oh! I'd relax!"

Jade said, "Exactly. There's no doubt she has wards up, or something that will tell her if we try to sneak onto her property. So we sneak onto her property in a two-front assault." She pointed to the map. "A small group will go in through the southeast gate. At the same time, a large group will go in through the main gate. It will look like we're trying to sneak that smaller group past her while the main group is a distraction."

Charlie said, "So Raven will focus on the smaller group? Won't she also try to stop the larger group?"

Jade smiled. "Yes, but if she thinks you and I are in the smaller group, that's where her main focus will be. She tried to take you before, and she seems to like messing with me. Anything she throws at the group entering the main gate will be less focused, and we might actually have a better chance of getting past her defenses. That's where we'll be. We'll do a cloning spell and a cloak at the same time. The clone will send our image to the smaller group, and the cloak will hide our being in the larger. She will be so impressed with herself for catching us sneaking in the small gate, she won't second-guess what she sees."

Selene said, "I don't know, Jade. That sounds pretty risky to me. What if she doesn't buy it?"

"Well, then at least we'll be in the larger group, and maybe the numbers will help us. Now, the only question is what to do when we're finally face to face with her."

Charlie said, "You aren't going to blow her to smithereens, are you?" He winked at her.

"No, I'm not. Though it would be satisfying."

"Of course we'll bind her and bring her to trial," Sophia said.

"I'm more concerned with the moment just before we bind her. Every time we've clashed, when it looked like she might lose, she's portaled away. We can't let that happen again."

"She can't portal if she's dead." All eyes turned to Charlie. He looked around surprised. "What? It's true. I'm not saying she should be killed outright without a trial. Of course that would be wrong. What I'm saying is, let's try her, right now. And then, when she's found guilty, we can attack and don't even have to worry about capturing her. We just carry out judgement."

Confused silence settled over the coven. A moment in time, frozen by the indecisive. Jade knew he was wrong, knew something was off about the way he was speaking, but she couldn't convince herself that it mattered. He was right. In a fair trial, Raven had no defense. She'd manipulated, tortured, and even killed to get what she wanted. She'd threatened to take over a coven by force. She had no doubt the coven would find her guilty, and then they'd be free to take her down, whatever it took.

Within a few moments the entire room had erupted into arguments. Katie wanted the abbey to take over now. Selene said she didn't come to this country to take part in more tyranny and injustice. Mr. Flannerly said a fair trial was more than Raven deserved.

While the coven continued arguing, Jade pulled Charlie aside. "I'm with you on this, but the last thing we need now is for the coven to be fighting among themselves. You need to take back what you said."

"Why? You agree with me, the coven has to follow us."

"Yes, but if they're doubting us, they're weak. One little thing could splinter their allegiance, and then we're going after Raven with a fractured coven."

Charlie rolled his eyes and whispered, "Fine." He stepped back to the front of the room and raised his hands. "All right, all right, let's all calm down." The arguing stopped but no one looked very content. "Our coven laws are clear. We don't just kill people. Hard as it may be, we need to take Raven alive." There was a loud knock at the front door. Jade motioned Charlie to keep going while she went to open it. "Once she's safely restrained we can come to an agreement on what justice looks like."

Jade opened the door. Three drones hovered over Inspector Caldwell's head, their red lights staring her down. He held a cuff in his hands, the cold metal circlet that would block Jade's magic the moment it snapped shut around her neck.

She was out of time.

CHAPTER 15

Jade was frozen to the spot. She gripped the open door, the only thing holding her up. Inspector Caldwell raised his head, the brim of his hat revealing a slight smile on his lips. When his eyes met hers, he frowned. "Miss Cerridwen?" He looked over her and the smile returned. He pushed past Jade and stated, "Mayor Charlie Jordan, I am officially arresting you for the disappearance and possible murder of Miss April Goodrich."

The floor tilted under Jade's feet. "What?" She couldn't have heard that right. He was investigating Jade.

The inspector approached Charlie, reaching for his arm. Jade's world spun out of her control. All this time she'd been worried for herself. She'd been a fool. Of course he wouldn't arrest her. Jade was well-known and respected in Sun City's higher circles. If news she was a Witch got out, it wouldn't just lead to war, it would destabilize the government and call everything into question. A Witch township mayor was a much neater option, one that played into Citizens' fears without threatening their feeling of safety. She should have seen it coming.

Ms. Scrivener stepped forward. "As Mr. Jordan's lawyer, I demand to know on what grounds you're basing this arrest."

"Demand?" He leaned toward her, his right hand gripping Charlie's arm. "You may be their representative in our legal system, but you're still just a Witch. I am the law. You don't get to demand anything from me." He turned back toward Charlie and quickly placed the cuff around Charlie's neck. The metal circle was hinged in the center. It snapped tight, a small green light blinking twice before turning red.

"Charlie Jordan, you are hereby stripped of your title of mayor and remanded into Sun City custody for suspicion of kidnapping and murder. You now have twenty-four hours to settle your personal affairs before the accusation is filed and judgment is carried out. This collar is currently set to the Sugar Hill border. Any attempt to pass its limits will result in your immediate paralyzation. Any attempt to remove it will result in immediate judgment. Since you aren't a Citizen, I'll spell it out for you. You will die."

The room erupted, everyone arguing with the inspector, but it was all just background noise. Jade stared at the red light on Charlie's cuff. It didn't matter what evidence they had, it didn't matter what she said. A lawkeeper's word was law, and this one had just condemned Charlie.

A voice boomed all around them. "Oh no. This won't do at all. I have plans for this one."

Raven materialized in front of Charlie and placed her hand on his chest. His face lost all emotion, and he stared straight ahead as the brief chaos ensued.

She touched the collar, it beeped twice and released his neck. Jade pulled the tension in the room into a tangible electricity, but before she could do anything with it, Raven tossed the collar at her. It snapped around her neck, and the charge she'd built dissolved into nothing. The inspector's drones approached Raven from either side, but just before they reached her, they fell to the floor. Their small, eye-like lenses black as death. Aiden charged, pushing a shield of fire before him. Raven waved her hand, and a force field crashed into him and his shield, sending Aiden flying backwards, knocking over Selene, and spreading the fire. Katie whistled and a water faerie darted through the room, putting out the flames as she went. The inspector removed the cuff from Jade.

Raven tutted. "So rude. I trust you'll behave now. I'd hate to spill blood all over this lovely marble." She gave everyone a warning glare as she ran her hands over Charlie's chest, inches away, as if feeling his energy. Charlie leaned toward her ever so slightly, though the expression on his face was as blank as ever.

When it was clear no one would attack, Raven turned toward Charlie and sniffed him deeply. "My, you are ripening nicely. You're becoming even stronger than I thought you would. How lovely."

The inspector held the open cuff as if preparing to Frisbee throw it. "Who are you and how did you release my collar?"

Raven looked him up and down while keeping her hands near Charlie. "Well, who do we have here? The pesky little inspector, I presume? I've heard all about you. Been annoying the heck out of Jade? Love it. Keep doing that. But I'm afraid this little puppy's off-limits."

The inspector slowly opened his coat, revealing a gun in a holster at his right hip. Once Raven looked at it, he said, "You would do well to answer my question. Underestimating me is ill-advised."

Raven smirked at him. "I never underestimate anyone." Her posture shifted, relaxing, a genuine smile and soft gaze lightened her expression. "Inspector, sir. I fully intend to cooperate with your investigation." Her smile was so bright and innocent, despite her dark overall look. She gave Jade a quick wink, and it was then she realized Raven had morphed her features. Not by much, but enough to fool the IDV.

"I'm glad to hear that, Miss . . . ?"

"Oh, you can call me Raven."

He frowned at her, then shook his head. "You . . . . you still didn't answer my question." He pulled his weapon and pointed it at her in the space of a blink. "How did you release the collar?"

Raven tilted her head at the weapon pointed at her. "Hm. Not fully buying my glamor, are we? Fine." She flicked a finger, and his gun flew out of his hands. She stepped up to him and lifted his hat, purring close to his mouth, "Why don't you go back where you came from?" As she stepped back to Charlie's side, the inspector and his drones disappeared.

Jade looked all around. "What did you do to him?"

"Oh don't worry, lamb. He's perfectly healthy. He and his little robot buddies just took a quick trip home. He was starting to bore me." She slithered up to Charlie and draped herself on him. "Now, lover, where were we?"

Jade wanted to try casting again, but she didn't want to risk hitting Charlie. Maybe she could try another precise spell like she had when they'd found Raven in her room. She looked to her coven, standing only a few feet away. Selene caught her eye and raised her head slightly. The message was clear to Jade: she need only say the word and they would attack.

"Jade, no." Charlie stepped in front of her, blocking her view of the coven.

She looked up into his eyes. Their usual bright blue was muted, flat somehow, and he had deep circles under his eyes. He looked so different than he had before Raven showed up.

"What has she done to you?" She reached out and caressed the side of his face.

For just a moment, he leaned into her palm, his eyes closed. "We had a good run, didn't we?" He straightened then and Jade saw determination in his eyes. His jaw flared as he clenched it. "She didn't really do anything to me. At least, nothing that wasn't already happening."

"What are you saying?" As he pulled out of her grasp and moved back to Raven's side, Jade's heart lurched. She was losing him. "No. What are you doing, Charlie? This is our chance."

"Our chance?" He looked at Jade with a malice she'd never seen in his eyes before. "We never had a chance." He advanced on her slowly. "All those years you left me here, I had to take up the slack for you. What chance did you give me? I was just a kid."

"So was I." She could feel herself shrinking before him, his cold darkness assaulting her.

"I didn't have your gift for magic. I had to work and struggle to do the simplest spell. I had to lead the coven and take on all the responsibility that should have been yours."

"I know, but I'm here now." Part of her screamed that it wasn't enough. She should have been there.

"Sure, you came back, but it's because of you that I'm like this now. If you had stayed, if you had been here, continued training, you would have been strong enough to lead the coven and I would have been safe. It's. All. Your. Fault." He spit the words at her, and each was like its own slap in her face.

He was right. Her tears blurred her world. She should never have left. His shadowed heart was her fault, his betrayal her own doing. "I'm sorry," she whispered. Her heart ached with regret she could never fix.

He turned his back on her and took his place by Raven's side. Looking down his nose at her, his heartless voice grated on Jade. "Let's go."

Raven looked from Jade to Charlie, then back again. "Well, what do you know? I thought I'd have to drag him from you kicking and screaming." She laughed, the sound for the first time seeming like a genuine laugh. She put her arm around him, and he returned the gesture.

Charlie's voice was chilling, mimicking Raven's condescending tone. "Don't worry, Jade. You'll see me again, soon."

Raven snapped her fingers, and both she and Charlie disappeared.

CHAPTER 16

Jade slid to the floor. Her tears fell on empty hands, listless in her lap. A coldness surrounded her. It wasn't dark and menacing like Charlie's shadow; it was a gray thing, like slate in winter. It was hard and painful. She replayed what had happened over and over in her mind. Those last moments from when Raven touched Charlie and his face turned to stone, to his arm around Raven as she portaled them away with a snap. She'd lost him.

Gentle hands lifted her up, steadying her, guiding her through the coven members. Like a tragic slideshow, each face she passed displayed a different worry: Katie's anxious frown as she wrung her hands, Selene and Aiden's concern contrasting Mrs. Keepsake's mask of cheerful determination. "Don't fret, dear. We'll—"

We'll what? Jade wondered as her face passed by, replaced by the face of someone simply bothered by yet another problem to add to the list: Mr. Flannerly. Not only had she lost Charlie, she'd probably lose the coven too. They deserved a leader who didn't mess up as royally as she had. She'd failed them.

A fresh wave of tears and her world was a blur again. She was guided to sit on the edge of a chair. Wiping her eyes, she looked around. She was back in the study. The walls of books, dim lighting, and comfortable furniture usually welcomed her in. But now she felt like an intruder. She looked down at her hands. If only she'd done something to save him.

"Stop that. Feeling sorry never did anyone any good, least of all a Witch." Willow stood in front of her, tall and regal. Her white dreadlocks piled high on her head, her white eyes contrasting her dark skin, staring right at Jade as if she could see her. She looked like her old self. Only the white of her blind eyes showed any sign she wasn't in full form.

Jade numbly stood and walked to Willow's side, meaning to take her hand and guide her to a seat. Instead, Willow pulled her into an embrace. The warmth of ginger and honeysuckle enveloped her, and Jade sank gratefully into Willow's soft form. There was something healing in that space, and Jade felt much of her anxiety and sorrow flow out of her.

After a moment, Willow pushed her back and led her to the chairs. "That's quite enough of that. It's time to deal with things. Have a seat." She pointed to the chair Jade had been sitting in and lowered herself onto the one next to it.

Jade sat next to her. "Why do you do that?"

"Do what, child?"

"Act as if you can't see."

"What makes you think I can?"

"Can't you? You just walked over to these chairs and pointed. That has to mean your sight's returning, doesn't it?"

"My dear child, you should know by now that we have six senses at our disposal. Any one of which is capable of guiding us through the physical world without incident. While my eyes may not be working, all my other senses are better than ever. I simply refuse to focus on what I can't see, and make careful study of what I can."

Jade asked quietly, "Does everyone in the coven hate me now?"

"Hate you? Child, why on Earth would you think that?"

"Oh, I don't know. Maybe because I let their High Priest be infected by dark magic and align with a Witch who wants to take over the coven. On top of that, an inspector is probably going to return with a Citizen army and throw us all in the stocks for breaking the Accords." Jade swallowed against the lump in her throat.

Willow smiled. "Child, you know what I think of pity parties."

"But—"

"No buts. They're a waste of time. Let's talk strategy, shall we?"

"I don't even know where to begin."

"I often find the best place to begin is with what you already know to be true."

"Well, Charlie's working with Raven now, the inspector got a front row seat to a Witch's fight, and even though I don't think he believes I killed April, he's sure to spill the beans to Sun City about our ability to possess people, so . . . I'd say what's true is that we're screwed."

"First of all, you have no idea what the inspector does or does not believe, nor what he will tell Sun City. Raven didn't look much like April, so it would be quite the leap of logic for him to know she's possessed. Don't let your anxious, fearful mind get carried away."

"I appreciate that, but if there's one thing I learned living in Sun City, it's that they're terrified of us. They have been since the beginning. We've kept the peace by staying in our separate corners, for the most part. A Witch casting on a Citizen breaks that peace. Thanks to Raven's portal spell, when the inspector comes back, it won't just be to investigate April's disappearance. When he returns it will probably be with an entire squadron of lawkeepers. They'll take over the entire town until they get to the truth about everything. They'll eventually find out Raven's possessing April's body. There are people in power who will not hesitate to react to that with fear and violence. They're gonna declare war. They have for less."

The itch to run away was creeping in on her. She stood and began pacing. "There is one thing that would solve everything though: getting rid of Raven. Kill her and suddenly there's no possession. A dead Citizen, sure, but not possessed." She plopped back down next to Willow. "But then we're right back at the issue with the lawkeeper, and the only way out of that is for April to be alive." She looked down at her hands in her lap. She wished desperately for April to take her hand like she used to, but that was a comfort she'd never feel again.

"Jade, do you think April was the first Citizen to ever die at the hands of a Witch? Those in power in the cities would love to think they are holding all the cards. But peace is a two-way street. There have always been Citizens who cared for Witches and vice versa. Over the years both sides have lost people to mistakes, carelessness, and accidents."

"Yes, but this wasn't an accident."

"Yes, and a Witch didn't actually kill a Citizen. Richard did. Citizen-on-Citizen violence is tragic, but it's dealt with by Citizens."

"Unfortunately, none of that changes the fact that Raven has raised an army of the dead and has Charlie on her side." The tears threatened to break free, but she stubbornly refused to let them fall. "If only I hadn't let Charlie teach me dark magic, this wouldn't have happened. It was because of that his heart went dark so fast." Willow's expression had shifted, and Jade could feel the scolding coming. "I know, dark magic is forbidden. I shouldn't have pressed him, but I felt like it was the only way to beat Raven. She's just so much stronger than me."

"Stronger than you maybe, but not stronger than us. You have no idea what our coven is capable of when we come together with singular purpose."

"But—"

"No!" Willow so rarely raised her voice, it startled Jade into submission. She returned to her usual calm tone and continued, "You need to learn that it's not all about you. Covens have thirteen members for a reason, child. Otherwise the High Priestess and High Priest could run everything on their own." She stood and reached out for Jade, gripping her hands tightly and pulling her to her feet. "Now, I thank you to stop all this business about how you should have this and could have that. The past is past, leave it be. Charlie may be gone for now, but your coven is still here and they are waiting for you to lead them." She walked to the door and paused with her hand on the doorknob. "Take a minute to find the High Priestess within you, then come lead your people."

***

When Jade asked the inspector to meet her, she half expected him to turn up with every lawkeeper from Sun City behind him. She was surprised when he arrived in one car and was the only person to step out of it.

"Inspector Caldwell. Thank you for meeting with me. I'm surprised you came alone."

"I considered bringing reinforcements, but something about your tone—I thought this would be better. Be assured, my drones are streaming everything straight to headquarters, and an entire battalion can be here in a matter of minutes. Your township wouldn't survive."

"Of course." She smiled at the nearest drone. "May I ask how you explained your sudden return to Sun City?"

"I told them the truth: I returned to gather resources and prepare for the final phase of the investigation."

"Well, then, let's not hold up the wheels of justice. I have a confession to make. I have been hiding something from you. I intend to come clean, but to do so, I need to ask for your trust."

"You ask for my trust after admitting that you've kept evidence from me? How am I to reconcile those?"

It was strange he didn't mention being portaled against his will, but he also returned to meet her alone. The whisper of hope told her to tread lightly. She took a step forward. Caldwell backed up, raising his hands. She raised hers as well, palms up. When he seemed to relax a little, she took another slower step until she was right in front of him.

"Inspector Caldwell, relations between Citizens and Witches have never been easy. But in every new discourse, someone has to be the first to trust. I called you here without any backup of my own. I'm asking you to return that trust. Let me show you the evidence you're missing." She looked directly into his cyborg eye. "Please."

CHAPTER 17

The ride to Siobhan Abbey was long and silent, the only noise coming from the electric vehicle, humming along as the miles of dirt road rolled by. Sophia sat in the passenger seat, giving Caldwell occasional directions. His drones were powered down and tucked back into their compartments in his jacket. He'd insisted they come back out when they arrived, but he promised he would not livestream without notifying her first. Jade sat in back, staring out the window, the blur of green-and-brown forest reminding her of the ride to Sugar Hill, when April was by her side. She was risking everything now, and the people she'd always relied on to support her were gone. There was a strange power that came from that, relying on only your own strength.

But Willow was right, she had a whole coven to support her now. She wasn't alone. It was an odd contradiction she was wrestling with, feeling her own individual strength as well as the power that came from the support of those around her. But she'd decided to lean into it. To use all the resources she possessed and follow her intuition. It was that intuition that told her it was time the inspector learned the truth about Richard and what he did to April.

The thought of portaling him to the abbey had crossed Jade's mind, but the inspector already seemed on edge about Raven's ability to defeat his technology so easily, not to mention portaling him and his drones miles away. Better to play it safe and keep things as simple and nonmagic as possible.

While waiting for him to arrive in Sugar Hill, Jade had told Sophia her plan to spill all the beans to him, but in a controlled environment. That way, they could wait out whatever initial reaction he had and temper it into something that wouldn't result in calling in all of Sun City to war. She agreed easily, explaining that she had just heard from the abbey moments before. They wanted to speak with her. And so, the unlikely trio were on their way to Sophia's alma mater.

The abbey was an expansive castle, high in the mountains. There was a small dirt road leading to it, but it was overgrown, as most people who visited were Witches and arrived by other means. Jade had never been there, but as the coven's main healer, Sophia had trained at the abbey for years and was very familiar. The inspector had insisted on taking his own vehicle, and the electric engine was nearly silent as it climbed the final pass to the abbey.

As they crested the hill, the castle came into view. Carved from the same stone as the mountain, it sat on the edge of a cliff, as if nestled in the range's arms. Five great towers rose from the outside wall, allowing vantage points from all directions. Centered within the ring of towers was a large dome of stone and glass. It shone brightly, glittering like a jewel as the sunlight bounced off the many panes of glass. Jade felt the calming energy as soon as she saw it. It was a shame the cloak kept non-Witches from seeing it. Jade would have loved to witness Inspector Caldwell's reaction.

Sophia cautioned the lawkeeper to slow down, and a moment later they found out why. The road they were following abruptly stopped, with only a small sign to warn them. The inspector slammed on the brakes, and they skidded to a stop before a huge ravine.

He looked at them from under the brim of his hat that he never seemed to remove. "That. Is dangerous."

Sophia smiled cordially. "Why yes it is. I guess people who don't belong here might want to be careful."

"Is that a threat?"

"Of course not. I'm just stating the obvious, aren't I?" Sophia's smile was warm and kind, but the energy she was giving off warned to tread lightly. Jade wondered if the inspector could feel it.

He glared at her momentarily, then pulled the car over to the side, away from the cliff face and off the road, and they all got out.

"Now what?" he asked, looking hesitantly over the side.

"Now we wait for our escorts. It should only be a few minutes. You might want to take this time to put away your technological contraptions." Sophia pointed to the ever-present drones hovering around his head.

"That's not gonna happen. Sun City law requires continuous recording of all events during an investigation. No exceptions."

"Well. That's unfortunate." She walked back to the car and got into the front passenger seat.

After a moment the inspector sighed and walked over to the window. "What are you doing?"

"You said you have to use those machines to record everything, no exceptions. Right?"

"Yes . . ."

"Well, Siobhan Abbey has a 'no exception' rule as well. No Citizen technology is allowed within the abbey's outer wall. Their rule has stood unbroken since the Burning Times. If you won't budge and they won't either, it seems we wasted a trip."

"You couldn't have told me this before we left?"

"I could have, but I didn't anticipate you being so stubborn."

The inspector lowered his head, looking down and to his left, away from Sophia. He sighed and lifted his head. "This is ridiculous. I'm not being stubborn, I'm following the law."

Jade said, "Inspector, you remember our talk about trust? This is the time. If you want to go further, you need to trust me. I promise, you will not be harmed."

He considered it a moment. "Fine." He spoke into the main drone. "In accordance with Statute 1, I'm going to take the drones off-line, temporarily, in the pursuit of justice. I will record all conversations by primitive means"—he looked at Sophia askance, and when she nodded, he continued—"and transcribe all events to the official record upon returning from this place." He moved to the trunk of the car and opened the lid. Within was a large case, which he opened, and the three drones immediately flew into indentations within it. He pressed his thumb to each one, just above the lens, and they shut off in turn.

He closed the case and started to close the trunk when Sophia said, "Uh uh. Aren't you forgetting something?" She pointed at the inspector's left eye.

"You've got to be kidding me. I can't remove this."

"No. But you can disable it."

He squinted at her, his cyborg eye whirring. "Disable it?"

"Only temporarily. Or we could just head back and you'll never get the evidence you're after."

"All right, all right. You have to turn your backs though."

Jade couldn't resist. "Why, are you shy?"

Without humor, he said, "Ha ha. No. Letting you see how this is done is a security breach I am not willing or able to commit."

Sophia and Jade turned their backs without another word, and after a few moments of silence, he said, "Okay. It's done."

He stood there looking like a scolded puppy. Head hung low, he fiddled with the corner of his notebook. "Can we go now?"

Sophia looked at him cautiously. "Do you have any other implants, or technology? They'll not come if you do."

"No. Not even a Band. The drones and my eye are all I need. All I needed." He sounded so discouraged.

Jade asked, "How do we know it's really disabled?"

He looked up at her. If the sorrowful and angry expression on his face wasn't enough of an answer, his eye was. It was dark and still. No whirring to signal it was focusing, no golden glow in the center. She reached out tentatively with her magic and felt nothing. A cold void where his dead eye was. His body was tense though. He stood rigid and still, not the relaxed pose of someone at ease in their skin.

"Does it hurt?"

His eyes widened momentarily, then his expression hardened again. "That's no concern of yours. Let's just get this over with." He stormed past them, toward the end of the road where it met the cliff.

Jade and Sophia caught up to him and looked over the edge at a footbridge. It was attached to two stone pillars on the edge of the cliff, the boards and rope disappearing into the foggy distance.

"When did that get here?" Inspector Caldwell frowned at the bridge.

Someone was crossing from the other side. A tall woman dressed in a flowing hooded wrap of some kind. It reached the floor, and Jade couldn't tell if she was walking very smoothly or floating just above the bridge's surface.

As she reached them and stepped off, she said, "It's perfectly safe, I assure you. But before you cross there's something we need to take care of." She lifted her hand toward the inspector's face and he backed up, raising his hands as if to fight.

The woman spoke in a very soft, soothing voice. "Hush now, Benjamin. You are safe in my care."

The inspector instantly dropped his hands to his sides. He stood completely still, facing her as she approached with her hand outstretched, her palm glowing slightly. She hovered her hand over his eye for a few moments. As she did so, his whole demeanor relaxed, and a small smile tugged at the corner of his mouth.

"Better?" she asked, stepping back.

The inspector frowned. "You may call me Inspector or Mr. Caldwell."

"Of course, Mr. Caldwell." She turned to Sophia. "Merry meet, Healer Sophia."

"Merry meet, Abbess Brigid. Thank you so much for hosting us on such short notice."

"Not at all. You are always welcome to return any time. Your companions . . . well, that depends on this encounter." She smiled kindly at Jade and the inspector. "Come. Mother Abbess is looking forward to seeing you again."

She led them across the bridge, which didn't move at all. When they arrived on the other side of the canyon, a towering wall appeared a few feet from the cliff face. A section of it shimmered and disappeared. Abbess Brigid walked through without hesitation and they followed.

As Jade passed the outer wall, a feeling of peace washed over her. The area just inside the wall was forest. A narrow dirt path led forward. Occasionally, a leafy branch would reach out and brush against them as they passed. It reminded her of entering Madame Belle's backyard. Each leaf pulled more stress from her, until she was feeling relaxed and confident.

"This is amazing," she said to Sophia. "I feel amazing. I need to have this setup on my property." She smiled as she looked around.

Sophia chuckled. "You could have it, Jade. It just takes decades of dedication to healing, commitment to proper tending of the plants, and a degree from the university."

"Does that mean Madame Belle attended Siobhan Abbey too? It feels a lot like this when you go into her backyard."

Abbess Brigid said, "Madame Belle was indeed a student here, but she left the order to pursue other talents."

Jade raised an eyebrow at Sophia. "I'd like to hear that story someday."

"Then you should ask her, dear. It's her story to tell."

When they reached the edge of the forest, they stepped out of the tree line into a clearing that contained several small houses, each with a garden taking up an area of nearly the same size as the building. Jade and Sophia caught up to the inspector and Abbess Brigid.

Abbess Brigid waved her hand as they passed between two of the structures. "These are our herb gardens. Students are assigned to a plot and cultivate it throughout their semester before moving on to the next."

The inspector had his notebook out and was scribbling in it as they walked. "So this is a school of sorts as well as a chapel?"

Abbess Brigid smiled kindly at him. "I wouldn't exactly categorize our building as something so quaint as a chapel." She motioned ahead.

In the distance, over the roofline of the long two-story building before them was a huge dome. It stretched nearly to the clouds. The same dome Jade had seen from the other side of the canyon, it looked much bigger now, like a mountain with fragments of clouds catching on the peak and dragging as they passed. There were parapets and towers all around, but the main dome stretched uninterrupted. A golden glow emanated from within. It was stunning.

The inspector seemed unaffected and simply said, "Indeed. Cathedral then," before writing in his notebook.

She continued leading the way. "It is a central place of study, healing, and law."

"Law? I thought the covens were the ones who made the laws for themselves."

"You are mistaken. The covens do make laws for their own townships, but those are mundane rules to help govern their people on a daily basis. We are in charge of interpreting the divine laws that rule over all Witches, covens, and townships. When your little Accords were thought up and brought to Sugar Hill to be signed, we were consulted first to be sure none of your requests would violate our divine laws. Those that did were refused, and your lawkeepers had to rewrite them. Those that didn't, then passed through the Sugar Hill coven members to be sure they did not violate their township laws."

"I see. We were not aware you were actually the spokespeople for the Witches, or we would have negotiated with you instead."

"We would not have negotiated with you. Citizens are not our concern. The Witches came to us to make sure they were not agreeing to something that went against divine law." She stopped and looked squarely at him. "Do Citizens not have a hierarchy?"

"Of course."

"Well then, know that you are not in ours. You are only here out of a courtesy bestowed to Sophia as a graduate of our university. Were it not for her, you would not be here."

She turned and continued walking through the maze of streets. The inspector looked at Sophia. She was smiling at him, kind and gentle. She glided past him and let out a little laugh, no more than a pip, but the inspector seemed to receive the message. He nodded, then turned and followed at a respectful distance. Jade grinned, laughing to herself about how quickly the tables could turn, and hurried to catch up.

They eventually came to a large building in the center of a street. The street split and flowed around it like a river. Abbess Brigid led them to the open doorway at the point of the building. "This is our Well-being Institute. Here we treat the sick in body, mind, and spirit. Your Mr. Whetstone is a resident here."

"How long will you be holding him for?"

"Holding him?"

"Yes. When will you release him back to our custody, and what, or who, do you request in exchange?"

"He is not a prisoner. He is free to leave whenever he wants. His only mandatory stay was for the first week after he arrived, in order to assess his danger to the Witch community and heal him enough to be taken out of critical condition. It was during this time we decided he was no threat to us. He has remained here at his own request, and we have obliged, as we see the need in him to continue the healing process."

Jade bristled at this. She would have preferred him dead, after what he did to April.

The inspector asked, "You will help him even though he's a Citizen?"

"We are Witches, Mr. Caldwell. We help all living things." She turned and strode down the hall, and they hurried to catch up.

She stopped at a closed door at the very end of the hall. "This is a space of quiet and peace. Please keep your voices low and your movements calm." She opened the door slowly and padded inside.

The room was large and completely empty except for a scrying pool in the center. It was dimly lit, and the ceiling, walls, and floor were a pale, calming blue. Richard was sitting on the edge of the scrying pool, staring into it. He was wearing a white hooded cloak, and one sandaled foot peeked out from the hem.

As they approached, their footsteps crunched quietly on the sand path. He looked up with a content smile on his face at Abbess Brigid. When he made eye contact with Jade, his smile disappeared, replaced by a grimace. He quickly looked back to the pool and pulled the cloak's hood up over his head.

Abbess Brigid said quietly, "Richard, you have some visitors." He began rocking slightly and mumbling something. She gently placed a hand on his shoulder and he stopped rocking. "Remember your therapy. You knew this day would come, and you have prepared for it. This is a good thing for you."

He shook his head and mumbled, "No. I'm not ready. I need more time." He looked up at her pleadingly. "Please, just a little more time."

She shook her head. "No. It is time." Her voice was so gentle, like a mother comforting her child.

"Will you stay?"

"Of course. But not because you need me to. I'm staying because I'm proud of you for taking this next step. I want to witness it." She smiled down at him another moment, then stepped back and nodded at the inspector. "Ask your questions, respectfully."

Inspector Caldwell approached Richard with head down. His voice was soft. "Mr. Whetstone, my name is Inspector Caldwell. I'm here to ask you a few questions about what happened last month. Is that okay?"

Richard nodded but turned back to the pool. Jade stepped a bit closer and looked into it. A young girl of about four, with long brown hair, was jumping around a grassy field, chasing a small puppy. She was laughing, but Jade couldn't hear her.

The inspector leaned over, as if to get into Richard's line of sight. When that didn't work, he sat down on the pool's edge, facing him. "Richard?" He glanced up for a moment, then looked back down to the pool. A flash of disappointment crossed the inspector's face, then he opened his notebook to a blank page. "I have a few questions, is that okay?"

Richard nodded.

"Do you remember leaving Sun City to come to Sugar Hill last month?" He nodded, so the inspector continued. "Could you tell me why you did that?"

He began rocking again, then steadied himself. "I missed her."

"Missed who?"

"She called to me, you know?" He looked up at the inspector. "She said she was afraid. Needed my help." He paused and looked at his hands. "It was the only way, she said. She just wanted to come home."

"Who?"

"Abigail. My sweet Abigail." He looked back to the pool again. The little girl was sitting at a table, drawing. Richard tilted his head as he watched her. "She said she would come back to me. That we could be a family again. She promised it would all be okay. I should have known. It was my job to protect her." He looked up at the inspector again, this time with anger. "The parent protects the child. I was supposed to protect her."

He glared at Jade. "You! If you had helped me, none of this would have happened. She said you could have brought her back without killing anyone." Tears began to flow down his cheeks then. "I didn't want to kill April" He looked pleadingly at the inspector, "I didn't want to, I had to. You understand?"

He glared at Jade again "Because of you. You should have helped me. April would still be alive."

Abbess Brigid stepped forward and placed a hand on his back. "We talked about this, Richard. You remember?"

He seemed to shake himself out of it. "Yes. A life for a life. Always a life for a life." He turned back to the pool, mumbling, "Life for life. Life for life." He was rocking again, repeating the mantra over and over.

The abbess said, "You won't get anything else out of him, I'm afraid. He has good days and bad days. Unfortunately, today is a bad one. I'm surprised he even spoke that much."

The inspector stood. "I have more questions for him. You're saying there's nothing you can do to make him more lucid?"

"Not without setting back all the progress he's made so far."

"Progress? He's a mumbling mess! The Richard I—" He stopped. After taking a moment to compose himself, he continued. "This is not Richard Whetstone. He was a strong and powerful businessman. He obviously needs better care than you are able to deliver here. I'm taking him back to Sun City for proper medical attention."

She said, "If that is what Richard wants, we will allow it, but he is in no condition to make any decisions right now. Perhaps if you return tomorr—"

"No. I'm not leaving here without him. He is a Citizen of Sun City, and as lawkeeper it is my duty to see he's returned safely home. No exceptions."

"Understood. We will not interfere with Citizen matters, but he is in no danger. You should wait a short time to allow him to speak for himself. If he has not become lucid by sundown, you may leave with him then, no harm done."

He thought about it a moment before replying, "Agreed." He sat back down and faced Richard. "But I'm not leaving his side."

"You are welcome to stay as long as you wish. Jade, if you and Sophia will accompany me, the Mother Abbess would like to speak with you."

They followed her to the door, and Jade turned back to look at the inspector and Richard one more time. Richard was just sitting there, rocking slightly and tapping his knee. The inspector sat facing him. His face slowly shed the steely, expressionless facade. Within moments he was looking at Richard with concern and compassion.

Jade spun and hurried to catch up to Sophia and the abbess, angry at herself for feeling any sympathy toward them. Richard had made his bed when he killed April. Now he had to lie in it.

The abbess led Jade and Sophia through the abbey's grounds. Sophia was cheerful, reminiscing on everything they passed.

"Oh, there's the observatory! I got to take my astrology class with Dr. Bennett. She was a marvel, made everything so clear and easy. A shame she passed so young. Oh, the cafeteria. They make the best apple crisp." She took Jade's arm in confidence as they walked. "My friend and I were in charge of the apples one year. I think we ate more than we sliced." Her giggle wormed its way into Jade, and she began to relax. "Down that alley are the most beautiful nightshades. Their nighttime fragrance and blooms are quite intoxicating." She whispered, "I won't tell you how I know that. Oh, and here's the administration complex. Do you know, I almost became a lawyer?"

They had reached huge double doors made of stone. The abbess stopped and turned toward them. "You would have made a wonderful lawyer, Sophia, but I'm happy you followed your heart."

She motioned to the doors, and they swung open just enough for a person to fit through. Jade couldn't help but wonder why they needed such a large opening.

"Mother Abbess asked to speak with you alone, so Sophia and I will wait here for you."

Sophia took Jade's hands. "Don't be intimidated by her, but do show respect. And whatever she asks, do not lie. She is a soothsayer, among other things." She patted her hand, then released her.

Jade took a deep breath and stepped through the massive doors.

CHAPTER 18

The first thing Jade noticed, before she'd even fully entered the room, was the smell of books. Old, dusty, and leather bound. She looked around the space which was dimly lit. A few hanging lanterns and candelabras shed just enough light so she could see her path. Beyond that was darkness, but she knew they were there, rows and rows of books. The biggest library she'd ever been in. And the darkest.

A raspy voice called out from the shadows ahead, "Step lively if you please. I'm a busy woman."

Strength and power pulled Jade to hurry through the room. She quickly wove through the handful of scattered tables and chairs and came to a stop at the end. Before her were two shallow steps forming a raised section, which held a long banquet-style table. There were only two chairs, one before her, and one facing it on the opposite side. There sat the Mother Abbess.

"Don't be shy, child. Have a seat." She was tall and frail, but sat straight, with a regal air about her. Her smile was comforting though, and she wore a blue-and-green-paisley flowered dress beneath her long white robes. As Jade took her seat, Mother Abbess said, "Now, tell me all about Raven."

Jade suddenly felt compelled to tell her everything, not just about Raven but all about her parents' deaths, her growing up in Sun City, even her tumultuous relationship with Charlie. The words just spilled out of her, without filter.

Mother Abbess sat and listened attentively, nodding occasionally and frowning at the right places. When Jade was finished, she sat back and closed her eyes, seeming to mull it over.

Time ticked by and Jade was beginning to wonder if she'd fallen asleep. She began to get uncomfortable with the silence and had just thought she should say something when Mother Abbess opened her eyes.

"Still working on our impatience, are we?" She smiled a moment before leaning forward. "Your theory of Raven inhabiting the mansion on the town's edge is correct. Send an emissary there to invite her to defend herself."

"And if she refuses? If she attacks and kills us? What then?"

"*Then* hasn't happened yet. Stop living in the future and the past. I know your visions can make that difficult sometimes, but remember," she raised one finger, "the only time truly under your control is the present."

Abbess Brigid strode in the room, and Mother Abbess turned toward her.

"Mr. Whetstone is lucid."

"Thank you. Please escort Miss Cerridwen to see him. If he wishes to leave, take them to the border."

Jade jumped out of the chair. "That's it? All the struggling we've gone through and you're not going to do anything?"

Mother Abbess paused a moment before answering. Her voice was low and measured. "Have you not heard me?" There was a warning to it.

Jade couldn't help herself. "Yes, but . . . we've been trying. She keeps portaling away or—now she has Charlie—I need help. We are asking for your help."

The Mother Abbess smiled, a proud grandmother beaming over her grandchild. "You have all the help you need. Trust in your coven. Trust in yourself." She eyed Jade for a moment, then sighed. "You must not only believe in your power, but act as if you do. If you promise to do that, I will promise to watch over you and your coven while you resolve the situation with Raven."

Jade considered this. She didn't exactly say she would help, but having them observe the struggles they went through might be enough to change her mind. "Thank you, Mother Abbess. I will do my best to be the leader you seem to believe I am." She smirked at her attempt to speak with confidence when she didn't feel it. She'd changed a lot in the last month, but apparently she still had work to do.

**

Richard did want to return to Sun City, but he had asked to speak with Jade alone first. The inspector seemed very reluctant, but agreed, assuring Richard he would be waiting outside if needed.

After he'd left and they were alone, Richard sat on the pool's edge and motioned Jade to sit next to him. She did, but farther away than he wanted, based on his sorrowful look at the space between them.

"Thank you for agreeing to speak with me. I know this isn't easy for you. I betrayed your trust. My actions . . . well, saying they're unforgivable doesn't even do them justice, does it?" He tried to smile at her, but it faltered. He looked down at his hands in his lap, one finger tapping the center of his other palm. "I don't have much time before my mind slips again. If there's anything you want to say, you should say it now."

When he looked up at her, his eyes were so kind, it was like she had him back. Richard, the kind, strong man who'd been like a father to her since she was twelve. The man who had watched over her, given her a place to belong when doing so threatened everything he held dear.

There was so much she wanted to say. She tried to tell him she wished he was dead, but she couldn't make a sound. She opened her mouth to ask him why, but nothing came out. All the pain, all the betrayal, everything she'd endured, April's death—it was all his fault. Raven may have been the mastermind, but he was the one who had lied to her. His hand had held the knife. He was the one to blame.

They stared into each other's eyes. Neither said a word, but Jade could feel he understood. Her energy, her posture, the expression on her face, it told him everything she was feeling and thinking.

He crumpled before her, head down, while sobs wracked his frame. "Saying I'm sorry isn't enough. But I am. I'm so sorry, Jade. For the rest of my life, I'll make it my mission to make up for it . . . No, that's not possible." He looked away from her, and his breathing slowed to normal. When he looked back to her, his eyes seemed more distant, glassy and unfocused. "Jade? Kill her."

Jade was taken aback by the anger in his voice. "What?"

"Please. What she did to me . . . I never would have touched April if it wasn't for her. She got in my head." Fear flashed across his face, and he reached out and grabbed her robe. "I can't do it, you have to. Kill Raven. For April."

Jade stared at the broken man before her. He sat back, mumbling apologies to himself again, lost somewhere in his own private hell. Unable to take back any of the horrible things he'd done, blaming both Raven and himself. He was nothing like the man she'd once known. She no longer hated him, but she no longer loved him. The most she could do was release him.

"I forgive you." She hadn't meant to say it out loud. She had meant to test the words in her mind first, but her voice drifted to him and his shoulders eased.

He looked up at her with a shattered smile. "Really?" he whispered.

As Jade's mind answered him, she felt a weight lift off her. It wouldn't bring April back, wouldn't cure the pain in her heart, wouldn't even absolve Richard. He would always carry what he'd done. The only thing it would do was set them free of each other. And Jade needed to be free. She needed to release the anger and vengeance she'd held in her heart and begin to heal. "Yes, Richard. I forgive you."

Richard's red-rimmed eyes overflowed with tears, brought on by the bittersweet anguish of being forgiven for the unforgivable. His sobs echoed off the walls, and the inspector burst through the door.

He rushed to Richard's side. "What did you do?" he accused Jade.

"I forgave him."

He stared at her, confusion and suspicion on his face. Turning back to Richard, he knelt next to him and leaned in, trying to catch his eyes, "Richard? It's me."

Jade felt for him. They'd obviously known each other well, and he seemed genuinely upset at his current state of distress. "I'll tell the abbess to prepare him to leave. We'll make for Sugar Hill within the hour." She turned and walked out of the room.

She felt unburdened, but also with new purpose. What was past was past. Her only thoughts now were for her coven and township. Protecting them from

Raven's threat was first priority. She would get her trial, one chance to do the right thing. If she refused, then Jade would serve justice. Her way.

CHAPTER 19

Sophia stayed behind to speak with Mother Abbess. She said it was a private matter, but it couldn't wait and she would portal back to Sugar Hill as soon as she was finished. Jade said her goodbyes and joined Inspector Caldwell and Richard by the path out. Abbess Brigid had insisted on escorting Richard herself. They walked slowly down the rope bridge, her arms wrapped gently around him, murmuring encouragement in his ear the whole way. He was calm, but didn't seem to be aware of what was going on.

The inspector and Jade followed close behind. His posture was tense, his face completely devoid of emotion, but his eyes never strayed from Richard. Jade wanted to ask how they knew each other, but it was not the right time. He could decide to arrest her at any moment for any number of crimes. She needed to know where they stood.

Richard was in no shape to stand trial, and there was a good chance he wouldn't. Whetstone Enterprises had connections around the globe, and Richard was on everyone's asset list in Sun City. Jade was sure someone would petition to get him excused from trial. Unfortunately, that meant they would accuse and convict some poor innocent in his place. The Citizens needed their scapegoat.

Whether or not that scapegoat was Jade really depended on what the inspector told them and how his drone footage was edited on replay. The hardcore newsies always caught the live feeds, but most Citizens relied on the edited replays to keep them updated on the news. Hours and days of investigations boiled down to sound bites and ten seconds of filtered footage.

"He won't stand trial." She waited impatiently for his reply.

"That's no concern of yours."

"It is. If he's not tried, someone has to be."

He looked at her, and his darkened eye gave her a chill. Jade wondered what could have persuaded him to give up that much of himself. He resumed his watch over Richard. "What do you want?"

"What will you tell them?"

"Tell them?"

"About us. About Sugar Hill and its coven. How much of a danger will the Citizens think we are?"

"I will tell them the truth."

She scoffed. "Which version of the truth? The one that hurts us, or the one that protects us?"

"My job is not to protect you."

"Isn't it? Regardless of where I was born, I took the oath when I came of age, just as you did. I am a Citizen."

"No!" He stopped walking and invaded her space. She grabbed the rope handrail for support, but stood her ground. "You are nothing like them." His gaze softened. "You may know them, you may even understand them, but you will never be one of them."

He resumed walking, and she hurried to take her place next to him. "You're just a Witch."

His words stung. It wasn't that she didn't want to be a Witch, but she couldn't imagine not belonging to Sun City either. Being a Citizen had been her purpose for most of her life. It was more than just the comforts and benefits high-tech living afforded her. She believed. Take away the politics and rhetoric, take away the bigotry toward Witches. At their core, Citizens believed they were a part of something bigger. They each knew their place in society and worked hard to make sure their contributions mattered.

That type of life was too strict and confining to some, but Jade had always found it comforting. There was never any question she was doing the right thing. As a Witch, that wasn't always the case. The simple tenant of "Harm None" left too much to interpretation.

They'd arrived at the end of the bridge. Abbess Brigid helped the inspector place Richard into the back of the car. Jade thought he'd resist, but once inside he curled up on the seat, as if he was home from a long trip.

The Abbess said they'd done all they could to heal him, but his mind refused to face reality for any length of time. She gave the inspector instructions on his routine, which seemed to help reduce the swings of his emotions, and explained the treatments they'd given him. She expressed hope that Sun City's doctors would have better luck then quickly turned and went back down the bridge and into the fog.

The inspector quickly got his drones out of the trunk and settled them into place on his coat, then got behind the wheel. By the time Jade was in her seat, he had already activated his eye implant. As soon as she shut the door, he took off down the road.

Jade watched the inspector scribbling in his little black notebook while the car's autodrive slowly picked its way along the route back to Sugar Hill. Richard was leaning against the door, staring out the window, occasionally murmuring something. Over the time it had taken them to get him to the car, he'd gone from lucid, to comatose, to screaming mad, and now he seemed to be having a sad conversation with his reflection.

They were almost back to the township and the inspector hadn't activated his drones yet. It was now or never. Jade turned in her seat and stared him down until he stopped writing and looked up. "What?"

She stared into his golden robotic eye for a moment, watching the iris grow and shrink. The color fluctuated slightly as he tried to read her. She found it strange that she was relieved he looked like his normal self again. "What, exactly, will you tell them?"

"Why do you want to know so bad?"

She raised an eyebrow at him. "Seriously? I may not be one of them, but I know how things work. A Citizen was killed, in a township. If Richard doesn't stand trial, Governor Bishop will be happy to accuse any Witch he can find. In fact, I bet he'd prefer a Witch to be convicted. It would serve his bigoted agenda better."

"And you want me to lie so he has no evidence to accuse a Witch."

"No, of course I would never ask a lawkeeper to lie."

"I'm not recording."

"I know. I meant what I said. Outright lying can come back to bite you, but there are different versions of the truth. Depending on the words you choose, the tone you use, you could have them mourning a horrible tragedy, or gearing up for a righteous war against all Witches."

He studied her a moment. "My report will show the truth. Mr. Whetstone killed Miss Goodrich in cold blood. It's unfortunate his mind was broken and he is not in a position to defend himself, but no one else was involved. That includes Witches. In fact, the Witches of Sugar Hill were instrumental in discovering his involvement and detaining him until I arrived to capture him. Good enough?"

"Thank you. That's more than I could have hoped for."

He glanced back at Richard, who smiled briefly, then frowned and turned away again. After a moment, the inspector asked, "What will you do about Raven? She's still out there somewhere, right?" The car pulled to a stop in front of Jade's house.

"Better if you don't know. She's a Witch, we'll deal with her in our own way." She got out of the car and bent down to make eye contact. "Thank you." When he replied with a nod, she closed the car door and walked up her front steps. She had a fleeting thought to look back at Richard, but reminded herself he was in her past.

She entered her living room to find Willow waiting for her. "About time."

Jade told her what happened at the abbey. "We need to gather the coven and make a plan. I'll tell everyone to meet at the mayor's house."

"No. This won't be a regular coven meeting. A battle meeting needs to be at a place of great ancient power, preferably on a ley line, central to the magical energy of the coven's township."

"The chapel." Jade nodded.

"No, child. We can't risk Raven, or anyone under her power, tracing the portal back into the chapel."

"Where then?"

Willow sighed and gripped Jade's arm tight. "This is going to be difficult for you, but as High Priestess it is your duty to do the difficult things and put your own feelings aside for the good of the coven."

Jade felt her entire body tense. "Mary's Tavern." If there was one place she wanted to go less than Charlie's house, it was there.

"Yes. Specifically, the well behind it."

A glimpse of bloodstained ground and April's pleading eyes flashed through Jade's mind. She pushed it aside and focused on what Willow was saying.

"The basement of the tavern has been the site for secret coven rituals for generations before Sugar Hill became a township. It is imbued with magic in a way no other place is. Not even the chapel."

"So why can't we meet there? Why do we have to go to the well?"

"Because, my child, the tavern is not where the portal is."

"You're telling me the well is a portal?"

"Yes. And because it's on a ley line that runs directly to the mansion, it's the best way for us to get into position."

"No. No, I can't. Asking me to go to the tavern is one thing, but the well? That's where . . ." That was the place April had died. It had been weeks now, but she still couldn't say the words. "I'm sorry, but I can't face that."

Willow sighed and was quiet for a moment. Then she stood and began pacing. "When I lost my sight, I thought that my world had ended. I pitied myself, wondering how I could function without my precious vision." She stopped just short of the wall and turned to retrace her steps. "When you came to see me at Sophia's, I almost didn't talk to you. I wanted to hide.

"Pity parties are comforting in the short term, but they don't solve anything. It's only when we stop thinking about ourselves and start thinking about others that we can break out of them." She stopped directly in front of Jade and turned to face her. "It's not about you."

She sat next to Jade again, taking her hand gently in her frail ones. "You have an entire coven and township to take care of. I know you're hurting, but we all go through tragedy in life. You don't get to choose the tragedies you face, but you do get to choose how you respond to them. Losing your best friend the way you did, well, it's not an easy thing to get through. But you have."

"I don't feel like that sometimes."

"The pains from past tragedy don't just disappear overnight. And even when we think they're gone, they come back to remind us, often when we least expect it. But we get through them the same way we get through the tragedy itself, one moment at a time." She squeezed Jade's hand. "We can meet in the tavern initially to make our plan. When we go to the well, you will not be alone. You will hurt, but your coven will be with you."

Jade sat still for several minutes, leaning on the calm, powerful energy she felt flowing from Willow. It wrapped around her like a warrior's cloak. Willow was right. She'd been through some tragedies, but she'd had April to lean on when her parents and aunt had died, and she'd had Charlie to lean on when she lost April. Now, she had her coven.

"Okay. I'll try."

"That's all anyone expects." Willow smiled.

She hugged Willow tightly. "Thank you so much. I wish you could be with me."

"I do too, then I could witness the powerful High Priestess in action."

Jade smiled, recognizing the same strategy Abbess Brigid had used on Richard. Even though she knew Willow was just saying that to help her confidence, it still had an impact. Jade knew what she had to do. And Willow was right; she wouldn't do it alone.

***

Sophia greeted them at the door of Mary's Tavern. "Thank the Goddess. When you agreed to go with the inspector, I had the brief worry I wouldn't see you again. What did he say?"

"He'll support us, Richard will be tried for April's death." She hung her robe by the front door next to several others of coven red. "Who's here?"

Sophia took Willow's cloak and hung it next to Jade's. They walked toward the cellar door. "The whole coven of course." She opened the door and voices floated up the stairway from the meeting room below. "If Sun City knows April's dead, I guess we won't be needing this after all." She reached into her dress pocket and pulled out a small metal disk that looked very much like the Earth Key. A raised pentagram spanned the surface. "Shame. Madame Belle and I had such fun designing it."

"That's not the Earth Key?"

"No, but I'm glad you think that. It's the enchantment for Raven. You'd have to be right next to her when you use it, so I wanted it to look like something she wouldn't suspect." She held it out to Jade in her palm. "All you'd have to do is press the center with your thumb and drop it near her. In just a moment, she'd think she's April."

"How accurate will it be?" She took the disk and stared at it. She wasn't sure she'd be able to handle seeing her best friend standing right in front of her, but they still didn't have a surefire way to keep Raven from portaling out when things looked bleak. Being able to turn Raven into April could give them precious seconds to stop her.

"Even her own mother would think it was her."

Jade backtracked to her cloak and put the grenade in her pocket. It was a desperate play, but they couldn't take any chances on her escaping again.

***

The basement of Mary's Tavern was humming with magical energy. The bare earth floors, stone walls, and simple timber ceiling were drenched with it. Willow was right, no other place in Sugar Hill felt quite like this.

While everyone chatted in small groups, Jade stood like a statue. She just wanted this night to be over, but knew her impulsivity wouldn't serve her. Each member had specific strengths. They needed to work out a plan that would take advantage of all of them. Katie was the wildcard. Untested in battle, her skills as a Marrow barely understood, Jade could only hope she would rise to the occasion. She waited patiently until everyone noticed her and stopped talking.

"Thank you all for coming so quickly, I'll get right to the point. The inspector has taken Richard to Sun City to be tried for April's death. Now that the investigation's not a concern, we can focus on Raven. First, we capture her. That means attacking the mansion she's been hiding out in. Once she's under our control she'll stand trial for all her crimes."

"Do we really have to try to capture her? Why don't we just call her?" Crystal hadn't spoken to Jade since the scrying fire. "She wouldn't want to come here for fear we'd harm her, and I doubt she'd let us get anywhere near her, so why don't we hold the trial at a distance? We could use a scrying fire. And yes, before you say anything, I see the irony. But this time would be different, we would be prepared. We could cast it from Bonfire Field and set up protection around it. It would be hard for her to contaminate it without us noticing."

"But not impossible," Jade said.

"No, but we'd be ready for it if she tries."

Sophia said, "But if she's found guilty, she'd have a good head start at escaping."

"Unless . . ." Jade began pacing. "If we use it as a distraction to give us time to get into position, when she's found guilty, we'd already have her in our sights. It would just be a matter of springing the trap." She turned to face them, hopeful they might have a real chance to end this without bloodshed.

Jade turned to Katie. "We need to make sure Raven's still at the mansion. How fast can one of your faeries get there and back?" Katie seemed to have stopped listening partway through and was arguing with her shoulder. "Katie?"

The young Witch faced Jade. "Sorry. Elida said she's definitely there. She said she's pacing in a room on the top floor. Seems agitated about something." She looked to her side and said in hushed tones, "I know, just next time wait until I say it's okay. What if she'd seen you?"

Jade prompted, "Are we sure she didn't? It's imperative that she doesn't know we're coming for our plan to work."

"Of course. She said there's no doubt. She wasn't there long enough to be seen."

"Good. So, here's the plan. We'll all portal to the mansion's property line in two groups. Everyone wait until we reach the other side before calling on your Elementals."

"But it will take time for them to reach us," Mr. Flannerly said.

"Yes, but we'll be able to get into position more stealthily if we don't have a bunch of magical animals trailing us. Soon as you exit the portal, call them. By the time you're in position at the main gate, they should be caught up. Crystal, you lead the main group to the front gate. I'll go in the side gate with Sophia, Katie, and Daisy. Mrs. Keepsake, can you enchant yourself to pass for me, long enough to fool Raven?"

"Of course, dear."

"Perfect. Soon as we're through the portal, Madame Belle, Ms. Scrivener, and Mrs. Keepsake will scry through to Raven. Try her for everything you can think of. Keep her occupied as long as you can. We'll sneak through the gates and into the mansion. There's no doubt the risen will try to protect her. Take them out as quickly and quietly as you can. Once we get inside, we need to find Raven as fast as possible and bind her. Then we need to rescue Charlie."

"He looked pretty happy to go with Raven to me," Mr. Flannerly mumbled to Aiden at his side. After a moment he looked up and caught Jade's silent glare. "But, of course we'll bring him home. If we can."

"All we need now is a way to communicate that Raven won't notice while she's talking to Ms. Scrivener and company."

"I can help with that." Katie stepped forward and held out two necklaces, one silver and one gold, each with a tiny birdcage pendant on the end. "Say hello to Elida and Flick. They're twin faeries who share a psychic bond. You keep Flick"—she gently handed Mrs. Keepsake the gold necklace—"and I'll keep Elida. They'll be able to communicate to each other telepathically and let me know when it's safe to move in. Then she can zip over to the main gate and let them know too. Won't take her more than a blink."

"Alright. We all know what we need to do."

Mrs. Keepsake stood and gave Jade a big hug. "It will all turn out alright, dear."

They all filtered out of the room, and Jade hung back with Willow. It was time to face the past again. Jade's throat tightened as she watched the last Witch start up the stairs. It was her turn, but her legs weren't moving. Willow gripped her hand firmly and pulled forward. They walked up the stairs together.

Jade's legs shook as she gripped the railing. She focused on steadying them as she stepped up one leg at a time. When she reached the top of the stairs Willow led her around toward the back door. The line of Witches before her blocked her view of the well, but she knew it was there, inching closer with every step.

"Child, if you don't loosen your grip . . ." Willow scolded.

Jade released her hold and focused on holding her hand as loosely as possible. "Sorry, Grandma Willow."

As they stepped out the back door and saw the well, memories of the night April was sacrificed came flooding back. Jade hadn't been anywhere near Mary's Tavern since that night. The last time she'd seen this patio, all the chairs were piled high to one side and a crazed Richard, driven mad by Raven's manipulations, had been pacing about, muttering to himself.

Jade didn't realize she'd stopped walking until Willow placed a reassuring hand on her shoulder. "You are strong. You are a High Priestess. The Goddess and God are with you. Take a deep breath and remember why you are here."

Jade wanted to find another way, walk there if need be, anything but using the well's portal. She knew there wasn't time. She focused on the task at hand, the plan to capture Raven.

She walked through the memories and toward the well, like she was walking through a ghostly apparition of the past, superimposed on her present.

April's blood covered the ground around the well. Jade looked into the eyes of her friend as she died.

She shook off the memory and concentrated on Willow, keeping pace by her side as they approached coven, waiting around the well.

A hand was gripping her head tight, and a whisper in her ear said, "My little lamb."

"The past is past," Jade whispered to herself. "The past is past."

They reached the coven and Jade turned toward Willow. "You'll be here when we get back, right?"

"Yes, child. I'm not going anywhere."

Jade took some small comfort in the fact that she'd be able to see Willow soon and that until then she'd still be safe here in the township. She gathered her strength and took her place in the circle. She whispered to herself, "The past is past. The past is past."

Mrs. Keepsake took on of her hands and Madame Belle the other. A wave of warm energy flowed through her and she relaxed, feeling protected. Surrounded by those who loved her. She looked around the circle of her coven and felt their support.

As each coven member joined hands, Jade immediately felt a subtle pulsing of power. With Charlie the coven would have been whole and the power stronger, but it was enough to raise her spirits. She led them in chanting, "Transportari." *Transport.*

The well glowed and soon the bricks and wooden structure that held the bucket shimmered, then disappeared. In the space where the well had been, a portal formed. Its eerie blue light shimmered on the faces of the coven members. One by one they each stepped forward and dropped out of sight.

As Madame Belle released her hand, she said, "Easy as pie, mon cher," and then she was gone too, leaving only Jade.

She stepped forward to the edge and stared into the void below her. Taking a deep breath, she lifted her foot outward and fell forward.

CHAPTER 20

The sun was still sleeping when Jade dropped out of the sky. Her boots landed with a muffled thud on the moss-covered ground. She crouched down and quickly called her Earth Elemental, then took a moment to gather her bearings.

The cool air was silent. Not even crickets sang, as if they knew what was about to happen and had hidden away. The night was dark, with only a sliver of moonlight to show the way. She was only a few feet from the side gate and the stone wall towered overhead. It was well worn, but in excellent condition. Various plants and bushes encroached on the boundary, but the trees stood several feet away. Although, some branches had reached over the wall with the lack of regular pruning.

Someone hissed from the bushes in front of her. Jade picked her way through to find Sophia and Katie with their Elementals huddled against the stone wall next to a small iron gate. A black panther sat next to Katie, its bright green eyes shining in the dark. A black-and-gray eagle perched on Sophia's shoulder.

Jade whispered to Sophia, "I thought you'd bring your phoenix."

"I considered it but decided on something a little more discreet." Sophia smiled up at the bird.

"Is Daisy here yet?" Jade asked.

"Right here." The whisper came from two feet to Katie's side.

Jade squinted and was just barely able to make out a shimmer. "Good. What about everyone else?" She looked at the tiny cage pendant dimly glowing around Katie's neck.

"They're almost there." The faint tinkling could have been leaves in the wind, but Katie was listening carefully between relaying the information. "Mrs. K's been enchanted . . . Flick's impressed, says she looks exactly like you. They're reading the charges against Raven and she's . . . she's laughing. Ugh, I really don't like her."

There was a rustling in the brush behind her, and she turned to see Tank slowly lumbering toward her. "Alright, get ready to move. Katie, let Flick know we're ready."

Katie listened for a moment, then relayed, "Okay, they're in position." A moment later a quiet, high-pitched chime came from her necklace. "We should go now."

Jade peeked through the gate. She could just make out the ends of the south and east wings lit by the full moonlight. The building itself was just a mixture of black and gray shadows that nearly blended in with the few clouds in the night sky.

She slowly crept through the side gate with her group close behind. There was a long stretch of field between the gate and side entrance. Nothing to hide behind or give them cover. Jade hesitated, wondering if it was a mistake. There were a handful of tall majestic trees, but they were at the front of the property. Here, they were completely exposed.

Katie's necklace glowed at the same time a commotion sounded from the main gate: shouting and rumbling punctuated by explosions. They were in a battle. Jade was less worried about being heard now that the main gate was full of the noise of Elementals clashing and fireballs.

She signaled them to move and took one step when Daisy materialized in front of her. She put one finger to her lips and stepped next to Jade. "There's something wrong here," she whispered.

"What is it?"

"Not sure. Just a bad feeling." Daisy faded away and her disembodied voice whispered, "I'll scout ahead of you."

Jade stood frozen in the pale moonlight, afraid to move forward or back, the sounds of battle echoing. Was her coven dying, or were they winning? She turned to ask Katie for an update when Daisy cried out somewhere in the darkness. In fear or pain, she couldn't tell.

After waiting a moment longer than Jade wanted to, she broke into a run, Katie and Sophia close on her heels. They hadn't gone far and Jade was about to check behind her for the others when she tripped and landed in something squishy. She lifted herself up to her hands and knees and looked down. The ground was squirming, bubbling as if something was moving under the surface.

She tried to back away, but the earth was like quicksand. The more she struggled, the more she sank. Her arms were completely underground when something gripped her forearm tightly, like a branch wrapping around it. Jade could feel the bruise forming.

A skeleton sat up abruptly, forcing her back. It had her forearm in its grasp and was raising its other hand toward her neck. Jade grabbed its hand, surprised at the strength it had. She was about to cast a curse at it when a huge boulder ran it over, ripping it away from Jade, leaving only its hands clasped harmlessly to her.

The boulder stopped several feet from Jade and turned toward her. Tank seemed to smile as she bobbed her head. The pile of bones at her side struggled to move. Without breaking eye contact with Jade, Tank simply stomped on it with one foot.

Jade looked around to find Sophia and Katie going through similar obstacles with help from their Elementals. They were making their way across an unmarked graveyard, and the dead were rising. Every few feet one would attempt to stop a Witch, and their Elemental would quickly put them back in the ground or scatter their bones.

They finally made it to the other side. Jade looked up at the darkened windows and balconies above them as she asked Katie, "What news from the main gate?"

"Flick says Raven disappeared soon as the fighting started. They're making good progress toward the mansion though. They're almost at the main entrance. They think Raven must be hiding out inside somewhere."

"Let them know to hold at the entrance once they reach it. We'll be inside any moment, and the last thing we need is to be caught in the cross fire."

While Katie relayed the message, Jade hurried to Daisy, a human-shaped shadow a few feet away. "What do you think?"

"The entrance here seems clear."

"Seems, or is? We can't just walk into a trap. We've come too far."

"I can only tell you what I sense. There's no one before me, living or dead. I don't have the same bad sense I did with the field. I think we're clear."

"Fine. We move forward, but slowly. Tank?" The reptile lumbered up next to her. "Enter here and slowly make your way in. We need to be sure there's no one hiding. Okay?"

Tank nodded slowly, then shrank to the size of a large dog. She trotted in through the doorway. Jade watched her disappear into the dark, sending a prayer to the Goddess for her safety. Moments ticked by.

Sophia tapped Jade on her shoulder. "Um, Jade dear. We have a problem."

Jade turned to see a small army marching toward them. There were apparently more dead in the field than they'd triggered on their way in. They were in various states of decay, some with tattered clothing still attached and hanging off them. They were moving slowly though.

"Alright, follow us in, then cast something to block them out once we're past the threshold. Katie, would Elida be willing to light our way?"

Without hesitation, the little golden light flew past her and floated a few feet in front. Jade entered with Katie close behind.

Tank was ahead of them, almost to the other side of the tunnel. Jade mentally called out for her to stop and she did, craning her head back to look at her.

When they got to the end, there was a locked door. Daisy made quick work of it and they entered.

Jade looked around the dim room. They were in a large antechamber with a low ceiling and no windows. The only light was from the faerie floating through the room.

As Sophia shut the door behind them, Jade had a moment of panic. The room had a musty smell to it like a basement, and the faerie's light was barely bright enough. The only door seemed to be the one they'd come through.

"That can't be right. Why would there be a room with only one exit here?" She crept around the room, passing through a cold draft, which sent a violent shiver down her back. Backtracking, she found it and followed it to a crack in the wall. The faerie drew closer, and Jade could see there was a latch. It was the same color and texture as the walls, which was why she'd almost missed it.

"Daisy?" she whispered.

Jade felt more than saw the Witch pass her and kneel at the hidden doorway. After a moment, she stood and said, "Stand back."

They all took a step back as Daisy placed her hand on the second crack opposite the one with the hinge. A rumbling and grinding signaled movement before the beam of light showed the door was opening.

It suddenly flew open, and something knocked Jade off her feet, taking the air from her lungs. She sat up, struggling to get her breath back. Dirt and sand kicked up into the air around her, blocking her vision. In the dust-filtered light from the doorway battled the silhouettes of two figures locked in hand-to-hand combat. One short and petite, the other thin and tall, their cloak's hood up over their head. Sophia quickly helped Jade to her feet and pulled her to the open doorway, where Katie was waiting.

They scrambled through and up the short flight of stairs. "What happened?" Jade asked, out of breath.

Katie was arguing with Elida, so Sophia answered, "Someone burst through the door and knocked you down. They went after Katie, but Daisy grabbed them and pulled them back. I only got a glimpse of them before they both disappeared. Whoever they were, they must be a Ghost, like Daisy."

"We have to go back and help her." She made a move to go down the stairs, but Sophia held her back.

"There's no time, Jade. She knew what she was doing, we have to trust that. Remember why we're here."

Jade didn't really need reminding. She'd been waiting for this day all month—they were finally moving on Raven. But she didn't want Daisy to be a casualty either. She didn't want any casualties. For this to be a true success, she needed everyone to be safe, but her plan was risky. The idea of anyone getting hurt was more than she could bear. So she pushed onward, focusing on the task at hand, and sent out another prayer to the Goddess.

They ran down the hall, which spilled out into a massive circular room. On their left was a wide staircase winding around and up to a domed ceiling several stories above them. Candelabras lined the walls, and a sourceless glowing light hung above the center of the room.

A loud explosion and scream drew Jade's attention. The front doors of the mansion were opened out onto the battlefield beyond. Smoke rose from the ruined roses on either side of the path. A fireball whizzed past the doorway, and in the background, two Witches were directing their Elementals to take out a small group of charging risen.

"Katie, Sophia, go see how you can help, then send anyone you can to help me find Raven and Charlie. But at all costs, keep the risen out of here. I need to face her on her own."

Katie was arguing with Elida in her pendant, which was glowing brighter than ever, "But she won't understand . . . I know. Ugh, fine." She removed the necklace and passed the chain over Jade's head. "Elida insists on going with you." She grabbed Jade's hand

and held it tight. "Trust your instinct with her. If you feel like she's telling you something, she probably is."

Katie followed Sophia out the door, leaving Jade to choose her path. An inviting, cozy library with a fireplace opened off the foyer, and Jade was tempted to start looking there. But Raven loved nothing more than being above everyone. She would be in the highest room. Jade sped up the stairway.

She reached the top floor, practically a room of glass. The landing continued around the edge and entered the left wing of the mansion. The hallway was as lit as the rest, but Jade shuddered as she stepped over the threshold. There was dark magic here. It clung like wallpaper and creeped over her head. She felt the need to shrink into herself to keep from touching it.

She pulled from the lightness of the feather in her cloak pocket to cast a shield around herself and crept down the hall. About halfway down, she heard quiet groans coming from a door next to her. A metal beam barred the heavy door. Jade lifted the heavy beam and laid it on the floor against the wall. Since it was locked from the outside, she doubted Raven was inside, but she was not sure it wasn't a trap. She pulled energy and held it ready as she opened the door.

The light from the hallway illuminated a person chained to the wall by their wrists, their head hanging limp.

Elida chimed softly, and the pendant vibrated. Jade opened the tiny cage and watched Elida flit around the room. She zoomed back to her, jingling loudly and shaking all over. Jade had no idea what the little faerie was trying to tell her, but the poor helpless person needed her help. They were no doubt someone who had angered Raven. Jade glanced around the room, looking for anything that could be hiding, waiting to pounce. The room was completely empty; only the eerie darkness hung in the air. As she got closer to the chained figure, she noticed curly dark hair, black jeans, and a copper bracelet.

"Charlie?"

Charlie slowly raised his head, and the light from Elida, hovering nearby, lit him up. His tears had streaked his face, tracing clean lines in the bloodstained bruises. Jade cringed at the swollen black-and-blue mess of his right eye and the gash that divided his lower lip. His expression was one of hopelessness.

Jade froze only a moment, her mind rebelling at a version of Charlie she never thought she'd see. She broke the chains with one swift spell, and Charlie collapsed to the floor, a pained grunt escaping him.

Jade gently raised his head and cradled it in her lap. "Charlie. What has she done to you? Can you hear me?"

He mumbled with eyes closed. "Jade? What're you doin' here? It's not safe. Not safe. She'll find you."

"Shhhh. It's going to be okay. We're going to get you out of here."

"We?"

"Yeah. The whole coven came to save you, Charlie."

Charlie lifted his head slowly and tried to look around the room. "Where . . . no. You're not real. No help. No help." His voice trailed off, and he weakly tried to push away from her, muttering and groaning in pain.

Jade's heart broke for him. Whatever mind games Raven had played were making him doubt her. She struggled to help lift him to his feet. "No, Charlie, I'm real. I promise you, we're here to help. You'll be safe, soon as we get you out of here." The sounds of battle had died down a bit, but there was still something going on outside. "Sophia, Katie, and I came through a back door. Come on, let's go." She tried to pull him to the doorway. His body was so heavy. Deep gashes covered one thigh, and his legs didn't seem to work right.

"That's all you have? I mean, there's no others here? It's not enough, she's too strong."

"The whole coven is here, Charlie. Once we get you out of here, they'll be more than enough to take her on." She pulled with all her might, but she wasn't making much ground. She stepped back to cast levitation on him and he stood straight, smiling at her. "Charlie?"

"Thank you. That's what I needed to know." He shoved his palms toward her.

The force threw Jade backward, her arms pinned to her sides as she landed on her back, mere inches from the floor. She struggled to move, but it was no use. She tried calling out to Tank, to any of her Elementals, but the connection was lost. She couldn't feel her magic anymore. Whatever spell Charlie had used on her not only immobilized her but also blocked her connection to magic. She stared at him in shock. How could he do this to her?

Charlie's face morphed back to normal, with no trace of injury. He pulled a crystal from his pocket and turned toward the window. He spoke into the crystal, "I have her. She's only brought the coven, so once you defeat them, it's just her. I'll take her to our room."

As soon as he'd turned, Elida had zipped back into her cage and dimmed her light. Charlie turned back to Jade and raised his hand, lifting her upright and setting her on her feet, then he pulled her from the room.

Jade stumbled after him in shock. She couldn't believe it. She tried reaching out, seeing if she could feel his heart, but there was nothing. It was as if she'd gone deaf, blind, and numb all at once. The realization of just how helpless she was chilled her soul.

Elida's cage was nearly dark, but Jade could feel her faint warmth against her chest. She clung to the feeling, focusing on it rather than the horrible truth: Charlie had betrayed her. He was delivering her to Raven.

They turned off the main hallway and up a short flight of stairs. An immense room opened off the landing, decked out in the finest furnishings and luxury items. A huge four-poster bed dominated the center of the room, sheer curtains draped around the corners, and a dozen pillows of various shapes and sizes scattered on the puffy duvet.

A fireplace large enough to stand in commandeered the left wall, the small bonfire within it warming the room. A chaise lounge sprawled in front of it on a fur rug. The right side was equally decadent, with a full-sized wardrobe next to a settee and mirror combo desk. A wide assortment of perfume and lotion bottles sat on the surface.

Charlie pulled Jade in and over to the corner to the right of the balcony windows. Here the tone changed drastically, one dark corner in the luxury. A lone rack stood guard, hung with chains and handcuffs on four corners. Dried blood painted the rack's wooden surface and pooled on the bare stone floor beneath. This was where Raven would torture Jade, just for fun. She didn't need a vision, she knew Raven too well.

Charlie dragged her to the rack and cuffed her quickly. He turned to look out the balcony doors.

Jade cried, "Charlie! What are you doing? Charlie, please talk to me."

"Why?"

"I need to know—"

"What's in it for me?" He looked at her with such empty eyes, as if he didn't even recognize her. "Don't you get it?" His sudden smile was so vile and sickly. "I don't care about you anymore. I've realized that the only thing that matters is yourself. Well, not 'your' self. I matter to me, you matter to you. But why should you matter to me? I have a High Priest's power now; I can have anything I want."

Jade glared at him. "None of it mattered? All the time we spent together, the years we were friends? None of it matters?"

He looked at her. "No. I'm . . . I'm sorry, but I come first. I have to." He nearly whispered the end, a frown briefly passing over his face.

Outside, the screams of battle died down. Flashes of light became less frequent, and the hum of magic in the air faded. The battle was over. Jade waited, wondering who won. Had they caught Raven? Was she being tried right now?

A shadow slid across the floor. Someone was rising up outside. They wore a flowing cape, but that's all Jade could tell from the dark shape that stretched out on the floor. The shadow expanded, filling the doorway. A black boot stepped into the room, the hem of a floor-length black cloak swinging over it. Raven rounded the corner. "Well, hello there, my little lamb."

A chill ran down Jade's spine. She had her answer. The silence outside was frightening. They had lost. She slouched back against the rack and let her head hang freely. Closing her eyes, she whispered, "I'm sorry." Her coven would never hear it, but she spoke the words anyway.

Raven smirked. "Why so glum, little one?" Jade forced her head up to see Raven slide a hand over Charlie's shoulder as she leaned against him. "Isn't this the reunion you were hoping for?" She turned her head and gave Charlie a long, deep kiss which he returned, wrapping his arms around her.

Jade's stomach turned. Being on Raven's side was one thing, but kissing her? Charlie's heart must be completely black for him to do something like that.

Raven and Charlie parted lips and turned toward Jade, arm in arm. Jade had never seen Charlie look so cold. Their eyes met, and it was as if she was looking at a stranger.

Raven waved a hand in front of Jade's face. "Hello? Anyone home?" She glanced at Charlie. "I do think we've broken the poor thing."

Charlie glanced out the balcony window. "Let's go."

"In a minute, lover." She sashayed over to Jade, watching her closely. "Are you broken, little lamb?"

Jade glared at Raven. "Is that what you want? To break me."

Raven looked shocked, hand on heart. "What? No, of course not." She smiled then. "At least, not yet. I mean not before I've given you the chance to join us." She glanced at Charlie. "I promised."

Her smile was snakelike. She was obviously hoping for exactly what Jade said next. "Are you joking? I'll never join you."

"Sorry, lover," she said to Charlie. "We do it my way." Her dark eyes searched Jade, as if deciding where to begin.

"Raven." Charlie's warning tone didn't even slow her down.

"Now, I could make this quick, but you know me. That's just not fun." She traced a finger down Jade's right temple. It left a thin trail of fire as her skin parted, and a trickle of hot blood dripped down. Jade refused to cry out, leaning her head back against the wood, smiling as she looked down her nose at Raven.

Raven grabbed Jade's hair and glared at her. "Do you remember what you did to me? I do. I remember those brief moments. They felt like years." Her eyes were dark with the shadow of remembered pain. "Here, let me show you what it felt like."

She stood back and raised her outstretched arm toward Jade. After a moment she clenched her fist tightly.

Jade hadn't noticed her heart beating, but she knew the moment it stopped. Her insides were slowing, freezing in place as her blood congealed. The pain began to build, every cell crying out. Then her lungs started to burn. She was in the grip of a blood magic spell, cast without a word spoken.

Charlie stepped next to Raven. "Stop. That's enough. You prom—"

His voice became muffled as the world went dark. Jade thought of her coven, of April, of the Charlie she used to know.

She gasped, panting heavily as the blood raced once again. Every inch of her skin burned as the oxygen-starved cells were revived.

Raven was yelling at Charlie, "… wouldn't hurt her if she surrendered. I gave her a chance, she said no. Now she's mine to do with as I please. If you can't take it, you can wait outside."

Charlie looked at Jade only a moment before whispering, "Sorry." He turned and strode out the door.

CHAPTER 21

Even when Charlie had left with Raven, Jade had held on to hope she would get him back. Rescue him from her. Somehow. Now, she knew he was gone for good. Now, he left with her last hope. Her Charlie was gone for good, and she was helpless to save him. She broke down, the tears mixing with sobs until she felt numb.

When she finally looked up, Raven was gazing out the balcony doors, saying something about how disappointed she was that Jade was falling apart over a man.

Raven flicked her hand, and the cuffs released from the rack, but Jade's hands were still bound to each other. The cuffs pulled her arms behind her back, and her wrists snapped together, painfully stretching her shoulders to their limits. Raven walked out to the balcony, dragging Jade behind her.

Raven stood to the side so Jade could go all the way to the balcony railing. She looked out at a battle zone. Small shrubs smoldered, several trees limbs lay broken, and impact scorch marks dotted the yard. Risen were scattered here and there, piles of bones or frozen skeletal statues. Many of them were standing around her coven, gathered in a tight group in the center of the front drive. A couple Witches were lying prone, and Jade sent a prayer to the Goddess that they were only unconscious.

"You see?" Raven gloated, "You have failed. Your coven is defeated. I've won."

Jade searched the group for Flick. He was there, a small blue light in the middle of the group. There was hope yet.

She couldn't keep the smile from her voice. "Yeah, it's a good thing we didn't imagine something like this might happen. Elida, now."

Elida glowed brightly as she signaled Flick. He flickered back, and after a moment, Katie stood up quickly and whistled.

"What did you do?" Raven asked, pulling Jade back from the ledge as she looked over it.

From the edges of the property, a thundering could be heard. Hooves, paws, and beating wings rushed toward them. A second wave of Elementals had been waiting out of sight of the property. They now came racing in, taking out the Risen as they went. The risen were no match for the Elementals. Jade watched the smile on Raven's face slip away.

"What's wrong, Raven?" she taunted. "Everything not going according to plan?"

Jade wanted desperately to take Raven out. She was right there, feet from her, shouting commands to the risen, trying to get them to fight against the attacking swarm.

Something brushed against Jade's fingers. Someone was unlocking her cuffs. She couldn't see anyone there, but she knew it must be Daisy. She felt the subtle click of the cuffs that bound her wrists opening, and with it the magic returned. She felt it run over her skin, blessed warmth chasing away the chill. This was it. If she didn't bind Raven now, she might never get another chance.

Jade bowed her head and focused inward. She had one shot at this. If she missed or messed up the spell, Raven wouldn't allow her another shot. It was all riding on her. Everything down to this one moment. She could feel her heart racing; her breath quickened; her arms buzzed; but it wasn't with magic. It was fear. She was starting to panic.

She heard Raven's muffled voice and her boots on the stone floor. Jade raised her head, to see a portal forming on her left. Raven was striding toward it from the balcony's railing on Jade's right, passing in front of her.

It was too late.

Or was it?

She looked down at her hand to see she had already pulled the enchantment grenade from the hidden pocket in her cloak. Raven was almost past her.

She pressed the center of the disk and tossed it in front of Raven. The ball of energy exploded outward like a wave from a pebble dropped in a pond. Raven stumbled back, away from the portal, which snapped shut.

Jade began pulling heat, but Raven was already starting to transform. Her eyes dimmed and took on a blank stare, her mind trapped in the enchantment. Her hair grew out and faded to a pale summer blonde. Her clothes changed, becoming softer and simpler. In mere moments, the enchantment completely dispelled the effects of Raven's glamor. It seemed April stood there, dazed, looking around like she was lost.

The more Raven had morphed into April, the more Jade's resolve left her. Her hatred for Raven fading, being replaced with the bittersweet sorrow at seeing April replace her. Jade dropped the energy she'd been building and reeled backwards, stumbling back against the door frame. She mumbled, "It's not her." She closed her eyes, struggling to push back the shock. She repeated it over and over in her head. *It's not her. It's not her.*

The enchantment was meant to simulate April using Jade's memories of how she spoke, moved, and even thought. But this was too much. Jade looked at her, tears flooding her eyes. This felt like April. That indescribable feeling you get with someone you know as well as yourself. Jade's mind knew better, but in her heart, this was April.

April-but-not-April turned and looked at Jade. "Jade? Are you okay?" She caught Jade's arm and steadied her. "What's going on? Where are we?"

Jade's heart broke. She grabbed April and hugged her tightly. It wasn't April; it was still Raven, locked away inside there somewhere. Before long, she would break free. Jade had to keep on task. No matter how much she just wanted to revel in the sight of her best friend, she knew it wasn't really her.

Jade pushed back, holding April at arm's length. She looked into her eyes; those same pale blue eyes she'd gazed into so many times before. The idea of killing or even binding her was too much to face. She couldn't do it.

Willow's voice echoed in her mind: *It's not about you. You will hurt, but your coven will be with you.*

Willow was right. She needed her coven.

"There's no time to explain," Jade said. "Do you trust me?"

A sympathetic smile formed on April's lips. "What kind of silly question is that? Of course I trust you."

"Then you need to listen carefully. I need you to follow me downstairs. Don't ask questions, don't even speak. Can you do that for me?"

April nodded solemnly.

Jade took her hand and dragged her through the mansion. It was best not to think about it, to not look back at the best friend she'd ever had, following her silently through the dark corridors and down the stairs.

They came to a stop on the front steps. The sky had gone dark, thick clouds smothering the full moon. Faeries flitted here and there, shedding light for the coven to work. As soon as the enchantment had changed Raven, the Risen were released from her command. Without a master, they collapsed. The coven was collecting them and placing them reverently in small piles. After it was all over, the coven would perform a ritual to cleanse the bones and property, releasing the spirits into the afterlife across the veil.

Jade glanced at April and pulled her down the drive. She needed her coven, needed their support to do what she couldn't bring herself to do. Several faeries hovered over Jade and April, lighting the way for them.

Sophia was by the open main gate, binding a wound on Katie's arm.

Jade slowed and walked toward her, about to call her name, when April tugged back on her hand. Jade turned to see why she'd stopped.

April looked at her fearfully. "Jade?" Her eyes glazed over, then cleared, and the slightest smile taunted her. "Nice try, lamby." She jerked out of Jade's grasp and began moving her hands in circles while she mumbled an incantation.

Jade was surprised her heart didn't break at seeing the dark Witch take over April's body again. Instead, she felt relief. The type of spell Raven was casting took time. It was a miscalculation that would cost her dearly.

Jade gathered moisture from what was left of the surrounding fog, quickly forming spikes of ice. She flung them at Raven in rapid succession then began stalking toward her, using the heat of her own fury to form a fireball.

Raven had just reached back, as if about to throw the spell she'd been casting, and her eyes widened at the onslaught of shards flying her way. She blocked most of them, but was overwhelmed and soon covered in minor cuts.

Raven's proud posture left her. She shoved her hand into her cloak pocket and withdrew a small coin. Slouching over it, she struggled to pull energy from it for a spell.

Jade yanked at the metal of Raven's token, whipping it out of her hands, then threw the fireball at her. Raven raised a shield at the last minute, barely blocking it, sending it careening into a giant tree just off the drive. Jade sent another, and it exploded on Raven's outstretched hand. She cried out and stumbled backward, gripping her injured hand to her chest as Jade approached.

Jade continued throwing fireballs. Raven struggled more with each one until she fell to the ground, holding her burnt and bleeding hands over her head for protection. The defensive wounds were painful to look at.

Jade stalked forward, trailing fire in her wake, a fireball in hand. Her anger was out of control, but she didn't care. She would put an end to this now.

When Jade reached her, she saw April's blue eyes looking up at her between shaking arms. She reminded herself that it was not April and that Raven was playing a disgusting trick on her. Jade raised her hand to cast the fireball. Within moments, it would all be over.

"Jade, wait!" Sophia shouted behind her. Jade didn't turn. She needed to finish this, make Raven pay, once and for all.

As she reached back to hurl the fireball at Raven, Selene grabbed her arm and doused the flame while Aiden seized her other arm. Sophia stepped into her line of sight, "Jade, stop."

Jade glared at Sophia. This was her last chance to defeat Raven, and she wouldn't even allow her coven to stop her. She drew from her own hatred of Raven, built it up within her, then unleashed it outward with a single word. "No." The shockwave sent all the coven members around her flying backward.

The corner of Raven's mouth was drawn up in that ugly smirk. Jade focused on it and imagined a spark. Raven screamed as her face burst into flames.

Selene stood and cast water at Raven, trying to put the fire out. Jade waved her hand, redirecting the stream back at Selene. Facing Raven, Jade raised a shield around them both. The energy pulsed within her like a heartbeat, fueling the impenetrable field. She wanted no interruptions for these final moments of Raven's life. This was what she'd waited for.

The flames were spreading. Raven clawed at her face and flung herself on the ground, desperate to put out the blaze. But it was fueled by Jade's emotions. It couldn't be doused or smothered. Bit by bit, Raven's body was covered by fire as she tried desperately to crawl away.

Jade stalked toward her. Watching her crawl was so satisfying. All pretense of power and pride were gone now. She was a wounded animal, desperately struggling to flee from the pain, crawling on her belly, screaming as her skin charred.

Jade had a moment of doubt. Maybe this was too much. The vision of April's last moments came to her, covered in blood, dying in her arms. Her face in shock as she looked to Jade for help. No, Raven deserved this and more.

Jade felt the sting of tears as her sorrow and anger welled. She let them flow freely, tracing hot tracks down her cheeks. Staring down at Raven, Jade kept pace with her slowly crawling form.

Raven's screams subsided, and she stopped moving. Her body lay smoking, black coal where a human once was. A fitting end, Jade thought. Justice not only for April, but Jade's parents as well. They'd died by fire at Raven's hands; now she had paid the same price.

Raven's spirit would cross over and be judged in the veil. Though Witches didn't believe in heaven or hell, they did believe in karma. Somehow, someway, the Goddess would make sure that in death, Raven paid for the harm she'd caused in life.

Jade sagged, exhausted from the battle. She wiped her face and released the toxic energy, grounding it into the earth below her. It was finally over.

She turned to find her coven staring at her in shock. Caldwell stood among them, brow furrowed in stern disappointment. Hovering around him were three red-eyed drones, recording everything.

Jade's head spun, and a cold ache settled in her chest as her worst fear was realized. She'd just been witnessed killing Raven. But she hadn't *looked* like Raven. The recording would show she'd just murdered April, a Citizen. a Citizen.

The drones swooped in to surround her as Caldwell stepped forward, cuff in hand. "Jade Cerridwen, you have been witnessed breaking Sun City laws. Stand fast and await judgment." He reached her quickly and placed the cuff around her neck, cold and metallic. Jade recognized the subtle click of the lock and the disconnect from her power. Caldwell looked into her eyes, and with a disappointment that was almost painful, he whispered, "You lied to me."

It was almost too quiet to hear, but it sent a shiver down Jade's back. She felt completely exposed. It wasn't just because her magic was cut off; she felt cut off from her coven as well. They were surrounding her now, only a few feet away, but the murder of a Citizen meant only one outcome: the death sentence, carried out swiftly by the arresting Lawkeeper. She was less concerned about her own death. What scared her more was that it meant her coven would be without their High Priestess. Again.

Ms. Scrivener leapt to her defense. "You have no right to arrest anyone in a township without first notifying—"

The inspector spun and advanced on her until they were nose to nose. "I have every right to serve justice. Wherever I am. On whoever I see fit. It would benefit you to stay out of my way."

Ms. Scrivener retreated to Jade's side and whispered, "We must tread lightly."

Jade's throat tightened. She'd never seen her back down like that. If Caldwell wasn't on their side and Ms. Scrivener couldn't find a loophole in the law, the death penalty was an absolute certainty.

He flipped through his little black notebook. It seemed like he was reading the evidence he'd gathered, but Jade was close enough to see his eyes, and they weren't moving. He was putting on a show for the Citizens.

He put the notebook back in his pocket and faced Jade. "Jade Cerridwen, it is my ruling that you are guilty of multiple crimes. Among them, the kidnapping and murder of Citizen April Goodrich. My judgment against you… is for you to be publicly terminated, effective immediately." As he raised his arm to signal the drones, his eyes flicked to Ms. Scrivener. A subtle movement, not easily caught by the cameras, but one Jade definitely saw as a sign. What was he trying to signal?

Ms. Scrivener regained her usual powerful posture. "My client appeals the judgment against her by requesting a formal trial, as per Article 3 of the Accords." She looked pointedly at Jade.

"Yes. Um, I do request a trial. As my council said."

The inspector paused for a moment, then lowered his arm. "I accept your request. Trial will commence in Sun City major court at the discretion of the Citizenship. Let's go." When Jade didn't move immediately, he said, "It would benefit you to follow my instructions without hesitation."

Ms. Scrivener took Jade's arm and moved her gently toward the gate with Caldwell close behind. She whispered, "Don't say anything else. This is the best we can hope for at this point. It gives me time to read the full charges and mount a defense. Do as you're told, keep silent, and know we will do everything we can to get you out of this."

At the gate, the inspector pushed Ms. Scrivener aside and stepped through with Jade in tow. They were headed for his car, parked across the road. Jade felt a momentary panic; her heart beat fast, and she had an overwhelming urge to run. She could hide in the woods if she could just make the tree line. But the inspector's grip on her arm was viselike. Even if she could break away, the drones would catch up to her nearly instantly. There was no way she could get out of it.

He shoved her into the back seat and slammed the door. Jade watched her coven gather outside the gate, helpless and worried. Katie cried on Mrs. Keepsake's shoulder. Sophia and Ms. Scrivener were deep in conversation, casting looks her way.

There was nothing any of them could do for Jade, but she realized that didn't matter. It was her job to protect the coven and its township, and she'd failed them. Sure, Raven was gone, but in a way, she'd still won. Soon Jade would be executed, leaving her coven without their High Priestess. Everything she'd been through was for nothing.

***

Hours later, Jade lay across the back seat of the inspector's car. The cuff around her neck fit loosely, but the stranglehold it had on her magic was palpable. Her breath hitched, and she half expected to start another round of crying. But her tears were all below her now, soaked into the seat's fabric and tangled in her hair. She sniffed and pushed herself upright.

The inspector glanced at her over his shoulder. "Almost there."

Sun City's main gate drew closer, the electric fence a barely visible line of bright blue in the distance.

Jade twisted round to look out the rear window. They were there somewhere, miles behind her. Sugar Hill's coven, left alone in the darkness.

***

Want to find out what will happen to Jade when she reaches Sun City? Get notified when the next book will be out before anyone else, by joining my newsletter at mwinklerbooks.com.

Whether you enjoyed Blood on the Raven or not, can you please leave an honest review? It's the best way to help it find readers who will love it.

ACKNOWLEDGMENTS

As always, I'm thankful for you, my readers. Without you my stories would be languishing in my brain. And I'm especially thankful for those of you who read book one and nagged me about when I'd get this one published. Your friendly reminders were the motivation I needed to keep going.

To my beta readers, you've helped me figure out what needed to be fixed before I embarrassed myself by sharing it with the world. Thank you so much. Any mistakes still present are my own.

About the Author

I was convinced by my husband to live in the Arizona desert. While skeptical at first, I realized if I could survive hitchhiking halfway cross country at 20 years old, spend eight years in the Navy, and raise two sons, as long as I had air-conditioning, I'd probably be okay.

Since my move I've: started a veggie garden, learned how to shoot a bow, completed three associate degrees, and become a kayak enthusiast. However, I still hate to cook and will absolutely run screaming from the room at the first sight of a bug. Because bugs are evil.

When writing, I'm usually supervised by my adorable pups; Zen, Pepper, Raven, and Skye.